D1152010

THE POSTMAN ALWAYS DIES TWICE

MOVIE CLUB MYSTERIES, BOOK 2

ZARA KEANE

BEAVERSTONE PRESS LLC

THE POSTMAN ALWAYS DIES TWICE
(Movie Club Mysteries, Book 2)

When former San Francisco cop, Maggie Doyle, extends her stay in Ireland, dealing with more murder and mayhem isn't on her to-do list. The instant Maggie and her UFO-enthusiast friend discover the dead body of the Whisper Island postman, Maggie's plans to chill for the next two months are put on ice.

After Police Sergeant Reynolds, Maggie's handsome neighbor, arrests Lenny's brother for the murder, her friend begs her to find the real killer. Meanwhile, Maggie is hired to investigate ghostly goings on at the Whisper Island Hotel. Can she solve two crimes before St. Patrick's Day? Or will the island's annual celebrations end in a glittery flame of green, white, and orange?

NOTE ON GAELIC TERMS

Certain Gaelic terms appear in this book. I have tried to use them sparingly and in contexts that should make their meaning clear to international readers. However, a couple of words require clarification.

The official name for the Irish police force is *An Garda Síochána* ("the Guardian of the Peace"). Police are *Gardaí* (plural) and *Garda* (singular). Irish police are commonly referred to as "the guards".

The official rank of a police officer such as Sergeant O'Shea is Garda Sergeant O'Shea. As the Irish frequently shorten this to Sergeant, I've chosen to use this version for all but the initial introduction to the character.

The official name for the Whisper Island police station would be Whisper Island Garda Station, but Maggie, being American, rarely thinks of it as such.

The Irish police do not, as a rule, carry firearms.

Permission to carry a gun is reserved to detectives and specialist units, such as the Emergency Response Unit. The police on Whisper Island would not have been issued with firearms.

Although this book follows American spelling conventions, I've chosen to use the common Irish spelling for proper names such as Carraig Harbour and the Whisper Island Medical Centre.

ONE

I'd encountered plenty of culture shocks since I'd swapped my cheating husband and my career in the San Francisco PD for a remote Irish island. Discovering that used car salesmen were the same slick sons-of-guns all over the world was almost a comfort.

I fixed the proprietor of Zippy Motors with a hard stare. "I'll give you three hundred bucks, and not a penny more."

"Aw, come on, Maggie. A man's gotta eat. This little beauty will zip you around—just like our slogan." Jack Logan treated me to the killer smile that had left a trail of broken hearts across Whisper Island in the years before he'd developed a beer belly and a comb-over. I remained unmoved.

"The car's fit for scrap metal," I said. "Before I shell out any money, never mind your insane asking price, I need to know the vehicle will survive the couple of months I'm staying on the island."

"Sure it will." Jack spread his palms wide in a gesture that was presumably designed to put his customers at ease. "Would I sell you a lemon? I value my reputation."

I rolled my eyes. "Your reputation stinks. You're still in business because you get an influx of clueless tourists every summer who are willing to rent one of your wrecks for the season."

The salesman's composure faltered. "Now that's a bit harsh."

"But true. I'm Lenny's friend, remember? Your cousin's told me all about you." And the parts Lenny hadn't told me, I could guess. Jack wore designer clothes and reeked of expensive aftershave. I glanced up at Zippy Motors' battered sign. Somehow, I doubted Jack funded his flash lifestyle with the money he made from selling and renting wrecks.

I strolled around the Ford Fiesta, examining it for obvious patches of rust. "Today's your lucky day, Jack. I'm in need of a cheap ride, and your establishment is on the island if there's any issue with my purchase." I made eye contact. "You do offer an after-purchase warranty, right?"

The man's Adam's apple bobbed. "Uh, sure, but nothing will go wrong with the car."

"For your sake, I hope not." I patted the ancient

vehicle, and it didn't fall apart under my touch. I took this to be a good sign. "Cash, I presume?"

Once I'd completed my transaction with Jack Logan, I slid behind the wheel of my new-to-me ride and drove out of Smuggler's Cove. I hung a left at the crossroads on the edge of town and headed in the direction of my new home—a sweet little holiday cottage on the far side of Whisper Island. As a thank-you for my help in solving a murder mystery, my aunts and friends had pooled their resources to pay for three months' rent on the cottage, thus treating me to an extended vacation on their island. I'd moved in last week. After spending six weeks living with my aunt Noreen and her menagerie of animals, I was still getting used to the silence.

The drive across the island took thirty minutes. I took it slow, soaking in the sights. The snow we'd had earlier in the winter hadn't lasted long, and now that it was early March, the first signs of spring were starting to show. The days were growing longer, and a few flowers had begun to bloom. As the road wound around the edge of the cliffs, I passed woodland and rolling green hills before finally reaching the gates of my new residence.

My cottage was part of a complex of eight holiday homes named Shamrock Cottages—although I had yet to see any evidence that shamrocks grew in the vicinity.

Built on a slope, the cottage boasted a spectacular view of the sea through my front windows. Each cottage in the complex had a fenced-in garden with just enough room for an outdoor table and chairs. There was also a communal playground, as well as a shared games room, neither of which I'd had reason to use.

When I drove through the gates of Shamrock Cottages, Noreen was waiting on my doorstep. She wore a wide smile on her face and balanced a tray of freshly baked scones in her arms. My mouth watered at the sight. Since moving out of her house, I'd started to skip breakfast. Not smart, but it had helped me lose a few of the pounds I'd gained while living with Noreen and eating her enormous portions. Bran, my aunt's lively Border collie-Labrador mix, danced by her side, tripping over Noreen's large bag in his excitement to see me.

The instant I stepped out of my car, Bran bounded over and treated me to an obligatory crotch sniff. "Cut that out," I said, bending down to pet his soft fur. "You've gotta learn manners."

"Too late for that, I'm afraid," my aunt said with a laugh. "I've tried everything. On the plus side, he only does it to people he likes."

I scratched Bran under his chin. "While I'm honored to be liked by you, Bran, I wish you'd show your affection for me in some other way."

As if he understood my words, the dog treated my hand to a generous lick. I gave him a last pat and drew my key from my jacket pocket.

My aunt squinted at the car and then leaped back in horror. "Please don't tell me you went to Zippy Motors."

"They're cheap, and I'm low on cash." I slammed the driver's door and strode toward the cottage door, Bran at my heels. "Mmm. Those scones smell divine."

My aunt clucked with disapproval. "Don't change the subject. Jack Logan is a snake. I buy cheap cars, but even I won't go near him. I'm convinced he's laundering money at that place."

"It's a done deal now," I said cheerfully. I unlocked the door and relieved my aunt of the tray. "Want to come in for a coffee? Because I'm totally eating one of these scones."

"That would be lovely." My aunt bounded into the cottage with an agility that belied her fifty-six years. "I have some housewarming gifts for you."

I raised an eyebrow. "More? You've already given me enough towels to dry a family of six."

Noreen bounced on the spot, making her jet-black curls dance. "These gifts are of a livelier nature. Literally."

I sucked in a breath. "Oh, no. Not the pet thing again."

"Just hear me out before you object. You could do with some company now that you're out here all alone. Bran can act as a guard dog."

I placed the tray on the kitchen counter and shook

my head emphatically. "You're not foisting the dog onto me. No way. Besides, I live next door to a policeman. What could be safer than that?"

My aunt clucked in disapproval. "Sure, Sergeant Reynolds hasn't moved in properly yet. Even when he does, he'll hardly ever be home. He's working crazy hours in pursuit of those eejits who keep sneaking onto farms and causing havoc. Did you hear about Paddy Driscoll's sheep?"

"Clearly, I'm behind on island gossip." I switched on the coffee machine and got out plates and coffee mugs. "What happened to Paddy's sheep?"

"They were given a makeover last night."

I looked at my aunt over my shoulder and slow-blinked. "What does a sheep makeover involve?"

"They were dressed in knitted outfits made out of acrylic yarn."

"Wow." I whistled. "An animal activist on a mission?"

"Maybe. At any rate, Paddy's chief issue was the fact that the pattern on the sheep's outfits was the Union Jack." Noreen's lips twitched with amusement. "Not a flag likely to please a man of Paddy's political persuasions."

I recalled the huge Irish flag painted on the wall of Paddy's barn, and the various pro-I.R.A. sentiments the grumpy farmer had uttered in my presence. No, he wouldn't be pleased to find his sheep wearing the British flag.

After I'd made a cappuccino for my aunt and a double espresso for me, I placed two of the scones on plates and put everything on the table. On autopilot, I retrieved one of the doggie snacks I kept for Bran's visits from the drawer under the sink.

"I'm serious about you adopting Bran," my aunt said, watching me feed the grateful dog his treat. "You're the one taking him on most of his walks these days."

"It's not fair to the dog. I'm only on Whisper Island until May."

"Until the end of May," my aunt corrected, as though the distinction made all the difference in the world. "Why don't you take him until then? He'll be great company for you and the cats."

"Cats?" My voice rose in a crescendo. I sucked in a breath and scanned the kitchen for evidence of feline habitation. My gaze came to rest on the big carrier bag at Noreen's feet, and I groaned out loud. "Oh, no."

Inside the carrier bag, six kittens snuggled against their mother, snoozing peacefully in a basket.

"Seeing as you rescued Poly's kittens, I thought you'd like to have a couple of them to keep you company. They're not ready to leave their mum permanently yet, so I brought her with them."

"A couple doesn't mean six. Besides, Sergeant Reynolds rescued one of the kittens. I just helped."

"Exactly." My aunt beamed at me. "Rosie is the

one on the far left. I'm sure she'd love to come and live with you."

"Not happening, Noreen. I love you to bits, but the animals are leaving when you do."

My aunt grinned across the table and spread a generous helping of strawberry jam over her scone. "I'll wear you down, Miss Maggie. You just see if I don't."

Before I could utter another protest, the familiar splutter of an old VW van drew my attention to the kitchen window. Through the glass, I saw my friend, Lenny, park his van at the entrance to Shamrock Cottages. Like my car, the van had seen better years, and better paint jobs. Lenny's recent decision to paint it psychedelic purple hadn't enhanced the vehicle's appeal.

"Lenny just pulled up," I told my aunt. "I'll go let him in."

When I opened my front door, Lenny was ambling toward me, carrying a large plastic bag. He stopped short when he saw my new car and circled it as one would a feral beast. "Aw, Maggie. You went to Jack's place? What did I tell you about that guy?"

"That he's a crook and a swindler and to run far and fast," I replied. "And although Jack's cons list outweighs his pros, he's cheap and easily intimidated."

"I wouldn't be so sure about the easily intimidated part," Lenny said, tugging on his scraggly beard. "He's bold enough to drive a brand-new Porsche around the island one minute, and plead poverty to the Inland Revenue the next."

"I take it Jack isn't keen on paying taxes?"

"That's one way of putting it. But enough about my idiot cousin. How are you doing? All settled into your new home?" My friend's easygoing smile lit up his thin face, transforming him from homely to kinda cute in a geeky sort of way. We'd been buddies since I'd spent my summers on Whisper Island as a child. Although we'd lost touch as adults, our friendship had picked up where we'd left off when I'd returned to the island in January.

"It's fab. I like it so much it'll be hard to leave when the lease is up." I nodded in the direction of the kitchen. "Want to come in for a coffee? Noreen's here, and she brought scones."

"I can't stay. I have to go to Paddy Driscoll's place to fix his computer." He held up the plastic carrier bag. "I thought I'd swing by yours on the way and give you your housewarming present."

"As long as it's not a pet, we're good," I quipped, remembering the basket of kittens with a sinking sensation in my stomach. I had a feeling Noreen would wear me down.

"No worries." Lenny's bony face split into a grin that brought a twinkle to his pale blue eyes. "I thought you needed a little greenery." He opened the bag and removed a leafy potted plant...a leafy potted cannabis plant. "I thought it'd liven up your new home."

"I can think of more legal ways to liven up my cottage." I shot him a look of exasperation. "Have you forgotten I live next door to a police officer?"

Lenny's grin faded. "Oops. I didn't think of Reynolds."

"You don't say," I said, deadpan. "Even if I was inclined to keep it, I have an unfortunate track record with plants."

Bran and my aunt emerged from the kitchen. Upon seeing Lenny, the dog gave an excited bark and raced over to give my friend a thorough crotch sniff.

"Maggie's not joking about her knack with plants," Noreen said, pulling on her coat. "She killed a cactus while she was staying with me."

I grimaced. "Guilty as charged."

Lenny laughed and scratched Bran under his chin. "Maybe you'll have better luck with this particular variety of plant."

When she'd buttoned up her duffel coat, Noreen squeezed my arm. "I'd best be off, love. I need to get to the café and relieve Kelly. I'll collect you at six-thirty for the Movie Club meeting. Will that suit you?"

"Six-thirty sounds good." I noticed a conspicuous absence of kittens in her carrier bag. "Whoa. You're not leaving me with the cats and—" Bran abandoned Lenny and rubbed against my legs, silencing me with the plaintive expression in his doggie eyes. I bit back a sigh. Who could resist that look? "Do you want to stay with me for a while, buddy?"

Bran's response was to lick my hand. Man, that dog knew how to pull at my heartstrings.

"If you're keeping Bran, you can hardly turf out the cats," Noreen said as if the matter was decided. She paused when she noticed the plant in my arms. "Oh, that's a beautiful bit of greenery."

I laughed. "A beautiful bit of greenery that's destined for the garbage can."

"Oh, no." My aunt looked horrified. "You can't do that. I'll take it home with me."

"Noreen, that's not a good idea."

"It'd look great in your house," Lenny said straight-faced. "It'd add class to the joint."

I shot him a warning look. "Don't listen to him. Take my advice and get rid of it."

"Nonsense," Noreen said. "I have loads of plants. It'll fit right in."

I opened my mouth to protest, but my words were drowned out by the roar of a motorcycle crunching up the gravel drive. Sergeant Liam Reynolds pulled up outside his cottage and leaped off his bike.

"Uh-oh," Lenny whispered beside me. "Now we're in for it."

The words I muttered beneath my breath were less polite. "What possessed you to show up here with a cannabis plant?" I whispered.

"I'm sorry," Lenny whispered back. "I thought it would give you a laugh."

Reynolds, also known as Sergeant Hottie—okay,

known as Sergeant Hottie *by me*—removed his helmet and revealed close-cropped dark blond hair and a face that would have been movie-star handsome but for a nose that had been broken more than once. To my annoyance, a jolt of desire set my blood humming.

"Cooee," my aunt called. To my horror, she held up the cannabis plant for Reynolds to see. "Look what Maggie gave me. Isn't it lovely?"

Oblivious to the policeman's slack-jawed expression, my aunt got into her car, waved to us, and drove off with the cannabis plant on her passenger seat.

TWO

Sergeant Hottie's gaze met mine. His dark blue eyes twinkled with merriment. "Your aunt cracks me up."

My shoulders tensed. I didn't think Reynolds was the type to freak out and accuse my aunt of deliberately growing cannabis, but he was still the legal representative of law and order on the island. "Noreen's lovely, but clueless at times."

Reynolds's smile widened, drawing my attention to his dimples. "You might want to drop her a hint to part company from the plant before I officially become your neighbor."

"Consider it done." I exhaled in relief. Had Reynolds's predecessor, Sergeant O'Shea, seen my aunt with the plant, he'd have hauled her down to the police station without stopping to think.

My new neighbor's focus shifted to Lenny, and his expression became markedly less friendly. "If I catch you cultivating or distributing controlled plants, Logan, I'll have you down to the station before you can blink. Understood?"

Lenny's gulp was audible. "Loud and clear, sergeant. I'd, uh, better make tracks. Paddy Driscoll is grumpy at the best of times, and he's in a foul mood today over his sheep."

"Noreen told me about the Union Jack coats," I said with a grin. "I'd love to have seen that."

Lenny laughed. "Paddy must have been livid."

"Incandescent with rage," Sergeant Reynolds drawled. "I had to deal with him. I'm still not sure if his sheep's new outfits or the British flag upset him more."

I chuckled and glanced at my watch. Eleven o'clock. The mail might have been delivered by now, and I was expecting papers from my divorce lawyer. "I'll walk down as far as the van with you," I said to Lenny. "I need to check my mailbox." I whistled, and Bran bounded over to my side, delighted to be included in whatever action might occur.

Reynolds petted the dog, deftly angling himself to avoid being subjected to a groin investigation. "Hey, mate. How's my favorite amateur sleuth? Caught any more criminals lately?"

"Nope. I'm hoping our days of crime solving on Whisper Island are behind us. Right, Bran?"

The dog barked and sped ahead of us.

"I'll join you," Reynolds said, and he fell into step with Lenny and me as we headed toward the gates. I say "fell into step", but I had to hurry to keep up with the policeman's long strides, and judging by the glance I exchanged with Lenny, he had to do the same.

We reached the mailboxes just as the postman's green van drew up. Eddie Ward, Whisper Island's wannabe Lothario, hopped out of the vehicle and subjected me to a visual strip search that made me want to scrub myself with Lysol.

The guy was a sight to behold. He was tanned an unnatural shade of mahogany with slicked back Elvis-style dark hair. Winter and summer, rain and shine, he wore his summer postal worker's uniform of shorts and a T-shirt. He added a splash of individuality to the ensemble with his trademark mirrored wraparound sunglasses, chained medallion, and the cigarette that was permanently clenched between his teeth.

"Good morning, love." The man's dazzling white smile was as blinding as it was insincere. He nodded at Reynolds. "Hey, Sarge."

Lenny, apparently, didn't warrant a greeting. My instinctual dislike of the postman increased a notch.

"Eddie," I muttered, aware my greeting was barely civil, but not caring. Noreen had her mail delivered to a box at the Smuggler's Cove post office, so I'd managed to avoid Whisper Island's resident sleaze while I'd been living with her. Since moving to Shamrock Cottages, I'd been subjected to the postman's leers on a daily basis.

After Eddie had handed Reynolds his mail, the

postman pressed a wad of envelopes into my hand, making sure to let his fingers brush over my skin in a predatory fashion. I yanked my hand back and glared at him. "Keep your paws to yourself."

Eddie smirked. "I'm just being friendly."

"More like overly friendly," Reynolds said in a warning tone. "Watch it, Ward."

The postman appeared to be unperturbed by this rebuke. "All I did was give her the post. Just doing my job."

"I'm pretty sure your job description doesn't involve making my skin crawl. Does your technique ever work on women?" I held up a hand. "No, don't answer that. There's plenty of fools desperate enough to overlook your slime factor."

Eddie's leer didn't falter. "Why won't you go out with me, Maggie? What's the harm in going for a drink?"

"How about because you make me want to hurl? A drink—or any other social arrangement that involves me being alone with you—is never going to happen."

"You've delivered the post, Ward." Reynolds's granite expression matched his voice. "Time to move on to the next house."

Chuckling, Eddie winked at me, and then gave Sergeant Reynolds a wave. "See you tomorrow, gorgeous," he said as he swaggered back to his van. "Bye, Sarge."

After Eddie's van had disappeared down the road,

Lenny muttered something in Gaelic that I couldn't understand but which made Reynolds laugh out loud.

"No love lost between you two, eh?" Reynolds asked in amusement.

"No." Lenny drew the word out to give it maximum impact. "I can't stand the man."

"He seems to be popular with the ladies, though." Reynolds turned to me and frowned. "Apart from Maggie. Is Ward hassling you? Do you want me to have a word with him?"

"He's reptilian, but I can handle him." I shuddered at the memory of his fingers on my hand. "I can't believe any woman would fall for his slick act. It positively oozes with practiced insincerity."

"Plenty of women do fall for Ward's act," Lenny said, an edge to his tone. "More's the pity. Anyway, I'd better get moving. I'll swing by the Movie Theater Café later to help you set up for the Movie Club meeting."

"Thanks. I'd appreciate some help. Julie has parent-teacher meetings and can't get there before eight."

"In that case, I'll report for duty at seven." Lenny gave me a mock salute, and Reynolds a sheepish grin. "See you later, folks."

After Lenny had left, Reynolds and I strolled back up the drive to the cottages while Bran shot up the drive, darting to and fro. I flicked through my mail, and my stomach clenched when I recognized Joe's handwriting. It was the third letter from him that I'd received since moving to Whisper Island, and I dreaded reading yet another insincere apology from my ex.

I shoved the letters into my jacket pocket and quickened my step to keep up with my new neighbor, although I suspected he'd already shortened his long stride to accommodate me. Joe's letter seemed to burn a hole in my pocket. I both itched to open it and dreaded what it might contain.

"How's the move going?" I asked Reynolds, conscious of an awkward silence between us now that we were on our own, and keen to focus on a topic that wasn't my divorce.

"Slowly but surely. I put most of my stuff in storage before I took the job in Galway. Now that I'm moving to Whisper Island on a permanent basis, it's time to get it and unpack properly."

"Is this your stuff from Dublin?"

"What?" Liam glanced up in surprise. "No, I'm from Dublin originally, but I was living in London until I moved to Galway in November."

"London?" It was my turn to be surprised. "Were you with the British police?"

"Yeah. I worked for the Met." He correctly interpreted my blank stare. "The Metropolitan Police Service. The HQ was at New Scotland Yard until their recent move."

I whistled. Even I'd heard of Scotland Yard. "What branch did you work for?"

"I started in vice and then moved to homicide."

"Wait a sec..." I stopped short and stared at him. "You were a detective?"

Reynolds shrugged. "For a while."

"Why on earth would you give that up for a transfer to Whisper Island?"

"I didn't transfer. It doesn't work like that. The British and Irish police forces are completely separate. I joined An Garda Síochána straight out of university, and I worked for them for a couple of years. When I moved to London, I had to go through the regular recruitment and training channels to join the Met. When I moved back to Ireland and reapplied for a position with the Gardaí, I had to complete a short retraining course to get my old rank back."

This speech was the longest I'd heard him make. Since his arrival on Whisper Island a few weeks ago, Reynolds had proved to be a man of mystery. Even Noreen hadn't managed to pump much personal information out of the island's new police officer. And knowing my aunt, it wasn't for lack of trying on her part. I was not-so-subtly fishing for info. "Were you tired of policing London?"

He looked down at me from his several inches height advantage and gave me a half-smile. "That's one way of putting it. You're very curious, Ms. Doyle."

"I take after my aunts," I replied, unperturbed by

his reluctance to open up. I'd get his story out of him eventually. My thoughts drifted back to the letter burning a hole in my pocket. Even though I was relieved to be rid of Joe and his overbearing mother, I still felt sick every time I received letters or email about our impending divorce. They reminded me of the mess I'd made of my life at home in San Francisco.

"Are you okay, Maggie?" Reynolds asked gently. "Is Eddie Ward's pestering bothering you?"

"What?" I'd forgotten all about the postman. "Oh, no. Well, yes," I amended, "but I can handle Eddie."

"So what's up?"

I grimaced. "I got a letter from my ex."

"Ah," he said. "Your aunt mentioned you were getting a divorce."

"Yeah. We're haggling over money. The usual story." Not to mention Joe's whining apologies for cheating on me with his paralegal that managed to descend into accusations and recriminations within a couple of paragraphs.

"Divorce is never pleasant," Reynolds said softly. "I hope it all works out for you."

We'd reached the front door of my cottage. We stood awkwardly for a few seconds, and I wondered if I should invite him inside. Reynolds must have sensed my hesitation, because he said, "I'd better get back to my place and finish unpacking."

"Don't you need to go to the station today?"

"Yeah, but not for another couple of hours. Sergeant O'Shea is on duty this morning."

I laughed at the mention of my old nemesis. "How are you two coping now that you're in charge?"

Reynolds slid me an ironic look. "About as well as I'd expected."

"I guess he's not thrilled that he can't spend his days on the golf course anymore."

"He's not a bad sort," Reynolds said diplomatically. "But we have a different work ethic."

"Oh, come on. He's useless. Before you came, he left most of the real police work to the reserve garda."

"Gardaí," Reynolds corrected. "Garda is singular."

I scrunched up my nose. "I'll never get the hang of Gaelic."

"Doesn't your cousin teach an Irish evening class at the school? I'm thinking of taking it."

"Julie teaches several Gaelic classes. Or Irish, as you call it around here." I frowned. "But why would you need an Irish class? Didn't you learn it at school?"

"I did, but that was a long time ago, and my parents never spoke Irish at home."

"If I were staying longer, I'd consider taking one of Julie's classes, but if I'm leaving at the end of May, it hardly seems worth it."

The corners of his mouth twitched. "I noticed an 'if' in your second sentence. Are you sure you want to go back to San Francisco?"

"I... I'm not sure." I swallowed past the lump in my

throat and cursed the hot tears that stung my eyes at the thought of the hot mess I'd left behind me in San Francisco. "I can't hide out here forever."

"Hiding out? Is that what you think you're doing? From where I'm standing, it looks like you're building a new life for yourself." His eyes moved from me to my new car. "Buying a car...that says commitment to me."

This made me laugh. "That vehicle is a heap of rust. I only bought it because it was cheaper than renting one for three months."

"Ah, we'll see if you stay or if you go, Miss Doyle." Reynolds's eyes twinkled. "I've a feeling we'll be neighbors for a while yet."

Was it my imagination, or was he flirting with me? My cheeks grew warm at the thought. The last thing I needed at the moment was a romantic entanglement. Look how well that had worked out for me the last time. On the other hand, I'd have had to be dead not to notice how good looking the sergeant was. "Are you planning to stay on Whisper Island for good?"

He shrugged. "I'll see how it goes. 'For good' is a long time, but I can see myself settling down here for a few years."

"Are you looking to buy a place of your own?"

"I've put out a few feelers. I've rented this place until the summer, and I'll see what properties turn up between now and then." He grinned at me. "I still have to survive my probationary period, remember?"

"You'll be fine. The district superintendent likes

you. Besides," I added with a cheeky smile, "how many policemen would be crazy enough to volunteer for a job on an island that's frequently inaccessible for part of the year?"

"True enough." Reynolds nodded in the direction of his cottage. "I'd better get back to my boxes. Unless those eejit activists decide to hold another sheep fashion show, I should make it to your aunt's café in time for the film tonight."

My heart skipped a beat. "You're coming to a Movie Club meeting? I didn't think it would be your scene." As I spoke the words, I realized I had no idea what the sergeant's scene was.

"Ah, sure, I figure if I want to stay on Whisper Island, I'd better get to know some of the locals."

"And there's not much to do in the evenings except go to the pub, or attend one of the numerous club meetings," I added for him.

"As you say, Whisper Island is a quiet place. That's exactly why I moved here." He took a step toward his front door and gave me a bone-melting smile. "Have a good day, Maggie."

"You, too." My cheeks burned like a love-struck teenager's and I bolted back into the safety of my cottage.

THREE

Several times a week, I worked at my aunt's café on Smuggler's Cove's main thoroughfare. Noreen had renovated the old movie theater and transformed it into a charming café. The foyer served as the café and sported comfortable leather chairs around wooden tables that were each named after a vintage movie star. The concession stand now served as a bar, and included an impressive Italian coffee machine to make patrons a variety of caffeinated drinks. One Friday evening per month, my aunt opened the doors to the old movie theater and screened a vintage movie for the Movie Club members. Tonight, unfortunately, our hopes of watching *The Postman Always Rings Twice* were dwindling.

My aunt stared at the broken projector with a dejected expression on her usually cheerful face. "Is there no chance of getting it to work?"

Lenny unfurled his skinny body and stood up from where he'd been working on the Movie Theater Café's one and only movie projector, which was stubbornly refusing to cooperate. "No chance, I'm afraid. I'll have to take it to the mainland to get it fixed."

"I could take it next week," I said. "I need to shop for spring clothes."

"Can't you order clothes online?" Lenny looked genuinely baffled. "That's how I buy mine."

I stifled a grin. Lenny had probably been ordering the same make and model of jeans since we'd been teenagers. "I looked online, but I find your Irish sizes confusing. I'd prefer to try on stuff."

Lenny scratched his scraggly beard. "When were you planning to go? We could make a day of it. Maybe see if Julie wants to come with us."

"Come with you where?" My cousin stood in the doorway of the Movie Theater Café's tiny projector room, carrying a tray of cocktails. She'd pulled her wavy auburn hair into a loose bun tonight, drawing attention to the light dusting of freckles that brought color to her milky-white complexion. She raised the tray. "I thought you could do with a drink."

"You were right." I took two martini glasses and handed one to my aunt. "The projector is a bust," I explained to Julie. "Lenny is taking it to the mainland next week for repairs, and I'm going to join him and go shopping. Want to come along?"

"If it's a day I'm not working, sure. When were you thinking of going?"

"Thursday is the only day that'll work for me," Lenny said, taking a glass of lemonade from the tray. "I have to work every other day at my parents' shop."

Lenny's parents ran Whisper Island's one and only electronics store. In addition to working at the family store, Lenny supplemented his income by repairing computers on the side.

"I have a half day on Thursday because it's the day before St. Patrick's Day," Julie mused. "I could make the one o'clock ferry. Would that work for you?"

I looked at my aunt. Since moving to Whisper Island, I'd worked at Noreen's café several times a week. Thursday afternoon and evening was currently one of my shifts. "Could I swap a day with you, Noreen?"

"Sure. How about the Saturday after St. Patrick's Day? You're due to serve the Unplugged Gamers that evening in any case for their annual contest night."

The Unplugged Gamers, of which Lenny was president, met at the café every other Thursday to play board games and other tabletop games. As a way to earn a little extra money, my aunt had hit upon the idea of offering her café to the island's various clubs every evening. In return for using her premises free of charge, the club members agreed to buy food and drinks. Since my arrival on the island, I'd covered several of these club evening shifts, and I was a participating member of three clubs: the Movie Club, the Unplugged Gamers, and the Book Club. The Saturday event was an extra meeting, allegedly to hold a contest. As far as I could tell, we were using it as an excuse to party.

"Saturday is perfect," I said. "Thanks, Noreen. If you need anything from the mainland, let me know."

My aunt clucked her tongue. "Never mind what *I* need. What *you* need is a date. It's a pity Sergeant Reynolds is a no-show."

My stomach sank at this unwanted reminder. My disappointment at the sergeant's absence annoyed me more than the man's failure to appear. A harmless flirtation was one thing, but developing feelings for the guy was out of the question. "He's my neighbor. No more and no less."

"I'm hoping you'll persuade him to be more than a neighbor." My aunt beamed at me. "In the meantime, Philomena and I made a list of all the eligible bachelors on the island. We'd like you to have a look at it and see if one of them strikes your fancy."

"Oh, no." I took a step back and held up my hands. "No more matchmaking. I'm still recovering from your attempt to throw me and Paddy Driscoll together at the town hall dance."

Lenny snorted with laughter. "Watching you two stagger around the dance floor was priceless."

Even when he wasn't freaking out about Union Jacks and sheep dressed in acrylic coats, Paddy was grumpy. In addition to his antisocial attitude, he was old enough to be my father. I'd pointed this out to my aunts many times, but as far as they were concerned, the man owned land, and this automatically made him a great catch.

Noreen pulled a piece of folded-up paper from her purse. "At least consider the list, love. You don't have to marry one of them, but it's time you got back in the dating game."

"It's been barely three months since I left Joe," I said. "That experience has put me off relationships for quite some time."

"Promise me you'll think about it. That's all I ask."

I sighed. If I didn't agree to look at the list, she'd hound me day and night. "Okay. I'll read it, but that's all I'm promising. Deal?"

My aunt's face stretched into a smile. She thrust the list at me, and I took it gingerly, wary of its contents. Noreen glanced at her watch. "Well, if we can't screen the promised film, we can at least serve the Movie Club members cocktails."

I took the hint. "I'll start mixing."

"I'll help you," Julie said.

Out in the café, the club members were getting restless. Philomena, Julie's mother, stood behind the drinks counter, shaking cocktails like a pro. Like Noreen, her curly hair was cut short and dyed a color nature hadn't given her. But where her sister had opted for jet black, Philomena had chosen platinum blond.

Few people could pull off the look, but Philomena could.

"Did Lenny manage to fix the projector?" she asked when Julie and I slid behind the counter to join her.

"Unfortunately, no." I tied my apron in place and washed my hands at the sink. "We'll have to hope the club members are satisfied with cocktails instead."

"That's a shame," Miss Flynn said from the other side of the counter. "Milly and I were looking forward to watching *The Postman Always Rings Twice* again. We haven't seen it in years."

Miss Flynn and her friend, Miss Murphy, were regular patrons of the Movie Theater Café and known as the Spinsters. Both in their sixties, the women wore their iron-gray hair pulled back into tight buns and favored tweed twinsets offset by pearl necklaces. The Spinsters were retired schoolteachers and shared a house in Smuggler's Cove. From my first days working at the café, I'd liked them, and I was grateful for their help in teaching me how to make a proper cup of tea.

"Lenny is bringing the projector to the mainland to be repaired," I said. "Hopefully, we'll be able to watch the film at the next meeting. In the meantime, can I make you a drink?"

Miss Flynn's lined face lit up. "I'd love one of those sidecar things you made me at the last meeting. And Millie likes the frothy white ones with the pineapple."

I smiled. "One sidecar and one pina colada coming right up."

The rest of the evening passed in a flurry of chopping fruit and shaking cocktails. Once they'd been supplied with drinks and Noreen's delicious sandwiches and baked goods, the Movie Club members were able to roll with the disappointment of the canceled movie. By the time the meeting broke up at ten, my arms were tired from shaking, and my feet ached in my high-heeled shoes. I loved making an effort and following the Movie Club's tradition of formal dress, but I wasn't used to standing in fancy shoes for long periods of time.

"That went well," my cousin said when we were loading the dishwasher.

"Yeah. We dodged a bullet through bribing them with sugar and alcohol. I only wish that trick worked to stop Noreen and your mother from trying to matchmake me with every single man on Whisper Island." Especially when the only man I was interested in hadn't bothered to show up. "Can you believe they made me a list? Why aren't they trying to matchmake you?"

Julie gave a half laugh. "They've given me up as a lost cause."

"No way. You're a much more likely candidate than me. You're settled on the island, and you want to stay."

My cousin rolled her eyes. "Mum's hoping I'll get

together with Günter. That will never fly."

"He's a nice guy," I said, "and intelligent."

She shrugged. "Günter and I rub each other the wrong way. Besides, the two times I gave in and let Mum and Noreen set me up on a date, they were disastrous. Never again. Maybe I'm not the relationship type."

"What about all the training you've been doing for the Runathon?" I asked, referring to the charity race that would be held on St. Patrick's Day. "Wasn't that for the hunky gym teacher's benefit?"

My cousin's face fell. "Oisin's gone on four dates with Mandy Keogh."

Ouch. "Is she the leggy blond barmaid from the pub?"

"Exactly," Julie said gloomily. "I don't stand a chance. She's everything I'm not: blond, tall, and thin."

"Don't give up. Oisin doesn't even know you're interested in him."

"That's not the point," she said. "I want him to be interested in *me*. I don't intend to run after him."

"Says the woman who goes out training every second morning for a race. If that's not running after Oisin, I don't know what is."

My cousin grinned. "Let's have a look at that list, just for a laugh."

"I'm not sure I want to know who's on there," I said, but handed it over.

Julie scanned the piece of paper and burst out

laughing. "Oh, no. Poor Maggie. There's not a man on the list who's under forty-five. They've even included Aaron Nesbitt."

"Ugh." I shuddered. The owner of Whisper Island's only law firm was a nice enough guy, but he had to be old enough to be my father. "Shred that list, please."

Still laughing, Julie put the list of not-so-eligible bachelors into the paper recycling container. "Listen, I was wondering if you wanted to join me at the hotel spa for a massage tomorrow afternoon. My parents got me a gift certificate for my last birthday. There's enough money on the card to cover two massages, and they had a cancellation."

I was touched that my cousin had thought of inviting me. Reconnecting with Julie and my other Irish relatives and friends had been the highlight of my stay on the island. Okay, given that a chunk of my time here had been spent investigating a murder, my friends and family hadn't exactly had stiff competition in the 'best-of' category. "I'd love to join you, but are you sure you don't want to save the second massage for yourself?"

Julie shook her head, making one of her curls escape the confines of the bun "I need to use the gift certificate before it expires. Besides, I'd rather have company. It'll make the whole experience more fun."

"In that case, I'd be honored to come along. What time have you booked the massages?"

"Four o'clock. That gives me enough time to pack up my stuff at the school and drive to the Whisper Island Hotel."

"You're working on a Saturday?"

Julie scrunched up her nose. "Yeah. I have a pile of paperwork to get through, and I'd rather not haul it all home. Plus I need to prep for my class's spring play. We should have started rehearsals last week, but I'm running behind."

"Sounds like you need the massage."

My cousin sighed. "Tell me about it. It's the typical scenario of more paperwork and extracurricular requirements for teachers, but no extra pay. So will the four o'clock slot work for you?"

"Perfectly. I'm at the café until three, and Kelly is due to stay until closing." I dropped my voice, in case Noreen overheard. "I'm actually looking around for another job, so if you hear of one, let me know."

Julie's eyes widened. "Do you want to quit the café? I thought you were happy working here."

"I am, but I suspect Noreen is inventing work for me. This time of year, the Movie Theater Café isn't busy enough to justify the number of shifts she's giving me. Besides, I could do with some extra cash. I spent the last of my savings on a car, and I'd like to pick up more work to make ends meet."

"I suppose," my cousin began carefully, "divorce doesn't come cheap."

"That's an understatement. At least my lawyer has

agreed to wait for the rest of her money until after Joe and I reach a settlement."

Julie frowned. "How long is that going to take?"

"Joe is fighting me over every cent. I'm pretty sure he thinks I'll roll over and agree to whatever lousy settlement he offers if he keeps up the pressure. Then the next minute, he's sending me maudlin love letters that contain more digs about my failings as a wife than apologies for cheating on me."

"Swine," Julie muttered.

"That's an insult to pigs everywhere," I said dryly. "But to sum up, until I get my divorce settlement, I'm low on funds. And frankly, I don't intend to rely on that money. I'd rather find a job."

"Aren't you supposed to be having a holiday? Some time to reassess your life?"

My lips twisted ironically. "I don't think I know how to take a real vacation. I like to be active, and I want to feel useful. And I can't let Noreen invent work for me. She can't afford it."

"Do you have any idea what sort of job you'd like to do?"

"I'm not picky. I'm not looking for a new and fulfilling career for the couple of months I have left on the island. Just a part-time job that'll bring in some cash and keep me busy."

"I can't think of anything off the top of my head," Julie said, "but I'll let you know if I hear of anyone looking to hire staff."

"I know it's a bad time of year to be looking for work on the island, but I can still try."

"Absolutely. You'd have better luck during the tourist season, but I'm sure something will turn up."

A knock drew my attention to the kitchen door. Lenny lounged in the doorway, wearing the ill-fitting suit he always wore to club meetings, and that I suspected had once been his father's—circa nineteen seventy-five. "Are you ready to go, Maggie?" he asked. "Noreen's decided to stay overnight with Philomena, so she's having another drink. I've offered to drive you home."

"Are you sure? I don't want to send you on a wild ride around the island when you live so close to the café."

"Actually, I told my grandfather I'd spend the night at his place, and he's not far from you. He's a bit freaked out after those activists broke into his cowshed."

"I can understand that, but don't your brother and cousin live nearby? Can't they look out for him?"

"Carl's working late at the hotel." Lenny pulled a face. "As for Jack...he comes and goes. Even when he's at home, he and granddad aren't close. The only reason they live near each other is that Jack inherited the land from his father. Up until his father died, he lived all over the place doing goodness knows what to earn a living."

"Jack strikes me as the kind of guy who's not fussy

about where his money comes from." I switched on the dishwasher and straightened. "Thanks for the offer of a ride. I'll just grab my bag from behind the counter, and I'll be ready to go."

After we'd said goodbye to my aunts and Julie, Lenny and I exited the Movie Theater Café and ran the short distance to where Lenny's VW van was parked in front of his parents' electronics store. A strong wind had blown in from the sea in the couple of hours since I'd arrived at the café, and rain lashed down, soaking us before we'd reached the van.

"Looks like the weather forecast got it wrong again," Lenny said when we were in the vehicle. "The storm wasn't supposed to hit the island until tomorrow afternoon."

A bolt of lightning zigzagged across the night sky, accompanied by a roar of thunder. Out in the bay, the waves crashed and foamed against the rocks with a ferocity I'd last seen the night Günter Hauptmann's houseboat had been destroyed.

"I'll be glad to be snug in my bed tonight," I said after I'd buckled my seat belt.

"Same here. Although my bed is likely to be a sleeping bag in granddad's spare room."

"What exactly did the activists do to your grandfather's cows?" I asked after we'd passed the school on the edge of town.

"They spray-painted the walls with anti-cattle farming slogans, and scared the cows. The eejits apparently can't tell the difference between dairy farming and beef farming."

"I'm sorry to hear they gave your grandfather a fright." Gerry Logan was another semi-permanent fixture at the café, along with his friend, also called Gerry. I was fond of the old man, and I hated to think of him being terrorized.

"That's the part that bothers me most," Lenny said. "I agree with many of the sentiments expressed by the activists, but I don't like them going around invading people's property and scaring old men."

We drove out of Smuggler's Cove and took the road that led to the other side of the island. The side I lived on was the less populated area of Whisper Island. Half of the population lived in the small town of Smuggler's Cove and its outskirts, and the rest of the island's inhabitants were scattered around the island on farms or other small homesteads. The cottage where I lived was in an area populated with sheep farmers, apart from Noreen. It took us thirty minutes to drive there, with Lenny's windshield wipers working overtime. When we reached a sharp curve in the winding cliffside road that led toward Shamrock Cottages, Lenny braked hard.

"Whoa," he said. "What lunatic parks in the middle of the road?"

I eyed the vehicle's lights with trepidation. "Pull over. I think something's wrong. Maybe they've broken down."

"They could at least have pushed the car to the side of the road," Lenny muttered. "I almost drove into them."

My friend pulled his van into the ditch and killed the engine. After tossing my high-heeled shoes into the back of the van, I jumped out and ran down the road. The heavy rain ran down my face in rivulets, and the wind almost blew me off my feet. When I neared the other vehicle, I recognized the logo of An Post, the Irish postal service. "Lenny," I shouted over the roar of the storm. "It's the mail van. No one's in the driver's seat."

The van's lights lit up the road, making me shield my eyes from their glare. An icy fear snaked down my spine. I had a bad feeling about this. I leaned in the open driver's door and scanned the vehicle. All I gleaned from my cursory search was that Eddie Ward kept his work van tidy and that he had a penchant for a particularly vile brand of chewing gum.

My brow furrowed, I straightened and edged my way toward the cliff. Cautious not to go too close to the edge, I peered down at the crashing waves below. Despite the storm, the full moon helped me to see more than I otherwise could have. I scanned the beach. And then I spotted the sight I'd hoped not to see. I tasted bile. "Call an ambulance, Lenny. And the police. There's a body at the bottom of the cliff."

FOUR

Despite his shocked expression, Lenny didn't waste time. He'd whipped out his phone and hit the button for emergency services before I'd had a chance to repeat myself. He explained the situation to the dispatcher and rattled off our location like a pro. After he'd disconnected, he came to join me at the edge of the cliff. We stared down at the broken remains of the Whisper Island postman. I shivered and drew my jacket tight around my chest. Even at this distance, the moonlight illuminated the man's familiar uniform. Who else would be crazy enough to wear shorts in Ireland in March?

Lenny swore beneath his breath. "He looks pretty dead to me."

"Yeah, but we still have to try to get down there," I said grimly. "The tide's coming in."

Lenny jerked around and stared at me in horror.

"Are you mad? We can't go climbing down the cliff. You're not even wearing shoes. Why don't we wait for the paramedics?"

"We can't risk the tide washing the body out to sea. Is there any way to get down the cliff fast?" I asked. "Excluding the route Eddie Ward took."

Lenny, used to my dry humor, didn't flinch. "If we walk farther along the road, there's a metal staircase the fishermen used to use. This spot was popular for mooring boats before Carraig Harbour was built in the Seventies."

I didn't hesitate. "Get the flashlight out of your van," I yelled over my shoulder while I sprinted toward the spot Lenny had pointed out. "And the first aid kit, just in case."

For a guy who didn't look particularly sporty, Lenny was surprisingly fast. I'd just reached the first step of the rickety staircase when he jogged over to join me, carrying a flashlight in one hand and a red first aid kit in the other. "This is madness, Maggie. The staircase doesn't look stable. I'm not sure it's still in use."

"Surely the council would have taken it down if it posed a risk?"

Lenny snorted. "This is Ireland. The wheels of bureaucracy turn slowly. For all we know, that staircase was condemned years ago, and no one's gotten around to removing it yet."

I peered down the metal staircase. I'd used a

similar staircase down to Carraig Harbour, but this one was visibly older, and a storm was raging. I took a cautious step onto the first landing, and it creaked in a menacing fashion beneath my stockinged feet. If I wore them down the steps, I'd slip. Swallowing past my fear, I pulled off the stockings and used one to tie my hair into a messy bun to stop the wind from blowing it into my face and blinding me.

"This is a bad idea, Maggie."

I shot Lenny a haughty look. "Then stay up here and wait for the emergency services. I'm going down." I held out a hand for the flashlight and first aid kit.

He sighed. "If you're going down, I'm coming with you. Just don't blame me if we're washed out to sea."

In my haste to reach the stairs, I'd shoved from my mind the potential danger of walking over the rocks while the tide was coming in. As we descended, the precariousness of the situation on the beach became more apparent with each step. I clung to the railings, exhaled my trepidation, and forced one foot in front of the other. Something about the death scene bugged me, and I couldn't pinpoint what. But when I had a hunch this strong, I was rarely wrong.

The climb down to the beach took us ten minutes, by which time the body was partially covered by water.

"We've got to get out of here," Lenny said the instant we stepped onto the slippery rocks. "The man's dead. There's nothing you or I can do for him until the ambulance gets here."

"I know he's dead," I said through chattering teeth, "but the sea is almost covering the body. He'll be washed away if we don't move him."

"Sergeant Reynolds will bust a gut if we go around moving dead bodies."

"In this case, I think he'll understand. If we don't shift him now, Reynolds will have to dispatch a search team, or wait and hope the body washes up on a beach somewhere. Besides, we don't know *how* Ward died."

"I'd say that's pretty obvious," Lenny said, frowning. "Dude jumped."

"Or slipped." I hesitated before voicing my true concern. "Or he was pushed. We can't rule anything out yet."

Lenny lost his footing and stumbled into me, almost sending us both crashing into the sea. My heart leaped in my chest, but we managed to stay upright.

"Seriously, Maggie. We need to turn around. Jeez, if *I'm* the voice of reason, you know it's got to be bad."

Despite the gravity of the situation, a bubble of laughter escaped me. Lenny had a point. An occasional stoner and a dedicated UFO spotter, he wasn't usually the kind of guy to shy away from the absurd.

"We'll move fast and be out of here in no time." I shone the flashlight over the beach and picked my way over wet rocks made slippier by seaweed. After a few minutes, and several stumbles, we reached the spot where the postman lay sprawled face down with his head at an unnatural angle.

"I think I'm going to be sick," Lenny said. Despite his obvious trepidation, he didn't slow down, and he didn't turn back. He might not be a typical alpha male, but the guy had guts.

I crouched down by the body and checked for vital signs on autopilot, even though I knew there'd be none. With the aid of the flashlight, I scanned the area around the body but could see no signs of a discarded weapon or any object that pointed to the postman's death not being the result of a fall from the cliff. Freezing seawater sloshed over my feet. "I'll use my phone to take photos, and then we'll move the body."

"I hate to break it to you, Maggie, but this isn't an Instagram moment."

"Don't you watch *CSI*? The photos are for the police. I want them to see where he fell."

"I'm more into the stuff they show on the Syfy channel," Lenny said. "Give me space ships and alien goo over cops and crime scenes any day."

"You're getting the real deal tonight, I'm afraid."

Lenny groaned. "Ugh. I can't imagine having a job where I had to look at those sorts of photos every day."

I took a few shots and then shoved my phone back into my pocket. "Grab a leg. We'll drag him farther up the beach."

Between us, Lenny and I managed to haul the sea-soaked body a few feet closer to the cliff wall. Over the roar of the waves and the wind, I identified the sound of approaching sirens.

"I think Mack is on duty tonight," Lenny said.

"I hope so. I'd be glad to see a friendly face after this experience." Mack McConnell, the town pharmacist and Lenny's longtime friend, volunteered with the island's paramedic service. "Can you give him a call and let him know we're down on the beach?"

"I can try. The signal out here can be dodgy at the best of times, and tonight is *not* the best of times."

But Lenny was in luck. By the time he finished filling in Mack as to our whereabouts, the tide was inching toward us.

"We can't wait for them to get down here." I nodded in the direction of the metal staircase. "Do you think we can manage to haul the body up to the first landing?"

Lenny exhaled in a sigh. "We can try, but the dude's a deadweight. Literally."

After much huffing and puffing, we dragged the postman up twenty steps to the first landing before collapsing in a heap.

"I'm going to need a shot of my grandfather's *poitín* after this," Lenny said, using the Gaelic pronunciation of poteen. "And a couple more before I call my sister."

"Your sister?" I blinked in confusion and dredged up a memory of a skinny little girl with braids. I hadn't seen her since I'd been back on Whisper Island, nor heard any mention of her whereabouts. To be honest, until Lenny had mentioned her tonight, I'd forgotten she existed. "Katie, isn't it? She must be in her early twenties by now."

"She's nineteen," Lenny muttered. "And a new mother."

"I take it that isn't good news?"

Lenny snorted. "Hardly. Katie was studying at the University of Bath in England, but she dropped out last summer." He glared down at Eddie Ward's corpse, which was currently wedged between us with his backside in the air in an undignified fashion. "That was after she found out she was pregnant by this sack of excrement."

My stomach lurched. "Oh, no."

"Oh, yes." Lenny's bitterness flavored every syllable. "And seeing as I'm the only family member she currently still speaks to, I'm going to have to break the bad news to her."

I performed a rapid calculation. "When was the baby born?"

Lenny nodded, and his expression under the pale moonlight was grim. "Two weeks ago. A little boy named Ryan."

I stole a glance at the corpse, and my stomach heaved at the sight of the now-smashed face that I'd seen whole just this morning. "Poor kid. Poor Katie."

"She'll cope," Lenny said. "She's strong. I just wish my parents hadn't fallen out with her. It wasn't so much the pregnancy that upset them but her decision to drop out of university."

"She can always go back once the baby is a little older."

He shot me a look. "We both know how hard that'll be."

"But not impossible."

A shout from above drew our attention to the clifftop. Two men in reflective gear waved down to us.

"Can you help us get the body up?" I yelled, but the wind whipped my words out to sea. I made hand gestures and pointed to the body.

"Looks like they got the message," Lenny said as the two men climbed down the rickety stairs.

The paramedics' descent seemed to take forever. Now that the adrenaline had worn off, I was shivering uncontrollably, and my damp coat wasn't doing its job. Although the weather was warmer than it had been when I'd first arrived on the island, the nights were still cold, and tonight's rain and wind had ensured that my bones now ached.

Mack was the first to reach us. I was so glad to see his familiar orange goatee that I could have hugged him. The pharmacist's eyes widened when he registered the body that lay slumped between Lenny and me. "What happened? Did you find him *here*?"

"He was at the bottom of the cliff. We had to move him," I said wearily, "or he'd have been washed out to sea."

"Smart thinking." Mack crouched by the body and

felt for a pulse. After a minute, he shook his head. "He's been dead for a while, I'd say."

"No kidding," I said dryly. "Only a superhero could survive a fall from that height."

The second paramedic loomed over Mack. To my astonishment, I recognized the man as Günter Hauptmann, the weird German guy who'd lived year-round on a houseboat until his home had been smashed during a storm a couple of weeks previously. He was currently sleeping in my aunt Philomena's spare room, much to Julie's annoyance.

"*You're* a paramedic?" The words had left my mouth before I became aware of how rude they sounded.

"Yeah. I trained as a nurse in Germany." Günter's gaze moved to the dead man. "Seeing as you've already moved him from the spot where he landed, let's get the body up to the top of the cliff. I got a text from Sergeant Reynolds to say he'd be here in five."

I breathed a sigh of relief when the two paramedics carried the postman the rest of the way up the staircase. Lenny and I staggered up behind them, with my teeth chattering from the cold. By the time we reached the top, Sergeant Reynolds had arrived. He kneeled by the corpse and examined the dead man carefully.

The fall had smashed Eddie Ward's tanned face beyond recognition. Acid burned in my stomach, and Lenny sidled closer to me, his Adam's apple bobbing.

Reynolds glanced up when Lenny and I approached, and our eyes locked. The policeman shook his head. "I should have known you would be involved, Maggie. You're a magnet for trouble."

In my drenched and frozen state, I was in no mood to be chastised for a situation that wasn't my fault. "Believe it or not, I don't plan to find dead bodies."

"And yet this is the second corpse you've tripped over in the two months you've been on Whisper Island."

All of Reynolds's flirty friendliness from this morning had evaporated, leaving a razor-sharp edge to his tone. He was doing his job. I knew that. Had our roles been reversed, I'd have also questioned the coincidence of the same person on a small island finding two dead bodies in short succession. All the same, his tone rankled.

"Given that I spotted Ward at the bottom of a cliff, I hardly tripped over his body." I put my hands on my hips and glared at the man. "Are you accusing me of something, sergeant? If not, I'd like to go home and get out of my wet clothes."

Liam Reynolds's hard expression softened, and he rubbed his stubbled jaw. Even under the moonlight, the shadows beneath his eyes were visible. "I'm sorry, Maggie. It's been a long day, and the last thing I expected was a dead body to deal with."

"Rough night?" I raised an eyebrow. "I thought you were pretty sure you'd make the Movie Club meeting."

His jaw clenched. "I was. Until Jimmy Wright found a young animal rights activist being chased by one of his prize bulls."

I wrapped my arms around my freezing body. "What happened?"

"The only way Wright could prevent the bull from trampling the young eejit to death was by shooting it."

I shuddered. "How horrible. The poor bull."

"Yeah. All because a young, privileged fool didn't have the sense to stay away from farm animals." Reynolds stood and eyed my damp clothes. His gaze moved to Lenny, who looked equally wet and uncomfortable. "You two had better go home and get dry. Could you drop by the station first thing tomorrow morning to give your statements? If the storm gets worse and I have to work through the night, one of the reserves will be there."

"Don't you need to question us right away?" I demanded. "After all, this could be a murder inquiry. I took photos before we moved Ward's body."

A hint of irritation tinged Sergeant Reynolds's weary expression. "It looks like a cut-and-dried case of suicide to me. Ward left a note in his van."

I frowned. "I didn't see a note in the van when I checked."

In the background, the animal rights activist started yelling in the police car. Liam muttered something rude under his breath and marched over to the car. He yanked the back door open to reveal a dreadlocked young man with pale, freckled skin, and a petulant pout that his lip ring only served to accentuate. "You can't keep me here all night," the guy shouted. "This is police brutality. I want to speak to my solicitor."

"You'll have plenty of time to speak to your solicitor when we get to the station," Liam said irritably. "Until then, I don't want to hear another word out of you."

"You can't leave me in the car while you swan off with your friends." The young man's whine reached a crescendo. "I have rights."

"Yeah," Reynolds said in a low growl, "and so does the man who was just brought up from the bottom of the cliff. Strange as it may sound to your entitled ears, you're not my number one priority right now. Deal with it." With these words, he slammed the car door and marched back to us, a deep frown line between his brows. "You say you didn't see the suicide note, Maggie. How closely did you look?"

I cast my mind back. Before I'd run to the staircase, I'd checked the postal van to see if someone was in there, but I hadn't opened the glove compartment or searched the side pockets. I'd been looking for a person, not a note. "Where did you find the note?"

"On the dashboard."

"That's weird." I scrunched up my forehead and replayed the moments before I saw the body at the bottom of the cliff. "I checked the van before we went down to the beach. I'm sure I'd have noticed a note."

"You can't have looked in the van for more than a few seconds," Lenny interjected. "You were moving pretty fast."

"I guess." But I wasn't convinced. Yes, I'd scanned the van quickly, but my years in the San Francisco PD had taught me to pick up pertinent details fast. I hadn't seen a note on the dashboard, and that was the sort of thing that should have stood out. "Isn't it possible that someone put the note in the van after Lenny and I went down to the beach?"

Reynolds squeezed his eyes shut and massaged his temples. "It's possible, but unlikely."

"You'll need to pursue it," I said, "and get the van dusted for fingerprints and checked for other evidence. Have you called Dr. Reilly?"

"Dr. Reilly is at a conference in Cork. Günter will have a look at the body when we get him to the Whisper Island Medical Centre."

"What about calling in a forensics team?"

The policeman sighed and shook his head. "Go home, Maggie, and let me do my job. I'll see you at the station tomorrow morning. You too, Logan."

I opened my mouth to protest, but Lenny cut me off before I could begin. "Let's go, Maggie. You have no shoes, and we're both freezing. We don't want to get sick."

"Okay, I'll go. If you want me to give my statement

tomorrow, it'll have to be early. I need to open the café at eight o'clock."

"In that case, come to the station at seven," Reynolds said. "And bring your phone with the photos. Can Kelly get the café set up without you?" Kelly was the schoolgirl who worked at the Movie Theater Café on Friday afternoons and on Saturdays, as well as on occasions when we needed extra staff.

"Yeah. She'll be okay." I cast a last look at the smashed remains of Eddie Ward. A memory nagged at me but remained an elusive sliver. Why did I feel something wasn't right about the body? Was it the position he'd been lying in at the bottom of the cliff? Something about the postal van when I'd looked in? How could I have missed seeing the note on the dashboard? It didn't make sense.

We said our goodbyes to Reynolds and the paramedics, and Lenny dragged me back in the direction of his VW van. On the way, we neared the abandoned postal van. Its headlights blazed a trail of light that made me shield my eyes.

"Don't even think about it, Maggie," Reynolds yelled after my retreating form. "Don't touch Ward's van."

I bit back a snappy retort and slid Lenny a look of exasperation. He was laughing silently. "Reynolds has your number, that's for sure."

I muttered something uncharitable about my new

neighbor under my breath, but followed Lenny back to his van.

A couple of minutes later, we resumed our interrupted journey to Shamrock Cottages. I slumped in the passenger seat, brooding over the evening's events. "Why was Ward still wearing his uniform? Surely he was off duty at this time of night?"

"I have no idea," Lenny said. "Maybe the storm delayed him. He usually goes over to the mainland on the ferry and catches the last one back to the island, but I doubt the ferry was running in this storm."

This was possible. Ward could have been delayed. I didn't know the rules of the Irish postal service, but there could well be a clause that Ward had to wear his uniform whenever he drove the postal van.

I moved to the next point that was troubling me. "Why did he leave his van in the middle of the road? It makes no sense. I can understand him leaving the lights on if he'd pulled over and didn't want anyone to run into him, but abandoning the van just around a bend is weird."

"Ah, Maggie. You're looking for intrigue where there is none. Why can't you accept that the man took his own life? Sergeant Reynolds said Ward left a note."

"Did he strike you as depressed when he was flirting with me earlier? Did he seem in any way out of character?"

"No, but maybe it was a spur-of-the-moment

decision." He sounded doubtful. "Some people hide their feelings well."

We drove through the gates of Shamrock Cottages. Lenny came to a halt outside my cottage and killed the engine. His eyebrows were drawn close together, and he appeared to be lost in thought.

I reached across the gearbox and squeezed his hand. "Are you going to call your sister tonight?"

He shook his head. "Tomorrow. I'll let her sleep. Insofar as any new mother can sleep."

"Was she still in love with Ward?"

Lenny shrugged. "Hard to tell. She says she hates him. Even if that's true, he was still the father of her child."

I opened the passenger door and climbed out. "Thanks for the ride. Say hi to your grandfather for me."

My friend forced a smile. "Will do. Talk tomorrow, Maggie."

I watched him drive away. When the van lights disappeared into the distance, I pulled my key from my purse and stepped toward my cottage. And froze. In the corner of my eye, an anomaly snagged my attention. I turned to my left and surveyed the semicircle of neatly spaced cottages, finally settling my attention on Number Four. I blinked slowly. Was it my imagination, or was the cottage's front door ajar? Apart from me in Number Eight and Reynolds in Number Seven, the cottages were empty.

Before prudency could conquer curiosity, I strode across the courtyard to Number Four. Sure enough, the front door was slightly open. I swallowed past my trepidation. "Hello?" I called. "Is anyone there?"

The only response was deafening silence.

Taking a deep breath, I pushed the door open and groped for the light switch I knew would be just inside the door—all the cottages in the complex had a layout identical to mine. Light flooded the hallway. I searched each room, but they were empty. Finally, I stepped into the kitchen. The back door was wide open, and the automatic floodlights illuminated the small backyard. My heart in my throat, I went out onto the deck and scanned my surroundings. The only movement was the trees swaying in the wind. I gave a last look around the yard and went back inside the cottage.

After I'd made sure that every door and window was closed, I left Number Four and headed back to my own cottage. Maybe the wind had blown open the doors. All the same, I'd let the rental company know tomorrow.

I unlocked my front door and stepped inside to the welcoming warmth of my new home. Bran raced to greet me. "Boy, am I glad to see you." I reached down to pet the dog. Although Noreen's determination to saddle me with a pet hadn't thrilled me at the time, tonight I was grateful not to be alone. I suspected I'd relent to Bran's inevitable whining and let him sleep at the foot of my bed.

Shivering, I stripped off my wet jacket. Time for a bath and a mug of hot chocolate to warm me up, followed by bed. I had a sinking feeling that my dreams would be haunted by the memory of Ward's crumpled body, and of cottage doors open when they should be locked.

FIVE

As I'd feared, I slept badly. The storm raged all night and contributed to my tossing and turning. In the morning, I dragged myself to the police station and went through the motions of giving the reserve policeman my statement. The man was alone at the station—the storm had kept Reynolds and the emergency services busy all night, dealing with fallen trees and car accidents. When I'd offered to give him the photos, he'd appeared flustered. In the end, I forwarded them to Reynolds's phone and left for my shift at the café.

The next seven hours passed in a blur of coffee cups and trays of scones. By the time I pulled into the parking lot of the Whisper Island Hotel at four o'clock, I was tired enough to fall asleep on the massage table. I found a free spot beside my cousin's car, unbuckled my seat belt, and stretched my neck from side to side. I couldn't remember the last time I'd treated myself to some pampering. On my honeymoon, probably.

When I got out of the Ford, Julie's eyes stood out on stalks. "Where on earth did you get that car?" Her eyes widened further when she registered the sticker I had yet to remove from the back windshield. "You went to Zippy Motors?"

"They're cheap, and I figure I can bully Jack Logan into replacing the car if it conks out on me."

My cousin blew out her cheeks. "What was wrong with the place you visited on the mainland? Kerrigan's Motors has an excellent reputation."

"They have prices to match their reputation," I said dryly. "Frankly, Zippy's sad and sorry fleet is all I can afford at the moment."

We crossed the gravel courtyard and went through the revolving door to the lobby. Although I'd been to the hotel a couple of times during a recent murder investigation, this was the first time that could be classified as a visit. The Whisper Island Hotel aspired to old-school elegance and had the five-star price tag to prove it. Located in an impressive nineteenth-century building, the hotel consisted of four floors over a basement. In addition to ornamental gardens, the hotel grounds boasted a lake, as well as access to a golf course that it shared with the Whisper Island Golf Club.

Inside, marble flooring stretched all the way to a winding staircase, whose cream-carpeted steps led to the guest rooms upstairs. The reception desk was polished mahogany with brass edgings. Except for the blond girl at reception, the place was deserted. Not surprising at this time of year, but probably not good news for the hotel's owners.

Julie strode up to the counter. "Hey, Lisa. We have aromatherapy massages booked for four."

Lisa's pink manicured nails clicked over the keyboard. "That's right," she said in a clipped English accent. "You're with Sven, and your cousin's with Marcus. Have you been to our spa and beauty center before?"

Julie and I shook our heads.

"I'll show you the way." The receptionist stood and led us out of the lobby and down a corridor to the right of the reception desk. "The spa is located in the east wing of the hotel, next to the swimming pool." Lisa's heels clicked over the marble floor. Despite her good looks and polished appearance, the receptionist's rigid posture and minimal facial expressions reminded me of the android in one of my favorite space opera novels.

As we followed Lisa, the tantalizing aroma of essential oils wafted down the hallway to greet us. The tension in my shoulders eased a fraction, and my breathing deepened.

Lisa ushered us into an elegant waiting room and gestured to a table topped with a porcelain teapot and matching cups and saucers. She gave us a tight smile, making me wonder how far up her behind she'd shoved the proverbial poker. "Marcus and Sven will be with you shortly," she said. "Help yourselves to some Ayurvedic tea while you wait."

"Talk about uptight," I said after Lisa had left. "She needs a massage more than we do."

Julie laughed. "Lisa's not a bad sort. She's taking my beginner's Irish class on Tuesday evenings, so I've gotten to know her a bit." My cousin poured us each a cup of the warm amber liquid and handed me one. "This place is fancier than I expected."

"Haven't you been inside the hotel before?"

"Only to the restaurant. One of Lenny's brothers is the head chef, and he gave Lenny a gift certificate last Christmas."

I cast my mind back to long-ago summers. "The brother with all the tattoos, right? Lenny said he worked at the hotel."

Julie blushed to the roots of her auburn hair. "Carl, yes."

"Hey, I saw that blush. Didn't you have a crush on Carl when we were teenagers?"

"Yes, but he never noticed I was alive." My cousin sat beside me on the low sofa and cradled her teacup. "Not much has changed."

"If I recall correctly, Carl went through women like most people go through hot dinners. I don't think you're missing much."

I took a sip of my tea. Not bad, even if I didn't like fancy brews. I'd barely had the chance to take three sips when two men strode through the door that separated the waiting area from the treatment rooms beyond. The first was tall and movie-star handsome. He treated us to a wide smile that revealed very white teeth. For an instant, an image of Eddie Ward's slick smile flashed through my mind, and my mood took a nosedive.

"I'm Marcus," the tall man said in halting English, extending a hand to me. "I'll be your massage therapist today."

When he held my hand a fraction of a second too long, the resemblance to the dead postman intensified. I looked longingly past Marcus to the dapper little man who was currently pumping Julie's hand and introducing himself as Sven. I wasn't in the mood to deal with a charmer today, especially one who reminded me of last night's traumatic events.

Julie glanced my way, and I forced a smile for her benefit. "Trust you to get the hot one," she whispered as Marcus and Sven led us down a narrow hallway.

"As far as I'm concerned, you can have him," I whispered back.

The men stopped in front of a door at the end of the hallway. Marcus opened the door to reveal a large room that was delicately scented with lavender and orange blossom. I exhaled in relief when I saw the two massage tables, side by side. With Julie lying next to me, deflecting Marcus's charm offensive would be easier.

Julie and I undressed in the changing cubicle and

returned to the massage therapists dressed in towels that felt far too short. I tugged at the hem of my towel, wishing it revealed less thigh. My cousin appeared to be unfazed at exposing so much flesh to two strange men. She jumped up on her massage table and lay on her stomach, an expectant smile on her face.

Shooting Marcus a wary glance, I followed suit.

Before the massage began, Julie and I chose the scent combination we wanted, and we both opted for a lavender and orange blossom blend.

"A good choice," Sven said. "We use only organic beauty products here, and that includes our essential oils. I'll only work at beauty centers that use natural products made from ethically obtained ingredients."

I tried to relax on the massage table, but failed. My reservations about the situation dimmed the instant Marcus began massaging my tense shoulders. "Mmm," I moaned, surrendering to the moment. Marcus might be a flirt, but the guy knew his stuff when it came to massage.

As he worked on my tight muscles, the sweet scent of the massage oil relaxed me. By the time Marcus had worked his magic on my shoulders and upper back, I was warming to him.

Sven proved to be the chattier of the two men and the one with superior English. He regaled us with entertaining stories from his time working at an upscale ski resort in his native Sweden.

"Where are you from?" Julie asked Marcus when there was a lull in the conversation.

"Germany," he replied in his heavy accent, and applied massage oil to my lower back. "I moved to Ireland three years ago, and I work here since two years."

"Do you have much to do this time of year?" I asked. "The hotel looks pretty empty."

"Not so much," Marcus replied. "More in summer. Like the hotel, the beauty center has a skeleton staff during the low season. But Sven and I, we are here year-round."

"This time of year is tough for businesses all over the island," Julie said. "Maggie's looking for part-time work, but it'll be hard."

"You want work?" Sven asked, his voice curious. "Maybe not so hard to arrange. The hotel has staffing problems at the moment. You should ask at reception if there's a vacancy."

"Really?" I asked, trying and failing to keep the curiosity out of my voice. The hotel manager and I had history, and not of the good kind. While I didn't wish Paul Greer ill, the fact that he had difficulties keeping staff didn't come as a surprise. Any employee who had to deal with Paul's wife, Melanie, had my sympathies.

"There's been strange...happenings," Marcus said, laboring over the last word. "People are quitting because they're afraid of the ghost."

"Ghost?" I jerked my head up and stared at him. "Like a banshee?"

Marcus shook his head. "More like a poltergeist."

"People are freaked out," Sven supplied in an excited voice. "They're saying the west wing of the hotel is haunted. Guests are leaving and staff members are quitting. You should find it no problem to get a job here."

I shared an amused glance with Julie. "A job at a haunted hotel run by my ex-boyfriend? What an enticing prospect."

"You know Mr. Greer?" It was Marcus's turn to be curious.

Yeah, I thought, *in the biblical sense.* Out loud, I said, "I used to know him, but that was a long time ago."

This was being economical with the truth. Our paths had crossed more than once a few weeks ago when I'd been investigating Paul's mother-in-law's murder. Since the murderer's arrest, I'd managed to avoid Paul and his odious wife, Melanie, and I got the impression they weren't too eager to hang out with me, especially after Melanie had confided in me about her unhappy marriage. From her attitude since that day, I suspected she regretted blurting out her grievances to me.

"What, exactly, does this poltergeist do?" I asked as Marcus applied pressure to my thighs.

"Moving stuff around. Wailing. Clanking chains.

Opening drawers," Sven replied. "Typical horror movie stuff, only without the gore."

I raised an eyebrow. "Surely people don't believe a ghost is doing all that? It's got to be a disgruntled member of staff, right?"

"I thought this," Marcus said, moving to my calves, "but then it happened during a staff meeting. Everyone was in the ballroom."

"Everyone? Are you sure? Even the cleaning staff?"

"Everyone," Sven assured me. "Mr. Greer was in the middle of his speech when a strange sound started, like a woman wailing through the walls. And then a picture fell off the wall with a crash. We all freaked out. Three of the maids quit on the spot."

Julie's amused glance met mine. "Paul won't like that," she said, "nor Queen Melanie—she might be expected to clean a room all by herself."

No, the Greers wouldn't be happy, and neither would the silent partner they were keen to appease. I settled my head on my arms while Marcus applied pressure to my reflex zones. The rest of the hour passed quickly. All too soon, Julie and I were dressed and retracing our steps to the hotel lobby.

"You're not seriously considering asking for work here?" Julie asked.

"If there's a vacancy that doesn't involve scrubbing toilets, I'd consider it."

"Working for Melanie would be a nightmare. Surely you're not that desperate for money."

"Not yet, but I will be if I don't find a way to bring in some extra cash. I can't let Noreen invent work for me. Besides, I like to keep busy. I got so desperate one evening that I borrowed wool and knitting needles from Noreen and watched an instructional video on the internet."

Julie laughed. "How did that work out?"

"About as well as can be expected from someone with two left hands. I knit the arm of a sweater around myself."

My cousin cracked up laughing. "Oh, Maggie. I'm going to miss you when you go back to the States."

"About that..." I hesitated, unsure whether to give voice to plans that were, at best, a quarter formed. "Don't tell Philomena or Noreen, but I'm considering extending the lease on the cottage and staying on Whisper Island over the summer."

My cousin's face lit up with delight. "That's wonderful. We'd love to have you stay longer."

"Nothing's certain yet," I cautioned. "I haven't even spoken to the rental company about my lease. And it all depends on me finding work." I'd been toying with the idea of staying for the summer since the day I'd moved into the cottage. It would be lovely to see the Whisper Island I remembered from childhood summers: lush green fields, warm sun, and the town alive with tourists. And it wasn't as if I had anything to look forward to at home.

"I guess it's not as if you have a job waiting for you in San Francisco." Julie's words echoed my thoughts.

"Exactly. I'm not even sure what I want to do when I go back. If...when...I return, I'll have to start my life from scratch." I slowed when we reached the reception desk. "I'm going to ask about job vacancies."

"You're looking for a job at the hotel?" The familiar female voice made me spin on my heels. Melanie Greer, my childhood nemesis, stood before me.

I stifled a groan. "Yeah," I said breezily. "Just a few hours work each week."

My stomach clenched in anticipation of a snide remark, but none came. Instead, Melanie's brow creased in thought. "It might just work," she murmured before noticing Julie's and my baffled expressions. "Do you have a moment, Maggie? Paul and I have a proposition for you. And it might be the answer to both our problems."

SIX

After saying goodbye to Julie, I followed Melanie past the robotic Lisa and into the manager's office. Although Melanie and I had reached a tentative truce when I'd been investigating her mother's murder, I was wary of the woman. However, her obvious desperation to talk to me intrigued me almost as much as Sven and Marcus's ghost story, and I had a hunch they were connected.

When Melanie led me into the office, Paul was seated behind his desk, looking dapper as always in a designer suit. He wore his fair hair slicked back and his face clean-shaven. At the moment, he was frowning at his computer screen. He glanced up, and his jaw dropped when he saw me. "Maggie? What are you doing here?"

I shrugged. "Ask your wife. She seems to think I'm the answer to your prayers."

"I said we might be able to come to a mutually beneficial arrangement," Melanie said in a frosty tone. "Take a seat, Maggie."

I obeyed, amused by the loaded looks Paul exchanged with Melanie. "Okay, cut to the chase. Why are you so keen to hire me? Even with staff quitting in droves, I'd have thought I'd be the last person you'd want hanging around the hotel."

Paul winced at my reference to his staffing crisis. "Where did you hear about that?"

"Word travels," I said vaguely, not wanting to get Sven and Marcus in trouble for gossiping. "You know what it's like on the island."

"If you already know about it, I'll come to the point," Melanie said. "We want to hire you to investigate whatever's going on at the hotel. I don't believe in ghosts, but I do believe in bank statements. We can't afford to let this continue."

Her husband reddened and loosened his tie, revealing the sheen of sweat around his neck. "Crazy as it sounds, people are spooked. We're losing staff and guests. We need you to debunk the ghost theory and solve the mystery before the holiday season starts, preferably by St. Patrick's Day."

I crossed my arms over my chest. Watching Paul squirm was fun. "Much as I loved *Ghostbusters* as a kid, hunting spooks isn't exactly my forte."

Melanie pressed her lips into a thin line. "I think we can all agree that whoever is behind the wailing and clanking chains is still very much in the land of the living."

"Have you spoken to the police?" I asked. "Isn't this a job for them?"

"We made a formal report to Sergeant Reynolds," Paul said, "but he says there's no evidence that a crime has been committed and his hands are tied. He's agreed to send a squad car by the hotel a couple of times a day, but I don't see what good that will do."

Melanie snorted. "This new guy is no better than Sergeant O'Shea. The least he could have done is agree to have a permanent police presence at the hotel. That would scare whoever is behind the pranks into stopping."

Just as I'd started to think Melanie had finally grown up and started to see the world beyond her own orbit, she came out with an idiotic statement. "You know that Reynolds is pretty much on his own, right? As you said, O'Shea is a waste of space, and the two reserve policemen only work a few hours a week. And at the moment, he's running all over the island in pursuit of these animal activists who are causing mayhem."

"Well, it's not good enough." Melanie glared at me as though I were personally responsible for her problems. "We were expecting an influx of guests for the St. Patrick's Day three-day weekend, but word of our...issues...has spread. Four reservations were canceled today."

Paul grimaced. "Make that five. I was responding to another cancellation email when you and Maggie arrived."

Melanie paled and swore beneath her breath. "This has to stop, especially with…" She trailed off and locked eyes with her husband.

"Especially with what?" I demanded.

Paul sighed. "The silent investor who owns the majority share of the hotel is planning to visit in the summer."

"Meaning you're under pressure to keep the hotel running smoothly," I added.

"And solvent." Melanie bit her red-stained lips. "Will you take the job?"

"That depends on what sort of financial arrangement we can come to." I looked at Melanie and then at Paul. "I might need a job, but you're not cheaping out on me. And I'm still working part-time at the café, so my hours here will have to fit around my shifts."

The Greers looked at one another for a long moment. "We'll pay you five thousand euros," Melanie said finally, "*if* you find out who's behind the poltergeist before St. Patrick's Day."

Five thousand euros for *a week's* work? Not bad. I performed a rapid calculation in my head. The money would pay for an extra two months' rent on my cottage —longer if I could strike a bargain with the real estate agent. "Make it six, and I'll start tomorrow."

"Five thousand five hundred," Melanie countered, "and that's my final offer. And we'll pay you *if* you get the job done."

Paul gaped at his wife. "Melanie, we can't—"

"I'll take it," I said, "but you pay two thousand in cash before I start, and the rest *when* I get the job done."

"Fair enough." Melanie tottered over to the painting behind Paul's desk and shoved it aside to reveal a safe underneath.

"Original," I drawled. "Just where no criminal would think to look."

Melanie gave me an ironic smile over her shoulder. "That's what I've been saying for years, but my father-in-law won't hear of replacing it. He even insists on paying the staff wages in cash."

Paul shifted uncomfortably in his seat. "Dad likes us to do things the way he did them. He doesn't like change."

I schooled my face into a serene smile. "I guess you cooking the books didn't go down too well with your folks, huh?"

Paul's face turned a fiery red and his lips parted as if to deliver an insult. Melanie cleared her throat and shot her husband a warning look. His jaw clenched, but he said nothing.

Melanie returned her attention to the safe and withdrew a wad of cash. She slipped it into an envelope and handed it to me. "Here's the first installment. I'd like you to be here at six sharp tomorrow morning. And don't tell the staff why you're here. As far as they're concerned, you'll just be a new employee."

I eyed her with suspicion. "What's my cover story?"

She smirked. "You'll be joining our cleaning crew. What better way for you to have access to every area of the hotel?"

I sucked air through my teeth. I loathed the idea of cleaning for Paul and Melanie. On the other hand, five and a half grand was a lot of money. I uncurled my fingers and extended my hand. "Deal."

By the time I left the hotel, darkness had fallen. I drove home to my cottage with music blaring from the car stereo, and I was still singing along to an old Bon Jovi song when I pulled up outside my cottage and killed the engine.

"Don't give up the day job," said a voice out of the darkness the instant I stepped out of the car.

My heart leaped in my chest. "Reynolds? Why are you lurking on my doorstep?"

The policeman moved out of the shadows and into the patch of light cast by the outdoor security lighting. "I wasn't lurking. I was ringing your doorbell."

"Need to borrow a cup of sugar?" I crossed my arms over my chest, still irritated by his dismissive attitude last night, even though I knew I'd have reacted the same way had I been the police officer in charge.

Reynolds shook his head, and I noticed the grim set of his mouth and the folder tucked under his arm. "This isn't a social call. I need to go over your statement from last night again."

I sucked in a breath. "I was right, wasn't I? The postman didn't jump."

"You were right." Reynolds stepped closer, and his grave expression sent a chill of apprehension through me. "Eddie Ward was dead before he ever went over that cliff."

SEVEN

My pulse kicked up a notch. "How was Eddie Ward killed?"

"Günter suspects he was poisoned. The pathologist backed up Günter's suspicion."

"Wait...Ward was poisoned and then thrown off the cliff?"

"Yes."

"Ugh." I shivered in the dark, and my grip tightened around my house key. "Did the pathologist come over to the island to examine the body?" The presence of a pathologist should have reached my ears at the café within minutes of the doctor setting foot on the island, yet I'd heard nothing.

"No. I escorted the body to the mainland this afternoon, on the down-low. With the chaos caused by the storm, Günter and I were busy all night. We didn't get a proper look at the body until this morning." The policeman rubbed his jaw. "Let's just say it quickly became clear we weren't dealing with an accident or suicide."

"I'm sorry, Liam. I'd hoped I was wrong."

Reynolds closed the space between us, and I could smell the aroma of his spicy aftershave. "Can we talk inside, Maggie? I need to go over your statement again. And I'd like your opinion on something."

My heart beat a little faster. "You want my help on the case?"

"Nice try, but no." His half smile warmed me from the inside out. "I just want to ask you a few questions, some of which are off the record. Okay by you?"

"Sure. And you're not fooling me, Sergeant Reynolds. Asking me off-the-record questions is totally getting me to help." With his low chuckle warming my neck, I unlocked the door and let us into the cottage. Standing awkwardly in my hallway, I groped for a topic that didn't involve murder and mayhem. "How's the unpacking going?" *Lame, Doyle.* Why couldn't I come up with something profound on the spot?

"The less said about my unpacking, the better." Reynolds followed me into my small living room. "My plans to unpack the last few boxes keep getting derailed by animal activists and murderers."

Over by the fireplace, Bran lolled in front of the kittens' basket, snoring. Some guard dog he'd make. Poly, the kittens' mother and my roommate when I lived at Noreen's, treated me to a disdainful stare before returning her attention to her offspring.

"Wow." Reynolds slow-blinked. "You've acquired some livestock."

"Blame Noreen." I gave him a rueful smile. "And I'm only keeping two of the kittens. They're all here at the moment because they're too young to be separated from their mom. By rights, you should have the tortoiseshell kitten. You saved her, after all."

The policeman kneeled before the basket and stroked the kitten. "Is that who this is? She's getting big."

"She sure is. Her name is Rosie."

The kitten investigated his large hand, sniffing his wrist. "The name suits her," he said. "Pretty but cheeky at the same time. She reminds me of my cat."

"You have a cat? No offense, but you don't strike me as the house pet kind of dude."

"Poppy is my daughter's cat."

It was on the tip of my tongue to say he didn't strike me as the sort of dude to have a kid, especially not one he casually dropped into the conversation six weeks after our first meeting. But then, what did I know about Liam Reynolds? "Do you want a drink?" I asked. "Frankly, I could use one after your news."

He inclined his neck. "Yes, please."

I went over to my drinks cabinet, recalling belatedly that I'd forgotten to stop off at the liquor store. I took stock of its meager contents. "On the alcohol front, all I have is rotgut whiskey that I bought for cooking, and an unchilled bottle of white so sweet it'll make your teeth hurt. Do either of those appeal to you?"

"You really know how to sell a man a drink," Reynolds said dryly. "A glass of water will be fine."

"On the snacks front, the situation is dire. I can offer you a dog treat."

Reynolds's mouth twitched, and his eyes twinkled with amusement. "I'll pass."

I poured sparkling water into two glasses and handed one to him. For an instant, my fingers brushed against his, and the now-familiar shock of awareness shot through me. I took a gulp of water and threw myself into the armchair next to Bran and the cats.

Reynolds placed his water glass on the coffee table and took the seat opposite. He drew a notepad and pen out of his shirt pocket and put the folder he'd been carrying on his lap. "I'd like to go over your statement again. You say you saw no one when you and Lenny stopped behind the post van."

"That's right, but as I said at the station, it was dark."

He raised an eyebrow. "It wasn't that dark. The headlights were on, and the moon was full."

"True, but there are plenty of places for a person to hide along that road. A stone wall runs along one side farther down, and the ditch is deep in parts. Once I looked over the edge of the cliff and saw the body, I was preoccupied with getting down to the beach."

"What made you look over the cliff? Why didn't you assume the driver had run out of petrol, or broken down, and then walked on in search of help?"

"The van was abandoned in the middle of the road with the driver's door open and the lights on. If my car broke down, I'd at least try to shove it to the side of the road, and I wouldn't leave the door wide open. The scene felt...wrong."

"And the cliff?" he prompted. "Why did you look over the edge instead of looking for the driver?"

"Because those cliffs give me the creeps every time I drive by. It's a steep drop, and there are no crash barriers. I wondered if he'd slipped and fallen."

Frowning, Reynolds skimmed my signed statement. "You insist that you didn't see a suicide note in the vehicle when you looked inside."

"Correct. I'm sure I'd have noticed one if it had been there."

"In light of the revelation that Eddie Ward was murdered, your suggestion that the note was planted in the lorry after you and Lenny had gone down to the beach seems more likely."

"You keep saying that he was murdered. Is there no chance he could have taken poison accidentally?"

Reynolds's mouth pulled into a frown. "Possible but unlikely. I'll get to the reason why in a sec. First, I want to finish going over your statement."

"Fine," I said, "but do it fast. I want to get to the good stuff."

"You're ghoulish, Ms. Doyle," Reynolds said, an amused twinkle in his eyes.

"Am I allowed to ask if you found any fingerprints on the alleged suicide note?"

Reynolds nodded. "We found Ward's. Given that the note was written on a sheet of official An Post paper, we can assume Ward handled it at some point."

I raised an eyebrow. "So we're dealing with a killer smart enough to hide his tracks."

Reynolds chuckled. "*We* are dealing with nothing. Leave the killer to me. As to his or her intelligence, the off-the-record part I'm about to share with you makes the whole situation confusing."

My ears pricked up. "Go on."

"I need your word that this information will go no further."

"My lips are sealed." I bounced in my seat. "Hurry up and tell me already. I'm intrigued."

He blew out his cheeks. "The pathologist found a stab wound through the left ventricle."

"Eddie Ward was stabbed in the heart?" I stared at him, slack-jawed. "But there was no blood on his clothes. We'd have noticed that, even in the dark. We all looked him over with flashlights—you, me, Lenny, and the paramedics."

"I know." Reynolds's mouth set in a grim line. "Ward was stabbed *after* he'd died."

My head jerked up. "What the heck? Who poisons, stabs, and then throws a man off a cliff? Talk about overkill—pun intended."

"The pathologist has yet to confirm the poison, but he suspects the cause of death was some sort of cyanide compound."

"Could it have started to take effect while he was driving, hence the haphazard way the van was left in the middle of the road?"

"That's the assumption I'm working on."

"So, Ward stops and staggers out of the van," I said, visualizing the scene in my head as if it were a movie reel. "At some point soon after, he succumbs to the poison. When does the stabbing occur? Before or after he goes over the cliff?"

"The pathologist couldn't say with certainty, but his educated guess was before."

"So our killer administers poison, waits for it to kill Ward, and then stabs him and throws the body over a cliff. He or she really wanted to make sure the guy was dead."

"Yeah," Reynolds said. "What I don't get is why the killer stabbed Ward if he wanted to stage a suicide. Why make the effort to write a suicide note and plant it in the van?"

I shook my head. "I don't know. I'm stumped."

"That makes two of us." Reynolds rubbed his jaw and sighed. "I took the position on Whisper Island on the assumption that murder and mayhem were unlikely to form a regular part of my working day. Maybe I let the easy pace of life make me lax last night. I should have noticed something was wrong before Günter and I examined the body."

"You had a lot to deal with between the storm and the shot bull. Whatever happened to your animal activist pal, anyway?"

Reynolds rolled his eyes. "His wealthy father caught the first ferry over from the mainland, with a fancy solicitor in tow. The guy appeared in court this afternoon and got bail. I expect he'll get off with a slap on the wrist."

I sifted through what Reynolds had told me about the murder victim. "Where was Ward's killer? Lying in wait for him along the road? But how could he have known when and where Ward would start feeling sick?"

"That's a good question," Reynolds said. "And not one I have an answer for, unfortunately. I had a team out searching earlier, and we'll go out again at first light."

"What about the van? Did it reveal any useful info?"

He shook his head. "I got forensics to look over the inside of the van. The problem with postal vans is they belong to a fleet. Ward didn't always drive the same one. The van Ward drove back to the island on Friday should have been cleaned before he collected it, but for some reason, it hadn't been, and it was covered in prints." Reynolds sighed. "We've taken control prints from the regular postal team, and the guys who occasionally help out with deliveries. We've identified Ward's prints, and those of his part-time helper's, and we're still wading through the rest."

"Do you need me to drop by the station tomorrow to be fingerprinted?"

"I'd appreciate it. We could get your prints from the San Francisco PD, but I'd rather not have to waste time putting in a formal request."

"No problem. I'll swing by after work tomorrow. Is there anything else I should know?" I asked. "Something else off the record?"

He met my gaze. "Nothing you *should* know, but there's something I'd like your opinion on."

"Shoot."

Reynolds's lips twitched. "Poor word choice. A firearm was about the only weapon *not* used to kill the man." He took a sip of his water and settled back in his chair, a line between his brows. "The pathologist is unsure about Ward's facial injuries. He said they could have been caused by the fall, or inflicted before he fell. We've sent the photos you took with your phone to our tech team in Galway for analysis, but they don't tell us much about how he received those injuries." Reynolds put his pen and notepad to the side and picked up the folder on his lap. "Would you mind having a look at the photos and giving me your thoughts? I've asked Sergeant O'Shea, but...well..."

He trailed off, but I got the hint. "But O'Shea's a pompous fool and unlikely to offer you a useful opinion, even if he had one." I opened the folder and flipped through the postmortem photos, scrutinizing each picture in turn. "I'm sorry. I have no idea if he got the injuries before or after the fall, but I can guess what's bugging you."

"Go on," he said. "Tell me what's on your mind."

"If Ward received injuries of this nature from his killer and not as the result of the fall, the killer wanted to disfigure his face. There are two main reasons for a killer to do that. One, he or she didn't want the victim to be easily identified, or two, the killer had a serious grudge against the victim and did it as an act of rage."

"Given that Ward was wearing his uniform," Reynolds said, "we're assuming we can rule out the first reason. We're waiting on dental records, but the body matches Ward's recorded height, build, and blood type on his medical chart at the Whisper Island Medical Centre."

"Which leaves us with the second reason. Someone hated Eddie Ward enough to stab him after death and disfigure his dead body."

Reynolds looked me straight in the eye. "Your family is from the island. Do you know of anyone with a grudge against Eddie Ward? From what Lenny said when Ward delivered our post yesterday, I guess he's not a fan."

A vision of Lenny's worried face floated before me.

If the postman had abandoned Lenny's pregnant sister, he and his family had plenty of reason to hate the guy. But enough to commit murder? I didn't buy it, and I certainly didn't want Reynolds latching onto Lenny's family as his prime suspects. "My dad is from Whisper Island, but I've only been here a few days longer than you. And I first met the postman last week when I moved into this cottage. I don't know who he hangs out with. For what it's worth, no one I've mentioned him to has a good word to say about Eddie Ward."

Reynolds sighed and ran a hand over his stubbled jaw. "Thanks, Maggie. I appreciate you acting as a sounding board." He stood. "I'll let myself out. Get a good night's sleep."

After he'd left, the pang of guilt gnawed at my stomach. I should have told him about Lenny's sister. He'd find out eventually, and then he'd be annoyed that I hadn't said anything. I bit my lip. Should I go after him? But what difference would it make if I kept silent for another day or so? Another twenty-four hours would give me time to dig for info about other potential suspects so that when I presented Reynolds with my findings, I'd have more names to offer him than the Logans'. If I'd believed for a second that they were responsible, I'd have told Reynolds right away. Nonetheless, the feeling I'd done wrong nagged me throughout a restless night, and hadn't dissipated by the time my alarm clock sounded the next morning.

EIGHT

I stared at my reflection in the full-length mirror and took in the full horror of my new uniform. In addition to the maid's cap that only fit when I drew my unruly red curls into a tight bun, I wore a frilly black skirt that barely skimmed my thighs, and a tight white shirt with a cleavage-baring V-neck slash. My indignity was further outraged by the addition of fishnet stockings and an incongruously innocent-looking pair of patent leather flats.

I turned to face Melanie. "You've got to be kidding."

My erstwhile nemesis smirked. "No joke, Maggie. This is the Whisper Island Hotel's official maid's uniform. The guests love it."

I snorted. "The male guests, sure. I look like the maid in the movie *Clue*."

"Don't blame me," Melanie said with a shrug. "My father-in-law designed the uniform. Besides, we agreed that the easiest way for you to work undercover at the hotel was as a maid."

"*You* decided to make me a maid," I corrected. "And when I agreed, I had no idea I'd be displaying my boobs to the world."

"It's not my fault you could do with losing a few pounds," Melanie said with a sniff.

"I'm busty, not fat," I snapped, irritated with myself for allowing her to goad me. "And the skirt's too short because I'm tall."

"I'm sorry you're not happy with your uniform, but you must agree that going undercover as a floater maid gives you an excellent excuse to be in various areas of the hotel."

I pulled up the V of my shirt in a vain attempt to retain some semblance of dignity, and muttered a noncommittal response. In truth, I agreed with her. As a maid, I could easily move from floor to floor without arousing suspicion. According to the cleaning schedule I'd flipped through in Paul's office after my arrival this morning, the cleaning staff was divided into teams that rotated between areas of the hotel on a monthly basis, presumably to reduce the monotony of the job. I'd been hired as one of the hotel's two floaters, meaning I didn't belong to any cleaning team, but was sent to help whichever area needed extra work done. Floaters were also expected to give assistance in areas beyond cleaning, such as helping the beauty center staff prepare a massage room for the next client, or chopping vegetables if a kitchen assistant was sick. This would give me the opportunity to be in the beauty center one day, and the executive suites the next.

Melanie swiped a finger over her tablet computer. "We'll start you in the kitchen this morning. They're short-staffed, especially with the demands of the Sunday brunch buffet, and they need someone to help with some basic food prep."

"Whoa," I said. "Cooking isn't my area of expertise. I can just about manage to warm up the food my aunt prepares at the Movie Theater Café, but that's the extent of my culinary talents."

Melanie rolled her eyes. "I said *basic* food prep. In a hotel kitchen, that means tasks like washing and chopping vegetables. Even you should be able to manage that."

"All while looking like a lady of the night," I muttered, tugging at the hem of my very short skirt.

The other woman laughed. "The kitchen staff will be too busy to care what you're wearing. Carl runs a tight ship."

"Carl Logan?" I asked, although I already knew the answer.

"That's right." A sneer marred the natural beauty of Melanie's face. "You're friends with his waste-of-space younger brother, aren't you?"

I bristled at this attack on my friend. "Lenny is highly intelligent and hardworking."

"At what?" I longed to wipe the smirk off her face at her words. "As far as I can tell, he helps out at his parents' shop and plays with computers on the side."

"What's wrong with that? It's an honest living." Actually, I wasn't entirely sure about the honest part. I had a sneaking suspicion Lenny wasn't quick to declare his sideline in computer repairs on his tax forms, but I wasn't about to share that tidbit with Melanie.

She tossed her glossy dark hair over her shoulder and pivoted on her elegant heels. "I'll show you to the kitchen and let Carl take over from there."

I shuffled through the hotel lobby in her wake, horribly self-conscious about my short skirt and low-cut top. When we passed a couple of elderly gentlemen dressed in golfing tweeds, they gawked at me. I tilted my chin and held my head high, as if looking like a stripper at six-thirty in the morning was no big deal.

The kitchen was located in the hotel basement. Even if Melanie hadn't been leading the way, the enticing aromas and clanging of pots would have tipped me off.

I followed her into a large open-plan kitchen. Like the spa area, it was ultra modern, and contrasted with the old-world sophistication of the rest of the hotel. Staff buzzed around, rushing with trays piled with breakfast food. At the center of the organized chaos stood a tall, dark-haired man with designer stubble and stylishly tousled hair. When he turned around, I recognized an older version of the Carl Logan I remembered from teenage summers spent on the island.

Carl was a taller, more handsome version of Lenny, but his air of confidence was tinged with an arrogance that his brother thankfully lacked. He gave me an obvious once-over and ended the examination with a wide smile. "Hello, there. Have you come to help us out?"

"This is Maggie Doyle," Melanie said before I'd had the chance to respond. "She's the new floater. I've asked her to help you prep the breakfasts."

Carl eyed me more closely. "Maggie Doyle...not Lenny's American friend?"

I nodded. "Guilty as charged."

The smile he gave me now was genuine. He stretched out a hand and subjected mine to a vigorous pumping. "Nice to meet you again, Maggie. Lenny's delighted to have you back on the island. There's few enough young folk left these days, and most are married with kids."

"Not a problem Maggie has," Melanie said archly. "She's getting divorced."

Cow. I bit my tongue before I delivered an acid retort and got fired before I'd had a chance to solve the mystery and pocket the rest of the promised five and a half thousand euros.

Carl cast me a sympathetic look. "Why don't I give

Maggie the grand tour before I put her to work? No need for you to stay, Melanie."

"I'm Mrs. Greer to you." Melanie glared at the chef and then at me before stalking out of the kitchen.

Carl grinned at me. "A lot has changed on Whisper Island since you and Lenny were kids, but Melanie hasn't."

I laughed. "I've noticed. So where do you want me to start?"

"The whole grand tour yarn was to get rid of Melanie. It'll take about thirty seconds to show you what you'll need to use to chop fruit for the breakfast buffet's fruit salad."

Within a few minutes, I'd been supplied with an apron that covered most of my scanty uniform—not difficult—and a sharp chopping knife. A mountain of washed fruit awaited my attention. For the next couple of hours, I sliced and diced, peeled and chopped. At ten o'clock, the breakfast buffet and à la carte service stopped, and I had a chance to take a short coffee break. Bernadette, the chef responsible for the vegetarian and vegan menu options, handed me an extra-large mug of cappuccino. We'd gotten talking earlier that morning, and I had the impression that she liked to gossip. Perfect for my purposes.

I took a sip of my drink and licked cocoa flavored froth from my lips. "Delicious," I said with a sigh. "I don't know how you do it. I thought working at my aunt's café could be frantic at times, but you guys are put through your paces."

Bernadette pulled a face. "Tell me about it. If the Greers don't find permanent staff to replace the people who've left, I don't know how we'll survive the summer season. Mind you, if this ghost nonsense keeps up, we might all be out of a job before then."

"I heard there'd been strange goings-on at the hotel."

"Of course you have. There are no secrets on Whisper Island. No wonder the hotel can't get new staff." She fixed her gaze on me and eyed me curiously. "Apart from you."

"I don't believe in ghosts."

"Neither do I, but whatever's going on is scaring guests and staff alike."

I smiled brightly. "I don't scare easily."

"You mustn't," Bernadette agreed. "Not if you chase down murderers and thieves." At my look of surprise, she laughed. "Like I said, everyone knows everyone else's business on this island. Now tell me, Maggie Doyle, how does an American cop end up chopping fruit in an Irish hotel kitchen?"

"It's a long story, but the short version is that I came here after my marriage broke up. My dad's from Whisper Island, and I had fond childhood memories of the island."

"Fair enough." Bernadette nodded, as if she found

my explanation satisfactory. "How long are you planning to stay?"

"Until the end of May. Maybe longer. I want to keep my options open, you know? That's why picking up some casual part-time work suits me."

"Well, good luck. I hope you last longer than the last floater Melanie hired. The poor girl encountered our pet poltergeist and fled without giving notice."

"This poltergeist business..." I began carefully. "Who do you think's behind it?"

"Hard to say." The woman screwed up her nose and gave the matter some thought. "Melanie Greer's a pain in the behind, but it's her husband who has a talent for upsetting people, especially those he feels are beneath him and not worth sucking up to."

"Can you be more specific? Has Paul annoyed anyone in particular recently?"

Bernadette frowned, and then shook her head. "Not that I can think of. He had a run-in with that old eejit of a policeman a while back. They had a shouting match in the hotel restaurant."

"Sergeant O'Shea?" I prompted.

Bernadette's lip curled. "Yeah. That's the one. An awful old fart, but he's been a regular at the restaurant for years. Or at least he was until that fight."

"Any idea what the argument was about?"

She shook her head. "Even with all the noise they were making, I never figured out that part. Something about golf and an unpaid bill, but I wasn't sure if O'Shea hadn't paid it or Greer."

Given his dubious history with the hotel accounts, my money was on Paul. According to Noreen, O'Shea had recently been appointed to the Whisper Island Golf Club's board of directors. Had Paul skipped out on paying his share of the golf course's maintenance? Or run up a tab at the golf club's bar? I knew the hotel shared the golf course with the golf club, but I didn't know the particulars of the arrangement. Even if Paul was in debt, why would he cause himself further financial grief by playing poltergeist? There had to be another solution.

I adopted an awed expression. "I heard the ghost clanks chains and causes havoc. Whoever's behind it must be pretty clever to fool so many people."

"I don't believe in the supernatural, but the noise and the flying objects are creepy. For all that Sergeant O'Shea is a loathsome toad, I can't imagine him pretending to be a poltergeist."

Neither could I. Which meant I was one morning into my time at the hotel and no closer to finding out who was terrorizing its inhabitants.

Over the next couple of hours, I worked alongside Carl Logan. He proved to be an efficient chef and, despite his bursts of temper when staff members weren't moving fast enough, Carl was surprisingly patient showing me the ropes.

After the lunchtime rush, he fixed me a delicious

dish of linguini with prawns and insisted I sit down to eat it. "I can't have our new member of staff collapsing with hunger."

I laughed. "After all I've been eating since I arrived on Whisper Island, I think I have enough reserves to last me for a while."

"Noreen's a good cook," Carl said. "Not up to my standard, of course, but not bad for an amateur."

I stifled a grin at his nonchalant arrogance. "How long have you worked at the hotel?"

The man puffed up with pride. "I recently had my tenth anniversary."

"Wow. Time flies. Have you ever considered looking for a job at another hotel?"

Carl shrugged. "From time to time, especially on a day the Greers annoy me, but I like living on the island. I have my boat and I can go sailing in my spare time. Besides, Granddad needs me."

"That's right," I said, as though the memory had just struck me. "You live with Gerry."

"Next door, actually." His wolfish grin returned. "I like my privacy, and living under the same roof as my grandfather would cramp my style."

"Still, it's nice for him to have you nearby."

"Yeah. Granddad's getting on in years, but his brain's all there. He just needs help with shopping, household repairs, and that sort of thing." Carl's face darkened. "Officially, my cousin, Jack, is supposed to chip in and help, but he's rarely to be found when we need him."

I smothered a laugh. "I encountered him when I was buying my car."

Carl's face transformed into a mask of horror. "Please tell me you didn't *buy* one of his vehicles?"

"It was cheap," I said with a shrug.

The chef grinned. "Want to take a bet on how long it keeps running?"

"Two months is all I need." Time to steer the conversation around to the ghost. "I keep hearing about the hotel being haunted, but that seems far-fetched. What's your take on the clanking and wailing?"

Carl's easy smile faded. Was it my imagination, or did I see a ripple of annoyance flash over his face before he got his emotions under control? "My take, as you put it, is that someone is taking the mickey."

I stared at him blankly. "Taking the what?"

"Taking the mickey means joking around. Not that this particular joke is making me laugh. The more guests who leave, the more likely it is we'll all be out of a job before the summer season starts."

"But why would anyone want to do that?"

Carl drained his coffee cup and stood. "Not everyone wants the hotel to thrive. The Greers aren't exactly contenders to win the Whisper Island Popularity Contest, and the hotel and golf course are sitting on prime real estate. Just last year, a guy from

England started an aggressive campaign to get the Greers to sell."

"What's the arrangement with the golf club? Who owns the land?"

"Officially, the golf course is on land belonging to the hotel. In return for sharing the cost of maintenance, the Whisper Island Golf Club is allowed to use the course."

"I'd imagine the golf club was pretty mad at the idea of the Greers selling the land. What did this aggressive investor from England intend to do with the land if they'd agreed to the sale?"

Carl snorted. "Raze the hotel and build a water park."

"Wow. That's quite a difference from a five-star golf hotel with spa facilities."

"I'll say," muttered Carl. "And to make matters worse, he wanted to build themed guest lodges for people who wanted to stay longer. I got a peek at the layouts, and they were awful. Definitely not what the island needs."

And definitely not the sort of place that would be in need of a chef of Carl's caliber. "Do you think this thwarted would-be buyer is on a vendetta to close down the hotel?"

Carl shrugged. "Who knows? It's a more likely explanation than the hotel having a resident poltergeist."

The guy had a point. I mulled over the

conversation while I worked, but came to no concrete conclusions. After I'd helped the kitchen staff clean up from lunch, Melanie reappeared in the kitchen. "One of our secretaries has called in sick," she said the instant we made eye contact. "I'd like you to take over for the rest of the day."

I took off my apron, once again exposing my cleavage. "Any chance I'll get to wear a different outfit?"

Melanie waved a hand in a dismissive gesture. "You'll be in a back room answering phones and booking appointments. No one will care what you're wearing."

With these not very reassuring words, she frog-marched me up the stairs. When we reached the lobby, our progress came to an abrupt halt.

Sergeant Liam Reynolds strode toward us, stony-faced, and flanked on either side by the island's two reserve policemen. My heart beat a little faster. That didn't bode well.

"Maggie Doyle," he said in a hard tone, surveying my outfit and pausing a second too long on the V on my shirt. "Got a new job?"

"Part-time," I replied nonchalantly, a betraying warmth creeping up my cheeks. "I'm still working at the Movie Theater Café."

His eyes flashed and I took a step back, surprised by his anger. "I'm looking for the kitchen," he ground out.

Melanie stared at him in surprise. "Why? Is something wrong?"

"Yes. I've come to arrest your head chef for murder." Sergeant Reynolds turned to me, a flash of anger in his dark blue eyes. "And I've a good mind to haul *you* down to the station for withholding information."

NINE

I swallowed hard. "I didn't—"

"Save it." Reynolds's jaw hardened. "I'll speak to you later."

"What do you mean? Is my chef a murderer?" Melanie's voice rose to a shriek.

Reynolds ignored her and marched to the stairs that led down to the basement. When he and the reserves disappeared from sight, Melanie and I stood rooted to the spot.

"What's going on, Maggie?" she demanded. "Clearly you know something I don't."

I released a long breath. "You've heard the postman died?"

She screwed up her nose. "Paul said something about it this morning. The silly man threw himself into the sea."

"Lenny and I found him at the bottom of a cliff."

Melanie rounded on me. "Again? Seriously, how many dead bodies can one woman find?"

I threw my arms up in defense. "Hey, Lenny was with me. And I don't plan to discover corpses. It just sort of happens."

A line appeared between Melanie's perfectly plucked eyebrows. "If Sergeant Reynolds wants to arrest Carl Logan for murder, the postman's death can't have been suicide. Do you know what happened?"

I was spared the necessity of answering by a raucous roar from the bowels of the hotel. A moment later, Sergeant Reynolds appeared at the top of the stairs, hauling a protesting Carl.

"Let me go," the chef yelled. "I didn't do anything. All I said was the man deserved to die. It doesn't mean I killed him."

The former cop in me winced. I stepped in front of them and blocked their path. "Shut up, Carl. Don't say a word until you have a lawyer present."

Reynolds's face turned an angry shade of red. "He's been read his rights. If he wants to shoot his mouth off, let him."

I ignored the policeman and focused on the sweating chef. "Carl," I said in a gentler tone. "I'm serious. Say nothing—and I mean nothing—until Jennifer Pearce gets to the station."

I pulled my phone from my pocket and located the lawyer's number from my list of contacts. Jennifer and

I weren't destined to become best buds, but we'd reached a mutual understanding after I'd helped her locate a valuable missing necklace. In short, she owed me one, and I intended to persuade her to deliver.

———

My twelve-hour shift at the hotel finished at six. Exhausted, I dragged myself into Smuggler's Cove and stocked up on groceries. After I'd finished shopping, I drove to the police station and dutifully allowed one of the reserves to take my fingerprints. Try as I might, I could glean no information from the man about what was going on with Carl Logan. Feeling grumpy, frustrated, and tired, I stomped out to the parking lot. I'd just slipped behind the wheel of my car when Lenny emerged from the police station. An anxious expression creased his bony face. My stomach clenched to see him so worried.

I rolled down my window. "Hey, Lenny."

His head jerked up at the sound of his name. A slow smile broke the tension on his face. He jogged over to my car. "Good to see you, Maggie."

"Has Jennifer arrived?"

"She got here an hour ago," Lenny said in a more subdued voice than I was used to from him. "She's talking to Carl now."

I reached across the gearbox and opened the passenger door. "Get in. We need to talk." Lenny slid onto the passenger seat and buckled his belt. I started the car and eased us into the evening traffic. "I thought it would be smarter if we talked away from the station."

He nodded. "Thanks for calling Jennifer. It's not like you know Carl well."

"But I know you. You're my friend, and Carl's your brother." I sighed. "Listen, I'm going to ask you a few questions, and I need you to tell me the truth." I glanced across at him, noting the grim set of his jaw.

"Okay," he said finally. "What do you want to know?"

"Do you think Carl killed Eddie Ward?"

Lenny stared at his hands for a long while before answering. "They found his knife at the top of the cliff. We must have missed it in the dark. It had Ward's blood on it."

"Back up for a sec. The police found a knife belonging to your brother near where Ward went over the cliff? When?"

He shrugged. "The following day, I guess. I didn't see a knife that night."

"Neither did I." I gritted my teeth. "And after the suicide note that conveniently appeared on the dashboard of the post van while you and I were down on the beach, I find that suspicious. Heck, Lenny. You, me, Reynolds, Mack, and Günter trampled all over that clifftop, and we all had flashlights. How big is this knife that supposedly belongs to Carl?"

Lenny averted his gaze, choosing to stare out the

passenger window. "Big enough. And there's no question that it's Carl's. It's part of a set of chopping knives that the hotel presented to him on his tenth anniversary. They have the Whisper Island Hotel's crest and his initials engraved on them."

"Isn't it mighty convenient that the postman was stabbed with a knife whose owner is easy to identify?"

"Yeah, but..." Lenny gulped for breath. "Carl was spitting mad when Ward dumped Katie."

"Mad enough to kill him?"

He sighed. "I don't know, Maggie. I hope not. Carl's my brother. I hate having this niggling doubt."

I didn't like him having *any* doubts. I'd hoped he'd leap to his brother's defense and produce a compelling argument for why Carl couldn't have done it.

Stifling a yawn, I forced my tired brain to concentrate. Sifting through what Reynolds had told me the previous evening, I considered the facts of the case. At some point before Lenny and I had discovered his body at the bottom of the cliff, Eddie Ward had been poisoned, stabbed, and hurled off the cliff. I knew from Reynolds that the stab wound wasn't the cause of death, although I was well aware that a cut of that nature to the heart would have proven fatal had the poison not done the job first. Even if Carl had stabbed the man in a fit of rage, could he have poisoned him? I didn't know Carl Logan well, but my gut told me that poison wouldn't be his weapon of choice, despite his profession. "Look, Reynolds shared some info with me that I'm not at liberty to pass on, but I can say that I'd be interested to know what evidence he has to link Carl to the murder beyond the knife."

"I have no idea. The reserve policeman on duty wouldn't let me see Carl, and Reynolds was on the phone." Lenny snorted. "I got stuck with O'Shea blathering on gleefully about how he'd always known my family was a bad lot."

"Ignore him. The man's a vindictive fool." I glanced at my watch. "I'm due to get the Movie Theater Café ready for the Unplugged Gamers. Do you want to cancel the meeting?"

"No." The word was adamant. "I need the distraction. Besides, I know Noreen relies on the extra trade she gets from the clubs. I don't want to let her down."

"Under the circumstances, she'd understand."

"I'd rather keep busy. Günter, Mack, and Julie aren't the type to press me to talk about Carl's arrest. All I want to do is play a game and get my mind off what's happened."

"Okay. Sounds good." I continued in the direction of the Movie Theater Café and pulled into my usual parking place outside.

Julie and Mack were already outside, bouncing up and down in an effort to keep warm. Farther down Main Street, I recognized Günter's loping stroll and German Army jacket.

I got out of the car and forced a smile. All I wanted

to do right now was crawl into bed and sleep for ten hours, but I'd promised my aunt I'd keep up with my shifts at the café, and I didn't intend to let her down. If Lenny wouldn't cancel, neither would I.

Julie and Mack's attention latched onto Lenny. "We heard about Carl," Julie said. "Is there anything we can do to help?"

Lenny gave her a weak smile. "You can distract me with a complicated strategy game. And Maggie can make me one of her legendary Irish coffees."

"Legendary only because of the amount of whiskey I put in them," I said dryly, opening the café's door and letting us in. "And that was an honest mistake the first time."

"A mistake we'll gladly ask you to repeat forever," Julie said with a laugh.

I took the hint and fixed strong Irish coffees for Julie, Lenny, and Günter, and regular coffees for Mack and me, the two designated drivers.

Günter, who prided himself on his skill at the more complicated strategy games, pulled *Agricola* out of his backpack.

Mack groaned. "No way. I come in last every time we play this game."

"You're such a showoff, Günter," Julie said with the hint of acid that she reserved for exchanges with our German friend. "You know most of us are terrible at that game."

Günter's expression remained benign. "It's Lenny's turn to choose. What does he think?"

"*Agricola* is exactly the sort of complicated distraction I need tonight," Lenny replied. "So suck it and help me set up the game."

Mack grumbled, but good-naturedly, while Julie shot Günter a look of venom. By the time the game was ready for us to play, I'd made the second round of Irish coffees.

Fifteen minutes into the game, Lenny's phone rang. He glanced at the display and shot out of his seat. "It's Mum. Sorry, I have to take this." He bounded over to the front of the café, the phone pressed against his ear. "Any news?" A brief silence. "What? You're not serious?" Lenny's pacing increased in speed. "Okay. I'll be there in ten." When he disconnected and turned to face us, his face was ashen. "Mum says Reynolds has taken Granddad in for questioning."

Oh, no. My stomach dropped like an elevator in free fall. "That's outrageous," I said. "Reynolds is crazy if he thinks Gerry had anything to do with the murder."

The words were out of my mouth before I'd had time to process the situation. My sluggish brain caught up with my emotions, and I tried to assess the situation with a degree of detachment. The Logans were a tight-knit bunch. They'd have taken Katie's abandonment hard, and the situation would have been made worse by Katie cutting ties with her family. Gerry Logan made a particularly potent version of poteen, Irish moonshine, and he'd worked as an electrician before his retirement. He wasn't scientifically clueless, but would he have access to cyanide?

Mack got up from his seat. "I'll drive you to the station, Lenny."

"I'm sorry to break up the game." Lenny's thin face looked suddenly older than his twenty-nine years.

"No need to apologize." I went over and gave him a hug. "If there's anything I can do, let me know."

"Thanks, Maggie. I'll call you when I have an update."

After Mack and Lenny had left, Günter and Julie helped me to put the game pieces back in the box, and then clean the café. The dramatic end to the game appeared to have pushed them to reach an unspoken truce, much to my relief. The tension between my cousin and our German friend had been building ever since Günter had taken temporary refuge at her parents' house after his houseboat had been destroyed in a storm. I couldn't understand Julie's objection to him staying there. She didn't live at her parents' house, and they were happy to have Günter as their guest. If Philomena was putting pressure on her daughter to date Günter, it still didn't account for the animosity she displayed toward him. Part of me wondered if Julie didn't object to Günter little too much for her dislike of the man to be credible.

"I can't see Mr. Logan killing anyone," Günter said

after he'd finished sweeping the floor. "He's very—" he paused as though searching for the correct word, "—proper."

"I don't buy it, either. Sergeant Reynolds is barking up the wrong tree."

"But why?" Julie demanded. "What evidence does he have against the Logans? We all know they hated Ward, but hating the man doesn't mean they killed him. They're not the sort of family to go around murdering people."

I gave her a wan smile. "You'd be surprised at the kind of people who commit murder. But I agree with you. It doesn't fit."

"Will you help Lenny figure out who killed Ward?" my cousin asked. "If Reynolds is determined to blame Lenny's brother and grandfather, it's up to you to set him right."

I sighed. "Why does everyone seem to think I'm the island's answer to Miss Marple?"

"Because you have an excellent reputation as a solver of crimes," Günter said, and then added, "and you play an excellent game of *Cluedo*."

I exchanged an amused glance with Julie. "Being able to play *Clue*," I said, using the American name for the game, "doesn't qualify me to solve crimes."

"But your work experience does," Julie insisted. "You're an ex-cop, Maggie. Who better to do a bit of investigating on the side? Surely your hotel work isn't taking up all of your spare time?"

I gave a silent laugh. Spare time? What spare time? Now that I was working for Paul and Melanie, I'd committed every second I wasn't at the café to catching their would-be ghost. "Actually, I'm going to be pretty busy over the next few days."

Julie crossed her arms over her chest and fixed me with a belligerent stare. "Lenny's our friend. Don't you want to help his family?"

I sighed. I'd sworn secrecy to Paul and Melanie, and I couldn't tell Julie and Günter what I was truly doing at the hotel. On the other hand, my cousin was right. Lenny was our friend, and he'd helped me out more than once. I owed it to him to be there when he needed my help. I blew out my cheeks. "Okay. I'll see what I can do."

Julie's face flooded with relief. "Thanks, Maggie. I appreciate it. I know you'll figure out who killed Eddie Ward."

"I can't promise anything," I cautioned. "I have no idea what new evidence Reynolds has turned up, and let's just say he's very unlikely to confide in me at the moment."

This was an understatement. Whatever tentative trust we'd built, I'd shattered by my failure to tell him of Eddie Ward's rift with Lenny's family. It wasn't fair, but I understood Reynolds's sense of betrayal that I'd held out on him, especially when he'd just confided in me. Had our roles been reversed, I'd have been livid.

"Is there anything we can do to help?" Julie asked.

"Maybe I can question people like I did when Sandra Walker was killed."

"Leave the heavy lifting to me," I said, thinking of the ferocity with which Ward had been killed. Whoever was behind the murder was ruthless as well as violent. "If you could ask around if anyone had a reason to want him dead, that would be cool."

My cousin beamed. "Consider it done."

Günter pulled on his jacket and trudged out of the café with us. "I, too, will do the asking," he said in heavily accented tones. "I have friends at the hotel who know Carl Logan."

"Sven and Marcus?" It was a guess, but there weren't many foreigners on Whisper Island, and even fewer for whom English wasn't their first language. I could imagine they'd stick together.

The German nodded. "Yes, they are both my friends, but I know Marcus a bit better because we can talk German to one another. Did you know Marcus worked with Eddie Ward?"

My ears pricked up at this unexpected information. "Ward moonlighted as a massage therapist?" A vision of the postman's slick smile and groping hands made me shudder.

Günter laughed. "Oh, no. The opposite way around. Marcus helped deliver post when Ward was on holiday or sick, and sometimes during busy periods like Christmas."

"So Marcus knew Ward pretty well?"

Günter shrugged. "I don't know about that. I didn't get the impression they were close friends, but they didn't dislike each other."

Interesting. I filed this information away for further consideration. "Thanks, Günter. I can arrange a moment to speak with Marcus tomorrow when I'm working at the hotel, but I'd appreciate it if you'd have a talk with him as well. His English isn't great, and I don't speak a word of German."

"No problem. I'll give him a call and arrange to meet him and Sven for a drink." At my wary look, he smiled and added, "Don't worry. I'll be discreet. They won't know I'm asking questions on your behalf."

"Thank you. Give me a call if you discover anything useful."

"I'll do that, Maggie."

Paul and Melanie would be furious if they knew I was digging for info about a case they weren't paying me to investigate, but I didn't care. As long as I delivered the goods before St. Patrick's Day, they shouldn't care what questions I asked. Besides, the beauty center was an area I hadn't yet worked, and it would give me the chance to ask the employees for more info about the hotel spook.

Feeling more cheerful than I had in over twenty-four hours, I locked up the Movie Theater Café and went home to plot my next move.

TEN

The next morning, my cunning plan to inveigle my way into a shift at the beauty center was torpedoed the moment I set foot inside the hotel.

A flustered Melanie met me in the lobby. She grabbed my arm and hauled me into the office. "Thank goodness you're here, Maggie. In addition to that fool of a chef getting arrested, we had another haunting last night, and two guests left as a result."

I frowned. "What did this 'haunting' involve?"

"The guests I mentioned were staying in one of our deluxe suites on the third floor. The fourth floor to you, I suppose. Don't Americans call the ground floor the first floor?" Melanie continued without waiting for me to respond. "Anyway, while the guests were in the hot tub drinking champagne, an eerie wailing came from the direction of their room."

"Eerie wailing? Like a banshee?"

Melanie nodded vigorously. "Exactly like a banshee."

"What happened next?" I demanded. "I need every detail."

"The man got out of the hot tub and went to investigate. The wailing stopped the instant he opened the bathroom door, but their stuff had been ransacked, and clothes lay everywhere." Melanie's hand fluttered to her throat. "They packed up and left immediately."

"So basically someone made wailing noises in their room while they were in the hot tub and threw their stuff around?"

"Yes."

I mulled over this information for a moment. "Do you have security cameras in the hotel?"

"Of course we do." Melanie looked indignant. "But we don't have them in the guests' rooms. That would be a gross invasion of privacy."

"I mean in the hallway," I said with ill-disguised impatience.

"We're not completely stupid," Melanie snapped. "Looking at the surveillance tape was the first thing we did. All we saw was what we expected to see: a maid delivering room service to another room, and one of our security guards doing his rounds. No one went into or left that suite at the time the guests claim they heard wailing."

"With the right technical knowledge, it's possible

to doctor surveillance footage so that only an expert could notice. Have you considered that possibility?"

Her tight expression turned rigid. "Our tech guy was one of the first employees to quit when this ghost nonsense started. There's no one left with the know-how to check if someone tampered with the footage."

"Lenny Logan is a whiz with computers and other tech equipment. I could ask him to take a look and give his opinion."

Melanie sneered. "I hardly think we need to involve a Logan in this affair. Carl being arrested is enough bad publicity for one week, not to mention the fact that we're now reliant on a skeleton kitchen staff. Between a ghost and a murderous cook, guests are canceling in droves."

"Carl hasn't been convicted of any crime," I said through gritted teeth. "Innocent until proven guilty, remember?"

"Carl Logan's knife was found at the scene of the crime. A knife that *we* gave him." Melanie pursed her lips and her sour expression reminded me of her late mother—and that wasn't a compliment. "I don't like the hotel being dragged into this sordid business."

"Unless you can think of an alternative, Lenny is the only person on Whisper Island with the technical knowledge to recognize a cleverly doctored surveillance tape." I crossed my arms over my chest and stood my ground. "We both agree that someone is deliberately scaring away your guests and employees.

Taking the supernatural out of the equation, we can assume whoever is behind the 'hauntings' is very much alive. And the living aren't invisible. Someone had to have entered that room and thrown the guests' belongings all over the place. And if they aren't on the surveillance tape, it points to something being wrong with the tape."

"Fine." A weary look crept over Melanie's face, erasing some of her hauteur. "Ask Logan if he'll take a look at the footage. We also have recordings saved from the other incidents."

"He'll need to be paid, of course," I said firmly. "I think five hundred is fair for an evening's work."

Her eyes snapped. "Are you trying to bankrupt us?"

"I'm trying to negotiate fair recompense for my friend. If you don't want him to look at the tapes, you can always get someone to come over from the mainland. But trust me, they'll charge a lot more than five hundred, and I'm willing to bet they won't be half as good as Lenny."

Melanie sighed. "Three hundred for his time looking through all the tapes, and an extra two hundred if he finds something useful."

I stretched out my hand. "Deal."

She brushed invisible lint from the front of her pantsuit, a sure sign that our meeting was at an end. "Given that we're terribly short-staffed in the kitchen, I'd like you to help out there again today."

My heart sank. So much for getting a chance to talk to Marcus about Eddie Ward. "I'd planned to talk to the beauty center staff."

Melanie's eyes narrowed. "Why? Do you suspect one of them of being responsible for the hauntings?"

"I have no idea who's behind the ghost," I said quickly, not wanting to get the beauty center staff into trouble. "I didn't have a chance to talk to them yesterday."

She practically vibrated with impatience. "You can work at the beauty center tomorrow. Right now, we need your help preparing breakfast."

"How am I supposed to get a feel for the hotel and its employees if I don't move around?" I demanded. "The whole point of me being here is to investigate your so-called spook, and I have less than a week to get the job done."

Melanie pointedly checked her watch. "You can 'move around' tomorrow. Unless we get the breakfast buffet ready, we'll have even fewer guests left at the hotel, and the whole point of you investigating will have been for nothing."

I swallowed a sigh. It looked like my double-duty questioning would have to wait.

———

When six o'clock finally rolled around and my shift ended, I dragged myself home and changed into my running gear. I'd arranged to meet my cousin and her mother for an evening jog. Bran, recognizing my running attire and knowing this meant an outing for him, barked excitedly and performed a little dance and tail waggling routine in front of the door. I checked the cats' food and water containers, and laced up my running shoes.

"Come on," I said, clipping Bran's lead to his collar. "I'll let you put me through my paces."

With an enthusiastic bark, Bran shot out the cottage door, dragging me in his wake.

"Slow down," I yelled, tugging on the lead. "You'll wear me out before we ever start our warmup."

The dog paid me no heed. I was obliged to run to keep up. When we reached the gates of Shamrock Cottages, Bran slowed to a trot, allowing me to catch my breath. Julie and Philomena had parked beside the entrance. Both wore their running gear and eyed Bran with a mixture of amusement and trepidation.

"Last time we brought him with us," Julie said, "it was more like a sprint than a jog."

"I'll take him off the lead and let him run ahead if he gets to be too much." I turned to my aunt and grinned. "Looking good, Philomena. I like the new running pants."

My aunt wore hot pink running tights and an equally tight purple long-sleeved running top. They emphasized her curves and showed how much weight she'd shed since she'd started training with Julie and me. She beamed at the compliment. "Thanks. John loves my new look."

"Uncle John is a smart man."

We set off down a winding path that led to one of our usual running routes, and we were soon jogging at a steady pace. As I'd anticipated, Bran was too impatient to wait for us, so I let him have his freedom.

"How's the job at the hotel going?" Philomena said in short gasps. "What are you doing, anyway?"

"I'm what they call a floater. I go wherever they're short-staffed." This, at least, was true, and didn't require me to lie to cover my true reason for being at the hotel.

"Have you seen the hotel ghost yet?" Julie asked. "Sven and Marcus's description of it was vivid."

I laughed. "No. I don't believe in ghosts."

"It's all nonsense," Philomena huffed. "If the hotel guests and employees are stupid enough to believe in ghosts, good riddance to them."

"I doubt the Greers agree," I said dryly. "They're worried about their bottom line."

My aunt snorted. "They're worried about not having the cash to build that awful new extension."

This was news to me. "Are they expanding the hotel again?"

"Oh, yes. And the news caused quite a stir. They've only just managed to get the planning permission approved after it was blocked."

"Who blocked it and why?"

"The Whisper Island Folklore and Heritage Society. Paul is determined to build an extension over some land at the back of the hotel. It'll be roughly the same size as the spa area only on the other side of the hotel."

"What's the society's objection?"

"The land he wants to build on has a fairy tree and an archaeological site on it."

A memory stirred. "Wait a sec. I remember climbing that tree. A hawthorn, isn't it?"

"That's right. The heritage society members are very upset over the idea of the tree being bulldozed. They managed to delay planning permission by arguing that the stones surrounding the tree are of historical significance, but the courts decided otherwise."

"So they have a known grudge against the Greers?"

"Yes," Philomena said, "but I can't see any of them messing around with clanking chains and banshees. They take themselves very seriously."

"But one of them could hold a grudge strong enough to persuade them to terrorize the hotel's inhabitants?" We'd slowed to a walk by now and were catching our breath.

"I suppose so." Philomena didn't look convinced. "But knowing the personalities involved, I can't see it. They'd be the sort to stage a sitting protest the day the bulldozers were due to arrive. Maybe hold up placards outside the hotel entrance and cause a scene. I can't imagine them resorting to organized terror."

"Where would I find the Folklore and Heritage Society?"

"They're one of the clubs that still meet at the library instead of the Movie Theater Café, so you probably haven't come across them before. Sheila Dunphy is their president. You might have served her in the café. An old lady who always wears her long, white hair in two plaits?"

An image formed in my head. "Yes. I'm sure I've seen her drinking tea with the Spinsters."

Philomena raised an eyebrow.

"She's not referring to me, Mum," Julie joked. "The Spinsters are Miss Flynn and Miss Murphy. They practically live at the Movie Theater Café."

I laughed. "Along with the Two Gerries, they keep the place afloat."

My aunt eyed me with a sly grin. "You say you've been employed at the hotel because they're short-staffed. Are you sure there's not another reason, Maggie?"

I schooled my face into a neutral expression. "Why would there be? I need the cash, and they need my help."

"Hmm..." My aunt didn't look convinced. "I'd have thought you had enough to do looking into this new murder case without running after ghosts."

"I didn't say I was doing either."

"And I didn't come down in the last shower, missy. Just promise me you'll be careful. And don't drag my Julie into any of this nonsense. It might be dangerous."

Julie flashed me a grin. "Don't worry, Mum. My main concern at the moment is not dying during the Runathon."

"I'm not saying I'm helping the Greers with the ghost business, but I do have a favor to ask," I said to my aunt. "Would you mind looking up the fairy tree and the history of the land Paul wants to build on? There might be some info at the library."

Philomena cast me a knowing look. "So you want to put your librarian aunt to work digging for information, but you won't admit to working for the Greers?"

"I can't admit to anything. If I was working for them, I'd have been asked to keep it confidential."

"All right. I'll have a look and see what I can find. Will you be working at the café during tomorrow night's Knitting Club meeting?"

I grinned, recalling that more gossip was exchanged during those meetings than knitting tips. "Yes."

"I'll give you whatever I've managed to find at the meeting."

"Thanks, Philomena. I appreciate it."

After our run, my aunt and cousin drove back to Smuggler's Cove, and Bran and I returned to Shamrock Cottages. "I'm having a bath," I told the dog on our way up the drive, "and I'm going all out. Bubbles galore, a good book, and a glass of red wine."

When we reached my cottage, Mack's car was parked outside. Mack leaned against the hood, a frown etched onto his forehead. Meanwhile, Lenny sat on my doorstep, chewing his nails. They both appeared to have the weight of the world on their shoulders. My heart sank. So much for my relaxing evening. "Hey, guys. You two look like the apocalypse just hit. What happened?"

Lenny leaped to his feet. "You've got to help me, Maggie. Granddad's been charged with being an accessory to murder."

ELEVEN

"Come into the cottage and I'll fix you a drink. I have a bottle of red wine, or I can make you a cocktail. I stocked up on ingredients for Brandy Alexanders."

Lenny's face brightened. "I'd love a Brandy Alexander."

"I'm driving," Mack said, but without real conviction.

"If you don't mind sharing with the cats, you guys are welcome to sleep in my spare room tonight."

I led them into the house and locked up for the night. Then I fetched the bottles of brandy and crème de cacao I'd purchased during yesterday's shopping trip and fixed three generous glasses of Brandy Alexander. When I served Lenny his cocktail, his stiff posture in the armchair was in sharp contrast to his usual lazy sprawl. I claimed the seat opposite Lenny, while Mack took the sofa.

I took a sip from my glass—tonight wasn't the night for toasts and pleasantries—and got straight to the point. "What evidence does Reynolds have to connect your grandfather with the crime?"

Lenny glowered into his cocktail glass. "Apparently, Ward's body tested positive for alcohol, and a bottle of my grandfather's *poitín* was found under the passenger seat of the postal van."

"Half the island has a bottle of your granddad's poteen rolling around somewhere."

Mack's mouth twisted. "Yeah, but this particular bottle contained an extra ingredient."

"Cyanide," I guessed instantly.

"How did you know that?" Lenny demanded. "Did Reynolds tell you?"

"Put it this way," I prevaricated. "Reynolds is unlikely to confide in me about *anything* at the moment. He's annoyed I didn't tip him off about Ward getting your sister pregnant."

"Well, you're right about the poison. According to Reynolds, the bottle of *poitín* was laced with a blood pressure medication that was found in my grandfather's bathroom. This particular medication contains a form of cyanide."

I contemplated this new information. "Man, this talk of poisons makes me feel like a character in an Agatha Christie novel. Did Reynolds tell you the cause of death?" The policeman had already shared the answer with me, but I needed to know what he'd told Lenny.

"Cyanide poisoning."

I whistled. "There must have been a lot of that stuff in the poteen for it to kill a man. I guess your granddad's medicine doesn't contain a strong dose."

"Here's where the story gets weird." Lenny's frown deepened. "Granddad swears he's never seen the medicine before. He takes blood pressure tablets, but those don't contain cyanide."

"What substance did the police find in his bathroom?"

"Sodium nitroprusside." Mack sat back on the sofa and thrust his hands deep into his pockets. "It's usually used during surgeries or medical emergencies. We have it at the pharmacy, and the Whisper Island Medical Centre also has it in stock."

"So it's not a medication Lenny's grandfather would have had easy access to?"

"No." Mack looked troubled and shot a glance at Lenny before continuing. "But he was at the medical center for an appointment last week when I made the weekly delivery of medications from the pharmacy."

"And the medications you delivered included sodium nitroprusside," I guessed.

"Bingo."

"And it gets worse," Lenny added. "Dr. Reilly claims a vial of sodium nitroprusside is missing from his medical supplies, and they were all accounted for when Mack made the delivery."

I turned to Lenny. "Your grandfather can't have been the only patient present at the clinic when Mack showed up. Anyone there might have taken the medicine, or it might have been stolen on another occasion."

"Sure, but it's circumstantial evidence. The more stuff like this the police dig up, the worse it looks for Granddad."

"Reynolds asked me for a list of people I'd seen at the clinic," Mack said, "and I'm sure he's asked Dr. Reilly for confirmation of all the patients he saw between my delivery last Wednesday and the night of the murder."

"I'd like to know who's on that list," I said, "but before we get to that, do you know when Dr. Reilly discovered the vial was missing?"

"Not until after the murder. Once the cause of death was confirmed, Reynolds asked both the pharmacy and the Whisper Island Medical Centre to check our supplies. We're the only places on the island that would have it in stock."

I took another sip of my cocktail and considered all I'd learned so far. "I'd like to see Dr. Reilly's list of patients, but I guess that won't happen. What about the people you saw in the waiting room the day you made the delivery?"

Mack pulled out his phone and made a few swipes

over the display. "I don't know all of them by name, but here's what I wrote down. Apart from Gerry Logan, Paddy Driscoll was there, as was Sister Pauline. There was a mother with two small kids. I think she's married to Pete McCarthy, one of the island's volunteer firemen, but I don't know her name."

"Sheila," Lenny supplied. "Who else is on the list?"

"Only two more. A blond woman around our age, and a dark-haired guy who I think works at the hotel, but I'm not sure."

My ears pricked up. "A guy from the hotel? Where have you seen him there?"

Mack frowned. "I can't remember. The bar, maybe? I'm not even sure why I thought he worked at the hotel. He might just have been at the bar one night."

"You have a good memory for faces," I said. "Most witnesses are vague when asked to make a list of people they saw a week ago."

He laughed. "Sheer luck. The medical assistant who helps me unpack the delivery was busy when I arrived and I had to wait. That's the only reason I paid any attention to who was in the waiting room."

"Returning to the medication, how easy is sodium nitroprusside to use for someone with no medical knowledge?"

The pharmacist considered my question for a moment before answering. "When he questioned me about the delivery, Reynolds mentioned that the sodium nitroprusside found in the poteen was used in its undiluted form. That would be easy enough for anyone to do." At my perplexed expression, the pharmacist elaborated. "The substance found in Gerry's bathroom is usually administered with an IV drip and diluted with saline solution. That would require some medical knowledge. But if it was just dumped into the poteen undiluted, anyone could do that."

"Is undiluted sodium nitroprusside always fatal?"

"It depends on the amount, of course, but yeah, it could lead to an overdose."

"And it was put into alcohol," Lenny added. "With Ward being a diabetic, it could have made the laced alcohol work faster on his system."

My eyebrows shot up. "Eddie Ward was diabetic? Are you sure?" For some reason, this detail bothered me, but at that moment, I couldn't pinpoint why.

Lenny shrugged. "I'm just going on what Reynolds told me. That's what's in the pathologist's report."

"The medication could have been taken by anyone, and we've already said that most people on the island have a bottle of his poteen. Does Reynolds have any other evidence against your grandfather?"

Lenny took a large gulp of his cocktail. "Unfortunately, yeah."

"Go on."

"You know the injuries to Ward's face?"

"Yeah…" My stomach lurched at what I was afraid Lenny would say next.

"The pathologist is convinced some of those injuries occurred after death but before the body went over the cliff." Lenny leaned forward in his seat, cradling his cocktail glass between the palms of his hands. "Reynolds found blood belonging to the dead man on the handle of Granddad's ax."

I exhaled in a hiss. This wasn't good news. The more evidence Reynolds amassed pointing to the Logans, the less likely he'd be to look elsewhere. "Lenny, I'm sorry I have to ask this, but—"

"No." He cut me off sharply. "Carl and Granddad say they had nothing to do with Ward's death. I believe them. And Gerry Two is adamant that he was with Granddad the night of the murder until I showed up. That's why Reynolds considers Granddad an accessory but not a murder suspect."

I held his gaze. "I have to ask these questions, Lenny. I want to help you clear their names, but if they did it and I find more evidence to help convict them, I'll give it to the police. I want to be clear on that point."

"They didn't do it."

"Okay. What about your middle brother? Or your parents? Any chance they might have been involved?"

Lenny shook his head. "Jake lives in Galway during the week. You know that."

"He could have caught the ferry over to the island before the storm blew in," I pointed out.

"But he didn't," Lenny said with emphasis. "Believe me, the police already checked, and Jake has an alibi. He was at the university delivering a lecture on fossils at the time of the murder. There are hundreds of witnesses to back up his story."

"Okay. Where were your parents on the night of the murder?"

"My parents were at a birthday party that evening. They arrived before Ward was killed, and left after we'd found the body."

"What does Jennifer Pearce say about Carl and Gerry's stories?"

Lenny shook his head. "She's not happy. I get the impression she'll be delighted to hand them off to her criminal defense solicitor friend once she arrives tomorrow."

"To be fair, criminal law isn't Jennifer's area," Mack said. "She's only standing in until a specialist can get to the island."

Lenny snorted. "In this case, it's more the fact that she doesn't believe Carl and Granddad's stories. It's obvious she's going through the motions."

"You've been watching too much TV, my friend," I said dryly. "I dealt with plenty of lawyers during my years on the force, and a defendant doesn't need an attorney that believes they're innocent. They need an attorney capable of mounting a convincing defense.

Jennifer might not be a criminal defense attorney, but she's good at her job. She'll take good care of them until her replacement arrives."

"I want them to have a lawyer who's on their side," Lenny repeated stubbornly. "I want someone who believes they're innocent. My cousin, Jack, says he knows a guy in Dublin who's a whizz at criminal defense, but I'm wary of anyone who considers Jack a pal."

I exchanged an amused glance with Mack. "Jack sold me my car."

Mack winced. "Ouch. Is it still moving?"

"At the moment, yeah. Any problems, I'm paying Jack another visit." I took a sip from my cocktail glass and regarded Lenny. His thin frame was rigid from tension, and his bony face had a pinched look I hadn't seen before. I wanted to help him, and I wanted to believe his relatives were innocent, but I had to admit that Reynolds was building a strong case against them. "You said your family disliked Ward. Can you remember any fights they had with him?"

Lenny's nod was a jerk of his head, and his pale skin grew ashen. "Granddad and Carl had a terrible row with Ward at the summer fair the week after he dumped Katie. Granddad said the man needed shooting, and Ward got up in his face about it, thus prompting Carl to throw a punch. The fight escalated, and ended with Sergeant O'Shea dragging Carl off Ward and throwing them both in a cell for fighting."

Yikes. A police record of the Logans fighting with Ward added an awkward slant to the situation. "A history of punch-ups doesn't look good, but it isn't proof that either your grandfather or Carl killed Ward." I paused before posing my next question. "Lenny, have you heard from your sister?"

A pained expression flickered across his face. "Katie texted me to say the baby was born, but that was it. I've been trying to contact her to let her know about Ward's death, but she's not answering her phone, and it's not the kind of news I want to deliver as a text message."

An uncomfortable thought slid through my brain. Judging by Mack's sudden preoccupation with his fingernails, the same thought had occurred to him. Could Katie have snuck back to the island to take revenge on her ex-lover? "If she's just had a baby, she's probably exhausted," I said in a hopeful tone.

Lenny frowned. "Yeah, but I'm starting to get worried about her. If she doesn't make contact within the next couple of days, I'm going to fly over to London to see her."

I glanced at Mack, but he studiously avoided my gaze. I took a deep breath and addressed Lenny. "You don't think—"

He held a hand up. "Don't say it, Maggie. I don't know how to answer you, and that bothers me."

"Of all your family, Katie had the most reason to hate Ward."

"Maggie has a point," Mack said, finally looking up from his nails. "Ward abandoned her."

"Do you think a woman who's just given birth is sneaking around Whisper Island murdering people?" Lenny sounded as though he was trying to convince himself.

I threw him a lifeline. "Katie would have had problems dragging Ward's body around and throwing it off the cliff."

"Of course she didn't do it. None of my family did it." Lenny put his head in his hands. "I just want to wake up from this nightmare and go back to fixing computers and hunting aliens. That's what I do best."

I refrained from voicing my suspicion that Lenny and Mack's UFO spotting trips owed their success to poteen and pot. In my presence, they'd only consumed poteen, but I was no fool. "Why don't you guys go on an emergency UFO hunt? You need the distraction."

"I guess." Lenny sounded doubtful. "We were due to go on Thursday, but I had to cancel because of our trip to the mainland to fix the Movie Club's projector."

"I can do tomorrow or Wednesday," Mack said.

"Sounds like an excellent plan." I drained my cocktail glass and stretched. "I'm going to hit the shower and then head to bed. Juggling multiple jobs is exhausting. I don't know how you two do it."

"The paramedic stuff is on a volunteer basis." Mack shrugged. "I enjoy it. Most of the time, we don't have to do much. The night of the storm was an exception."

"And I can fit my computer repair business around my day job," Lenny added. "It's not set shifts like you're working at the hotel and the café."

Not to mention the two mysteries I was investigating—one ridiculous and the other all too serious. Before I showered, I found spare bedclothes and helped Lenny and Mack to make the bed in the guest room. When we were done, Mack gave me one of his weird handshakes, and Lenny gave me a quick hug. "Thanks for letting us crash here, Maggie. I have a feeling that cocktail will help me sleep."

"If not, I can give you a sleeper." Mack patted his pocket.

Lenny reared back. "No way. The last time you gave me one of those, I woke up the next morning to discover I'd shaved my balls and uploaded the evidence to Snapchat."

"What?" I cried at the same time Mack demanded, "You're on Snapchat?"

"I didn't even know I had an account until people started messaging me." Lenny turned to me with an earnest expression. "The shaved-balls business wasn't a good look."

"I'm happy to take your word on that," I said, deadpan. "No need to show me the evidence. Sleep well, guys. And stay off the sleepers."

"You, too," they said in unison.

I forced a smile. "And don't worry, Lenny. It'll all work out."

I shut the guest room door behind me and hoped the doubt I felt at the veracity of my words hadn't shown on my face.

TWELVE

When I got back to the cottage after taking Bran for his morning walk, Lenny and Mack were still asleep. I fed the cats and dog, and left the guys the spare key with a note asking them to lock up when they left. As a postscript, I added that I had a potential paid job offer for Lenny and that he should call Melanie at the hotel. I'd intended to ask him about looking at the surveillance footage last night, but I'd been distracted by the news of Gerry Logan's arrest.

Still tired after a restless night, I jumped into my car and drove to the hotel to begin my morning shift. Today, I was in luck. Mclanie agreed to let me work in the beauty center, thus giving me the perfect opportunity to ask Marcus and Sven about Eddie Ward. The men were busy all morning with guests from a bachelorette party, but they joined me for a coffee break at eleven.

"You took our advice and asked for a job." Sven beamed at me. "This is good."

"And you know about the ghost already." Marcus added. "You won't run away when he comes clanking his chains."

I laughed. "No. I don't intend to be scared off by a poltergeist, real or imagined."

"These last few days, everyone has forgotten about the ghost," Sven said, his expression growing serious.

"I heard there was another incident on Sunday night," I said. "Didn't that upset the staff?"

"Only briefly." Sven's jaw tensed. "We're all upset about a different matter. Have you heard about our head chef being arrested for murder?"

Oh, yeah. "I was in the lobby when the police arrived."

"It's terrible," the Swede said. "I can't believe Carl would kill someone. He's hot-tempered, yes, but he's no murderer."

"Everyone knows he hated Eddie," Marcus added. "It's not so very strange that the police suspect him."

"Did you know Eddie Ward?" I asked in an innocent tone, even though I knew the answer.

Marcus shrugged. "Not well. I helped deliver post from time to time."

"He sometimes came to Murphy's Pub," Sven said. "We'd sit and chat for a while, but the conversations were always very superficial."

Marcus grinned. "Sven is not a football fan. He got bored when Eddie and I discussed our favorite teams."

Sven puffed out his not-inconsiderable chest. "I prefer philosophy and politics. Eddie was not an educated man."

"Snob," Marcus said, but with a good-natured laugh.

In my experience, the best way to get people to open up during an investigation was to use honesty to camouflage one's true purpose in asking specific questions. "I wasn't the postman's greatest fan," I said frankly. "I thought he was a slimeball."

"You weren't the only person to have that opinion," Sven said. "Eddie was popular with women, but he treated them badly. Always a new woman on his arm every week. That's why he preferred the hotel bar to the island's pubs. More turnover in the clientele."

"I heard he got a girl pregnant," I said, toying with the handle of my coffee cup.

The men exchanged glances. "We heard he got more than one woman pregnant," Sven said. "He had a son living in Galway."

"Really? Do the police know this?"

Marcus grabbed a banana from the staff's fruit basket and unpeeled it. "I don't know. Eddie said he wasn't named on the birth certificate."

I'd have to share this information with Liam Reynolds. If the postman had a vindictive ex living on the mainland, he needed to know. "Did he have any contact with the child?"

"Not that I know about." Sven's lips twisted into an ironic smile. "He said he'd seen the boy once, just after he was born, and then the mother banned all contact. Typical Eddie."

"Lemme guess...Ward didn't pay child support?"

Marcus snorted. "Eddie had moved on to another woman before the baby was born."

"Apart from the Logans and the ex with the kid, can you think of anyone else with a grudge against Ward?"

Marcus shook his head. "No. Like Sven said, Eddie wasn't a guy to share his feelings. We didn't talk about personal stuff."

"When I found the mail van abandoned, it was pretty late for Eddie to still be on the island. I thought he returned the van to the mainland every night." Actually, I hadn't a clue what Ward did with the van, but I figured Marcus would know.

"No, no. That's not how it worked," Marcus said. "Eddie had a cottage on the island. Every evening, he emptied the letter boxes all over the island and collected packages from the post office. The next morning, he drove the van to the mainland and brought the post to the main post depot in Galway. They'd give him the mail to deliver to the island, and back he'd come."

"Do you know where Eddie lived?"

"Near Carraig Harbour," Sven supplied. "Convenient for the ferry."

I scrunched up my forehead. There were very few houses in the vicinity of Carraig Harbour, and one of them was my cottage. "Was Ward's place the one with the bright blue door and the gnomes in the garden?"

"Yes." Marcus grinned. "I was very surprised to see he had garden gnomes. He was very proud of them and his garden."

"He used to grow raspberries and give them to Carl to make jam," Sven said. "In exchange for Carl's signature chocolate cake, of course. Ward always had a sweet tooth."

My stomach performed a flip and roll. "A sweet tooth? Wasn't Ward diabetic?"

Sven and Marcus stared at me. "I don't think so," Sven said. "Did he mention it to you?"

Marcus considered for a moment, and then shook his head. "No, but Eddie said his girlfriend liked Carl's cake. Maybe he got it for her."

"Which girlfriend?" Sven laughed. "Eddie got around."

Marcus smirked. "How should I know?"

"Maybe Eddie used Carl's cake as part of his seduction ritual," Sven said. "It would be the sort of thing he'd do. He probably told women he'd baked it himself."

The by-now-familiar clip clop of Melanie's high heels on the marble floor alerted us to her presence.

She marched into the salon with Lisa the receptionist at her side. "What are you doing sitting around?" Melanie demanded. "I don't pay you to drink coffee."

The men leaped to their feet. "We were on our coffee break," Sven said. "Just a few minutes."

"Something's wrong with the phone," Lisa said in her clipped monotone. "I can't get through to the beauty center from the reception."

Marcus took a step toward her. "I'll take a look. Last time, someone had hit a wrong key."

"Yes, do," Lisa said, sounding so like an android that I had to stifle a giggle.

The tall massage therapist flashed me a grin. "Bye, Maggie."

After he and Lisa had disappeared into the hallway, Melanie rounded on Sven. "Time to get back to work," she snapped, and then focused her attention on me. "We need you upstairs. One of the maids has taken ill and gone home early. I need someone to finish cleaning the rooms on the second floor."

Casting a conspiratorial wink at Sven, I followed Melanie out of the beauty center. In the hallway, we passed a vending machine that offered an array of snacks. My eyes fixed on the chewing gum. I sucked air through my teeth. So that was what had bothered me when I'd reviewed the contents of the mail van. The pack of chewing gum. I stepped closer to the machine and examined the package through the glass display.

The chewing gum I'd seen in Eddie Ward's van wasn't sugar-free.

———

Of all the tasks I'd tackled since starting work at the hotel, making beds was the one that almost finished me. After engaging in a wrestling match with a ridiculous number of sheets, I stood back panting and regarded my handiwork. And groaned. Somewhere in the middle of tucking in the requisite two sheets, two blankets, and an elaborately embroidered coverlet, I'd created a lump in the middle of the bed.

"Well, heck." I took a deep breath and hurled myself onto the bed. I rolled from side to side several times, but the lump stubbornly refused to flatten.

"What you do, Maggie?" Zuzanna, my Polish cleaning partner, emerged from the bathroom, rattling the cleaning cart. "Oh, no. That bed is mess."

"It's a hot mess," I agreed, still face-down on the bed. "I'm trying to get rid of the bulge. If I roll around on it for a while, maybe no one will notice."

Zuzanna clucked her tongue. "Mrs. Dennehy notice everything."

I pushed myself up and looked at the stubborn lump. Ingenious as it was, my lump-killing technique wasn't working. "Hey, I'm new. Maybe Mrs. Dennehy will give me a pass."

"That dragon give no one a pass. She rule her

kingdom with the iron rod." Zuzanna circled the bed and regarded my bed-making efforts with scorn. "You tuck all wrong. Do you never make bed before?"

"Sure I have," I said indignantly. "I shake out my quilt every morning. I've even been known to pummel my pillow back into shape."

Zuzanna shook her head. "You'll never make it as a maid."

"Well, shucks," I said. "I guess I'd better stick to burning scones."

"Do you take nothing seriously, Maggie?"

"Yeah, but apparently not the fine art of making beds with a thousand sheets." I swung myself off the bed and tugged at the hem of my ridiculously short skirt. "This fancy sheet is a waste of time. I bet half the guests pull off the whole shebang and use the spare quilt in the closet."

The girl shrugged. "I know they do, but this 'fancy business' is what guests expect. It's a five-star hotel after all."

I gave a derisive snort. "I bet most of the guests would prefer a regular quilt to getting tangled up in their bedclothes. I mean, for heaven's sake, you could strangle yourself in these sheets."

"The only person getting strangled is you if Mrs. Dennehy sees that lump." Zuzanna sighed. "Come on. I help you." Five minutes later, Zuzanna and I had wrestled the various layers back onto the bed and ensured it was a lump-free zone. My companion checked her watch. "Only one room left on this floor, and then we can eat lunch."

As if powered by rocket fuel, we zoomed through the last room. This time, I tackled the bathroom, while Zuzanna made up the bed. When we wheeled the supply cart out of the room and locked the door, it was after two o'clock. My stomach rumbled. I hadn't eaten since breakfast.

"We can see if the kitchen has leftovers," Zuzanna said. "They're not supposed to give to us, but Bernadette always does."

I remembered the good-natured chef from my first day on the job. Yeah, she'd be the type to sneak us a hot meal. I quickened my pace, my mouth already watering in anticipation of eating some of the delicious food I'd helped to prepare yesterday. We'd just passed one of the suites we'd cleaned earlier when an eerie wailing stopped me in my tracks. My pulse pounded, and a shot of adrenaline coursed through my body. Was this the infamous ghost?

Beside me, Zuzanna made the sign of the cross and muttered something in Polish.

The ghostly wailing increased in volume until it was eclipsed by the sound of a very human scream inside the suite. A woman charged out of the room, arms flailing, her face chalky white. "*Help me,*" she cried when she saw us, and clutched a towel around her ample bosom. "There's a ghost in my room. It's thrown my stuff everywhere."

"Nonsense," I said, and marched past her into the suite. "There's no such thing as— "

The final word froze on my tongue when I saw the state of the suite. The bed that I'd fought to make earlier was in disarray. Drawers and closets had been emptied, and their contents lay strewn around the room. A picture on the wall was askew, and the window had been thrown up. I ran to it and looked outside. The only place for someone to go was down the fire escape. If they'd used it as their exit route, they were long gone. I pulled my head back into the room and frowned. The wailing had stopped by now, but it had to have a source. I scoured the suite from top to bottom but found no evidence of a speaker.

"Come, Maggie," Zuzanna said with a touch of irritation. "There's nothing here."

"What on earth is going on?" The large form of Mrs. Dennehy, the hotel's head of housekeeping, loomed before me. She had her hands on her ample hips and a menacing expression on her homely face.

"A guest claims a ghost ransacked her room," I said. "I'm looking for a recording device or speaker. That wailing had to come from somewhere, and I don't buy the ghost theory."

"Not that nonsense again." Mrs. Dennehy glared at me as though I were personally responsible for the mayhem in the hotel. "People these days have no common sense."

I spread my arms wide. "Ghost or no ghost, the

room didn't trash itself. Someone was in here while the room's occupant was in the shower."

Mrs. Dennehy took a phone from her pocket and hit a number. "Mrs. Greer? You'd better come up to Room 245. There's been another incident."

"The half-naked woman streaking through the lobby probably tipped her off," I said dryly, earning another glare from the housekeeper.

I hunched down and scanned the perimeters of the room. And then I spotted the anomaly I'd been looking for. I took a Swiss Army knife from my pocket and unscrewed a section of the baseboard.

"What do you think you're doing?" Mrs. Dennehy screeched. "You're wrecking the place."

"The room's already wrecked," I said, unperturbed. "Me unscrewing a piece of baseboard that can easily be replaced isn't going to make a difference." I eased the baseboard away from the wall to reveal a small hole. I laid the wood paneling on the floor, took a tissue from my pocket, and reached inside the hole. The instant I grasped the object, I knew what I'd found. "Look," I said excitedly and opened my fingers to show Mrs. Dennehy the tiny speaker sitting on the tissue. "This is the source of the wailing."

The older woman pursed her lips. "I always said a mischief-maker was behind these shenanigans."

Zuzanna stepped into the room and stared at me in awe. "How you know where to look?"

I shrugged. "Whoever tampered with the

baseboard didn't put it back on straight. I figured some sort of speaker had to be hidden in the room."

A moment after I'd found the speaker, Melanie arrived on the scene, looking flustered. "Mrs. Blake wants to leave," she wailed, "and she wants a refund for her stay. She and her husband were booked through St. Patrick's Day."

"At least we know how the banshee wailing is being transmitted." I showed her the mini speaker.

Melanie examined the device and pursed her lips. "That's all very well, but we don't know who planted it, or who ransacked the Blakes' belongings."

I forced a smile and said through gritted teeth, "Give me a break, Melanie. I've made more progress than you or Paul."

She glanced around the room nervously, not meeting Mrs. Dennehy's curious gaze. After all, I wasn't supposed to be on a first-name basis with the boss. "Come downstairs, Maggie. Your technically inclined friend is waiting for you in the lobby."

My mood brightened. "Lenny's here?"

She nodded. "I told him you'd assist him with that little job we discussed. Now that the cleaning's finished, you can manage without Maggie, Mrs. Dennehy."

The housekeeper bristled. "But what about this mess? That Zuzanna's run off to eat her lunch."

"Then you'll just have to tidy the room yourself,

won't you?" Melanie swept out of the room and propelled me down to the lobby.

Lenny's easygoing grin was a welcome contrast to his tense expression last night. "Hey, Maggie." He nodded to my companion. "And Melanie."

"Let's go into the security room." Melanie gave the lobby a surreptitious scan and led us across to a locked door. She opened it using a key card and gestured for us to enter.

Inside, a gray-haired man hunched before a series of screens, his attention on none of them. He leaped out of his seat when we walked in, and made an ineffectual effort to shove the newspaper he'd been reading into a drawer.

"Stellar security guard," Lenny whispered to me. "That's Pat Inglis. He divides his free time between propping up the bar at Murphy's Pub and losing money at the races."

I stifled a giggle. Judging by Pat's red face, he wasn't happy at being caught in the act of not doing his job. "I was just—"

"Save it," Melanie said with a weary sigh. "I want you to show these people the surveillance footage from the days of the various hauntings."

Pat frowned. "But we've already looked at it several times. What will they see that we didn't?"

"I want to check if the footage was doctored." Lenny slung his backpack onto a desk. "If someone is staging the hauntings, there has to be evidence on the tapes. Otherwise, they've been tampered with. How many cameras do you have, total?"

Pat shifted uncomfortably in his seat and avoided looking at Melanie. "There are two rotating cameras on each floor, one outside the beauty center, one in the restaurant, one in the kitchen, one in the lobby, and, uh —" he counted on his fingers, "—four outside the hotel."

"Fourteen cameras and six screens." Lenny shook his head. "Shoddy setup, Melanie. You should at least have a separate screen per camera."

Pat snuck a look at his boss, who was staring resolutely into space, her mouth an uncompromising slash. "The thing is," he said, "a few of those cameras are on the blink."

I raised an eyebrow and looked at Lenny for an explanation.

"A few cameras are broken," he translated for me. "Why does that not surprise me?"

"We haven't been able to fix them." Melanie sounded curt. "I wanted to, but my father-in-law overruled me."

"Given that the hotel is being terrorized," I said, "I'd have thought Mr. Greer would want to fix the cameras pronto."

"I know, but replacing them costs money we don't have at the moment." Melanie opened a drawer in a filing cabinet and withdrew a piece of paper. "Here are the dates and times of the various 'hauntings.' I've saved the relevant days' surveillance footage on this laptop." She pointed to a battered-looking laptop on a corner desk. "Look through it and see what you think."

I took the piece of paper from Melanie and scanned the dates. One leaped out at me. "Hang on a sec. There was a haunting incident on the night the postman was murdered?"

Melanie raised an eyebrow. "Well, yes, but I can't see how that's significant."

Trouble was, neither could I. It was probably just a coincidence, but like all cops, former or active, I didn't care for coincidences.

Lenny exchanged a glance with me before addressing Melanie. "Is it okay if I copy the footage? I'd like to replay it at home where I've got all my gear."

"If you must," she replied with a sniff, "but only copy the relevant times."

"Fair enough." Lenny dropped into the chair in front of the laptop and gestured for me to take the one beside him.

"If you need anything, I'll be in my office." Melanie's heels clicked out of the room.

The instant she was gone, the security guard lumbered to his feet. "I'm going out for a smoke. Don't break anything while I'm gone."

"We'll do our best." Lenny shot me a wicked smile.

The security guard leaned over the laptop and muttered something indecipherable. "I don't know what you two think you'll find. We had a thorough look at those recordings, and there's nothing to see." With these discouraging words, the man stomped out of the room.

"Eejit," Lenny said after Pat had left. "Inglis is a lazy oaf. I doubt he looked through all the footage. And even if he did, he's too stupid to notice anything out of the ordinary."

"I hope you don't mind me recommending you to Melanie. I know you're busy at your parents' store."

"I'm delighted, Maggie, and Mum doesn't mind covering for me for a couple of hours. Frankly, serving customers doesn't require much brain power, and I could do with the distraction."

"Any news on your grandfather and Carl?"

"Nothing much. Carl's still locked up, but Granddad's been released on bail." He snorted. "Sure, where do they think he's going to run to? Carl did mention one interesting piece of info, though."

My ears pricked up. "What?"

"The knife used to stab our dead guy went missing on the evening of the murder. Carl remembers it clearly because there was a haunting in the restaurant, and total chaos in the hotel. He left the kitchen to see what the fuss was about—"

"And when he returned, the knife was gone," I finished for him and slapped my palm against my thigh. "I knew it couldn't be a coincidence."

"Do you think the haunting was staged deliberately to steal Carl's knife?"

"It's a possibility. The other option is someone took advantage of the chaos to take Carl's knife."

We both fell silent and looked at the laptop. Lenny tapped the keyboard. "If we locate the footage from that night, maybe we can see who took the knife. Assuming, of course, that the camera in the kitchen is one that works."

"It's worth a shot." I scooted my chair closer. "Okay, let's get to work."

Two painful hours later, Lenny removed the flash drive he'd inserted into the laptop and stood, stretching his neck from side to side. "Nothing more we can do here today. The footage was definitely doctored, but I want to take another look at home to be sure."

"I feel square-eyed," I said, getting to my feet. "I have no idea how tech forensics do this all day." We let ourselves out of the security room and I accompanied Lenny out to the car park. "Thanks for doing this, Lenny. I'm sorry we didn't find any info to help your brother."

"It was worth a try. And I'm happy to earn a bit of extra cash." He held up the flash drive. "At least this will help me earn the extra two hundred. It should be easy enough to prove the footage was doctored."

"Unfortunately for me, all it does is prove the Greers' terrible security system was hacked. It doesn't bring me any closer to finding out who is faking the poltergeist."

Lenny cocked his head to the side. "So...you're

finally admitting you're working undercover for Melanie and Paul?"

"There's no point in denying it now."

"I guess not." He slipped his keys from his pocket. "Want a lift into town?"

"No, thanks. I have to report back to Melanie. My shift doesn't finish until six. Listen, before you go..." I slipped the speaker out of my pocket and showed it to him. "Do you know what this is? I'm pretty sure it's some sort of wireless speaker."

Lenny took the device in his hand and whistled. "I'll bet this cost a pretty penny. Where did you get it?"

"Behind the wall in one of the hotel suites. It was the source of the wailing woman during a so-called haunting incident. Is this the sort of thing someone could order online?"

"Sure. You can order pretty much anything online if you know where to look."

I sighed. "That was what I was afraid of. If it was an online purchase, it'll be harder to trace the buyer. I can't imagine this is the sort of equipment you stock at your electronics store."

Lenny slipped a toothpick out of his pocket and chewed it carefully, a frown etched onto his forehead. "No, but I know a place where you can buy this stuff on a hush-hush basis."

My heart leaped and my body buzzed with anticipation of a useful lead. "Where? Can we go there today?"

"Don't you have to finish your shift at the hotel?"

"Yeah, but I can persuade Melanie to let me leave early if I have a lead to pursue."

Lenny shook his head. "Sorry, Maggie. You'll need me to approach Chivers. He's...prickly around strangers, but he knows me and he owes me a favor."

I bounced up and down on the spot. "So let's go. Where does this Chivers dude live?"

"Galway. And I don't have time to hop on the ferry today." At my crestfallen expression, he added, "We're supposed to go to the mainland on Thursday to get the projector fixed. While you and Julie hit the clothes shops, I'll take care of the projector and the black market tech dude."

I breathed out a sigh. "Yeah, okay. I guess I'll have to be patient."

"Don't get your hopes up. Chivers is the only guy I know who sells that sort of stuff on the down-low, but your ghost could have bought the equipment online or from another seller."

"I know. It's just the first concrete lead I've discovered since I started working here, and I have until St. Patrick's Day to solve the case. That's less than three days away."

"Chin up, Maggie. I have faith in your sleuthing skills." Lenny winked at me. "And watch out for ghosts."

THIRTEEN

Although I'd faithfully knocked on his door the moment I got home from work, I hadn't been able to relay my news about the murdered man's potentially vindictive ex to Sergeant Reynolds. No one was at home, and his cell phone number went straight to voice mail. I could have called the station's number, but I had no desire to deal with the odious Sergeant O'Shea or the clueless reserves.

Instead, I decided to go for a run. "This time, you can go as fast as you like," I told Bran, who danced around my feet the instant he saw me put on my running shoes. "We have to keep a sedate pace for Philomena, but tonight, you can fly."

The dog took me at my word. He shot out the door, forcing me to sprint to keep up. Once he'd burned off his initial energy, the dog slowed down enough for me to catch my breath and we settled into a nice steady tempo.

"Want to take your favorite route?" I asked when we neared the wall that separated Paddy Driscoll's farm from Shamrock Cottages.

Bran's answer was an enthusiastic bark. He tugged on the lead and took off toward the path through the woods. The dog's determination to explore every pile of leaves and behind every tree meant that I slowed to a brisk walk until we came out the other side. Although the days were growing longer, it was already seven in the evening and the sun had set. In anticipation of a run in the dark, I'd worn my running headlamp and put a flashlight into my jacket pocket. I switched on the flashlight and surveyed the terrain. In spite of my reflective gear and Bran's reflective dog coat, I was wary of cars this close to the road. The coast was clear and we crossed to the other side and strolled past the place we'd found Eddie's abandoned van. I'd never been fond of the cliff edge in this area of the island. Since Lenny's and my discovery, the place gave me the creeps. However, if Marcus and Sven were correct, we'd pass Eddie Ward's cottage farther along the road.

The information about the cake and the chewing gum bothered me. I didn't know much about diabetes, but if the pathologist said Ward had had the condition, the gum couldn't have been his. So who had been in the van with Ward? His murderer? But the police had searched the van for prints and other DNA evidence as soon as they'd established that Ward's death was no suicide, and the only prints they'd found were Ward's, mine, and those of other postal workers. If I hadn't lost Reynolds's trust, I could have asked him if he had more details. Instead, I'd have to get Lenny to pump Carl and Gerry's lawyer for the information.

Five minutes after crossing the road, I spotted the cottage with the gray slate roof and bright blue door—now navy in the moonlight. When I drew closer, my heart leaped in my chest. I jerked Bran's lead, indicating he should stop. Slowly, I angled the flashlight across the road. My hands grew clammy around the handle. I hadn't been mistaken. Someone was creeping around Eddie Ward's cottage. I stood frozen to the spot and watched as the dark-clad individual reached under a garden gnome and retrieved a small object. A moment later, they slipped what must have been a key into the lock and let themselves into the house. I switched off my flashlight and shrank back into the shadows.

Slipping my phone from my pocket, I hit speed dial. Once again, Reynolds's phone went straight to voice mail. Swearing under my breath, I hit the next number on my speed dial list.

"Maggie!" Lenny sounded drunk, stoned, or both. "What's up, dude?"

"What's up is you needing to get here quick. Someone just broke into Eddie Ward's cottage."

"Man, that's deep." A pause. "Do you think they

want to rob his gnome collection?"

Okay, he was definitely stoned. I bit back a sigh. "Lenny, this is serious. Whoever broke in might be the murderer. The gum in Eddie Ward's van wasn't sugar-free. The killer was very familiar with Ward's van and his routine."

He seemed to sober up at these words. "Mack and I are UFO spotting. We're not far from Ward's place. Meet you in five?"

"Okay, but park down the road. We don't want to draw attention to ourselves." At that moment, Bran let out a plaintive howl guaranteed to wake the dead. "Shh," I whispered. "I know you're bored standing around. We'll walk down the road and meet the guys."

A few minutes later, Lenny's beat-up VW van came into sight. It drew up in a cloud of exhaust fumes. Lenny drew down the window and grinned at me. "Dude," he said in a voice loud enough to be heard on the mainland. "Want a vegan scone? We bought the last of them at the café to keep us going. Granddad making bail was worthy of a celebration even if Carl's still locked up."

Mack rolled his eyes. "He made brownies to celebrate but forgot to bring them. I'd have preferred those over the scones. No offense to your aunt's baking skills," he added belatedly, "but Lenny's brownies are particularly good."

"Got it," I said dryly, trying not to think of what

ingredients Lenny's brownie recipe included. "Now let me into the van and I'll fill you in."

Mack slid open the door, and Bran and I clambered in. "Hang on a sec," the pharmacist said. "I need to move our costumes off the back seat."

"Costumes?" I looked from one to the other. "Please tell me you guys haven't started dressing up for your UFO spotting excursions."

"St. Patrick's Day, dude," Lenny drawled. "Mack and I always make an effort for the parade. Gotta show our national pride, you know?"

Mack and I shoved a box stuffed with St. Patrick's Day paraphernalia off the seat, and I buckled up.

"So what's the story?" Mack asked. "Lenny said something about a murderer breaking into Eddie Ward's house."

"A person—I'm pretty sure it was a man—just entered the cottage, but it wasn't a break-in. He used a key he found underneath one of the garden gnomes."

"Great security system there," Lenny drawled, easing the van into motion. "Maybe Ward got security tips from Pat Inglis."

I laughed. "By the way, I reminded Melanie that she owes you the two-hundred euro bonus for your work today. She was inclined to 'forget.'"

"Awesome. Thanks." Lenny's voice was still unnaturally high, and it occurred to me belatedly that I probably should have taken over at the wheel.

Before I could voice this thought, Lenny screeched

to a halt outside the postman's cottage. In an upstairs window, a light shone. Whoever Eddie Ward's posthumous visitor was, he was still in there.

Mack turned to me. "Do we have a plan?"

"Not really. I don't feel too happy about the idea of knocking on the door and being confronted by a potential murderer."

"Should we call the police?" Mack frowned. "I don't want to get into trouble for interfering in an ongoing investigation."

"For all we know, it's a burglar who's taking advantage of the fact that the house's owner is dead." I sighed. "Yeah, okay. Call the cops. The last person I want to see tonight is Sergeant O'Shea, and knowing my luck, he'll be the one to take the call."

"Whoa," Lenny said, and leaned over the steering wheel with enough force to accidentally sound the horn. "Looks like the dude's making his escape."

I swore under my breath. I unbuckled my belt and moved to open the door, my foot slamming against something as I did so. "Wait, you guys have pepper spray? Awesome." I bent down and picked up the canister. I was out of the car in an instant and sprinting across the road.

Lenny had been correct. The intruder was outside the cottage, walking down the path to the gate. His dark hoodie shielded his face. For a moment, doubt crept into my mind. What if this was a forensics guy sent by the police? I scanned the area but could see no car. If a forensics guy from the mainland had visited Eddie Ward's house, they wouldn't do it at night, and they sure wouldn't come without a mode of transportation.

"Maggie," Mack called from behind me. "Wait up. That's not—"

At the sound of Mack's voice, the man in front of me spun around, and the hoodie fell back to reveal his face. I let out a scream that put the hotel's fake banshee to shame and hit the pepper spray hard.

The man roared and covered his face with his hands. "Are you insane, woman?"

Mack and Lenny brought up the rear, and Mack's flashlight illuminated the intruder.

Breathing hard, I gave a little yelp and let the now-empty canister drop to the ground. "That wasn't pepper spray," I said redundantly, staring at the sparkly green face before me. "And you're not dead."

FOURTEEN

Eddie Ward stared at me slack-jawed. He pointed to his green face. "Was this stuff supposed to *kill* me?" He looked at Mack and Lenny for support. "She's nuts. You know that, right? As in totally loop-the-loop?"

"I'm perfectly sane," I said, circling him as one would a potentially rabid dog. "And you're perfectly alive."

"You're dead, dude," Lenny said. "As in toe-tagged-in-the-morgue kind of dead."

"Are you threatening me, Logan?" The postman's green face darkened. "I've had enough of your family making threats and throwing punches. The next time one of you comes near me, I'm calling the police." As if on cue, the sound of sirens floated toward us. Ward threw Mack a pleading look. "Are they on something? I know you and Lenny hunt aliens and smoke funny stuff. Tell me they're high."

"They're sober." Mack slid Lenny a look. Lenny beamed back at him as though he hadn't a care in the world. "Well, mostly," he amended.

"Never mind our sobriety," I said. "If you're alive, who's the dead dude?"

"*What* dead dude?" Ward was sounding desperate now, his eyes darting from side to side as if in search of an escape route. "High or sober, you're all whack jobs. I'm getting out of here."

The police car came over the hill, its blue lights flashing.

Ward bounded into the road and waved his arms over his head. "Help," he yelled. "They're over here." The car pulled over, and Sergeant O'Shea heaved himself out. Ward ran to greet him. "Thank goodness. That loony American woman sprayed something into my face, and Lenny Logan's making threats about putting me in the morgue. I don't know what they're on, but I want them away from me and my property."

Sergeant O'Shea's chins wobbled and his jaw descended as if in slow motion. "Eddie Ward?" he asked in a hoarse voice.

"Of course it's me," Ward said in an irritated tone. "We play golf together, you eejit. What did she put on my face that you can't recognize me?"

"Green spray," O'Shea said, scratching his head, "with some kind of glitter. But I recognize you all right. The only problem is, you're supposed to be dead."

Ward jerked back as if the policeman had shot him.

"Not you as well? Has the whole island gone mad in the few days I've been away?"

I leaped on this information. "You were away? When did you leave?"

He regarded me warily. "I took my boat to the mainland soon after I delivered your post on Friday. Why is that an issue? I'd put in for holidays."

"Not according to the post office," O'Shea piped up. "I know because Reynolds made me call them. As far as they were concerned, you were supposed to work on Monday."

"That's ridiculous," Ward snapped. "Check the system. I put in for three days free. I'm not due back until tomorrow."

"Believe me, I checked the system. There was no record of you taking leave."

Ward scratched his head. "That's bizarre. I filled in the form and handed it in with plenty of notice. I got an email confirming it and everything."

"You'll need to show that email to the police," I said. "Why didn't you take the van back to the mainland?"

"Because my leave started at noon on Friday," the postman said. "The post depot was to arrange for Marcus Kramer to cover for me. He should have taken the van back to the mainland on Friday evening."

"Kramer knew nothing about you taking a few days free," O'Shea interjected. "We've already spoken to him."

Ward scratched his head. "I don't think I discussed my leave with Marcus, but I haven't seen him recently. The boss should have contacted him, though."

"The more pertinent aspect to your reappearance on the island is the fact that a man wearing your uniform turned up dead on Friday night," I said, watching Ward's reactions carefully. "We all assumed he was you."

The postman whipped around to stare at us again before focusing on O'Shea. "So they're not talking nonsense?"

O'Shea glared at me and looked as though he'd love to tell Ward we were all destined for a psychiatric evaluation. He heaved a sigh. "A man was murdered on Friday night. As we haven't been able to track down your dental records yet, we've been working on the assumption that the dead man was you."

"And my brother is currently behind bars, charged with your murder," Lenny growled.

The postman looked alarmed. "Uh, I don't know what to say. Sorry I'm alive?"

"I'm going to have to ask you to come with me to the station, Mr. Ward," O'Shea said, a sly smile across his smug face. "My esteemed colleague Sergeant Reynolds is currently over on the mainland giving a press conference. He'll be dismayed when he has to tell the district superintendent that he's got the wrong corpse."

A pang of guilt hit me between the ribs. I should

have tried Reynolds's cell phone again the instant I'd realized Ward wasn't dead, but the shock of discovering I'd spray-painted the not-so-dead postman had numbed my senses. And now that O'Shea was on the scene, the whole farce had been set in motion.

As O'Shea led the postman to the police car, a thought struck me.

"Hang on a sec," I called to the postman. "Why did you open your front door with the key under your garden gnome?"

Ward glared at me. "Because someone stole my car from the Carraig Harbour car park and my house key was in the glove compartment. Whoever the joker is, they drove my car back to my house and it's now sitting in my garage."

"Where have you been for the last few days?" I persisted. "Why hasn't anyone been able to get in touch with you?"

"You don't have to answer her questions," O'Shea growled. "Just ignore her."

"If you must know, I was visiting *his* sister and our baby." Ward inclined his neck in Lenny's direction. "And leaving my phone wasn't part of the plan. It went missing on Friday afternoon."

"Do you have a tendency to lose your stuff? Your house key, and now your phone?"

Ward shot me a dirty look. If I'd known spray-painting his face would put an end to his flirtations, I'd have tried it the day I moved into Shamrock Cottages.

"No," he muttered. "I never lose my stuff. I don't know what's going on here."

"Enough questions, Ms. Doyle. This is a police matter." O'Shea propelled Ward to the car and practically shoved the man into the passenger side. A few seconds later, the police car roared down the road, leaving me, Mack, and Lenny staring after it.

"Dude." Lenny's grin was wide. "If that eejit is still alive, Carl and Granddad will be off the hook."

"I'll call Sergeant Reynolds," I said. "Knowing O'Shea, he'll leave it to the last second to tell him and wring maximum humiliation out of the situation."

"If they couldn't locate dental records and Ward's prints aren't on file, it's not Reynolds's fault he assumed what we all did. Why was the dead man wearing a postal uniform?" Mack asked. "Only Ward would be crazy enough to wear the summer uniform in March. It was his trademark."

"Exactly. Whoever killed the guy must have known Ward would be away," I mused, "and that means that the act of disfiguring the dead man's face wasn't an act of rage, but simply to disguise the fact that he wasn't Eddie Ward."

"Why go to all the trouble of dressing up as Ward?" Mack demanded. "Why not kill whoever he was and dispose of the body?"

I shook my head. "I'm as baffled as you are. Ward turning up alive poses more questions than answers.

For one, who stole Ward's car? Is the theft connected to the murder?"

"I don't give a toss about Ward's car. For all I care, Jack can sell it as one of his wrecks." Lenny bounced up and down on the spot. "This lets Carl and Granddad off the hook. Reynolds will have to let Carl go."

I stepped forward and gently pried the keys to the van out of Lenny's fingers and shoved him into the back seat with Bran. I slid behind the wheel and started the engine. "Don't get too excited, Lenny. All Ward's return from the dead proves is that he wasn't the victim. The police still have your grandfather's ax, his poteen, and the empty vial of sodium nitroprusside, not to mention Carl's knife."

"But why would the murderer kill a stranger? It makes no sense."

"We don't know who the dead man is. I don't think this was a random killing. The murderer knew his or her victim, and they've gone to a lot of trouble to frame your brother and grandfather. And that person is familiar with your family and their feud with Eddie Ward." I glanced into the back before turning my attention to the road. "Do you want me to drop you off at your grandfather's place? He deserves to know what's going on, and I doubt O'Shea will be in a hurry to tell him."

"Yes, please. Granddad needs to call his solicitor and get her to make a petition to get Carl out of jail."

Gerry Logan, also known as Gerry One to differentiate him from Geroid O'Sullivan, his friend and frequent companion at the Movie Theater Café, lived a short drive past Paddy Driscoll's farm. When we pulled up in front of the house, all the lights were blazing, and Fifties rock and roll was blaring through the windows.

"For an old guy, your grandfather sure likes to stay up late," Mack said with a chuckle. "Do you think he's playing Xbox again?"

My jaw gaped. "Gerry Logan plays Xbox?"

Mack grinned at my incredulous expression. "Oh, yeah. He and Geroid are addicted, especially when they've had a few shots of *poitín*. Lenny and I taught them how to play."

I laughed out loud at the mental image of the Two Gerries, drunk on moonshine and battling it out on Gerry Logan's widescreen TV. "Now that's a sight I'd like to see."

We piled out of the car and Bran raced ahead, barking to announce our arrival. The door swung open to reveal Gerry Logan wearing nothing but his birthday suit and a wide grin across his craggy face. His wild white hair stood up on end, and his bushy eyebrows and mustache added to his mad professor look.

"Hello, there, comrades," he drawled, sounding more like his grandson than his usual self. "Come on in."

I slow-blinked, but no, my mind wasn't playing

tricks on me. Gerry Logan stood before me naked and completely at peace with his lack of clothing.

I elbowed Mack in the ribs. "Remember me saying I wanted to see the Two Gerries drunk and gaming?"

"Uh-huh."

"You didn't tell me they'd be *naked*."

"I didn't know," Mack whispered. "They've never stripped off before."

Gerry swayed in the doorway. "Don't just stand there. Come on in and have a swig of my *poitín*. It's a new batch."

"And a potent one by the look of it," I muttered under my breath.

"Uh, Maggie, I don't think Gerry got naked on poteen alone."

My eyes shot to Mack's. "Oh, no," we said in unison.

"Dude," Lenny drawled, "do you think Granddad ate my brownies?"

"It sure looks like that," I said and followed Gerry into the house.

Lenny's grandfather led us into the kitchen, where we were greeted by an equally naked and equally stoned Geroid O'Sullivan, the second of the Two Gerries. Sure enough, a half-empty tray of brownies lay on the table.

"Uh-oh," Lenny said, surveying the scene. "Please tell me you guys didn't eat all of those brownies."

"There's a couple left," Gerry said, gesturing to the few brownies left on the tray. "Help yourselves."

I suppressed a giggle. "Thanks, but I'll pass."

Lenny, having grasped the gravitas of the situation, strode to the coffee maker. "We need to get you lads sober before the police arrive."

"Don't tell me those eejits are planning another visit." Gerry's expression darkened. "It's harassment, that's what it is. Police brutality."

"That Reynolds fella must have picked up a few dodgy ideas when he worked in England," his friend said. "Did you know he used to work for the British police?"

I nodded. "Yes, but I doubt that has anything to do with Gerry and Carl's arrests."

Lenny had just placed two steaming mugs of black coffee in front of the old men when the sound of a car crunching up the drive had me sprinting to the window.

"Yikes," I said. "It's Sergeant Reynolds."

"Quick," Mack yelled. "Hide the brownies."

"That's not very hospitable," Gerry said indignantly. "Reynolds might have arrested me, but I'll offer any guest in my house refreshment. If he agrees to let my grandson go, I'll even throw in a free bottle of *poitín*."

"I'd seriously advise against offering him one of those brownies," I said, "and the moonshine's better out of sight. And after you've gotten rid of the stuff, you might consider putting on clothes."

Gerry One stood up and stared down at his naked body—and at an area I'd been studiously avoiding looking at. "Well, I never. I was feeling a bit hot earlier. I guess they just fell off."

Riiiight...

Gerry Two pulled the brownie tray out of my reach and packed them into a storage container. "These are too good to waste. Lenny should set up business as a baker."

Mack, Lenny, and I, all thinking about the not-so-secret extra ingredient, avoided eye contact.

The doorbell rang, making us all jump. "Reynolds is going to bust a gut," Lenny said. "I guess I'd better let him in."

"Nonsense," his grandfather said, moving across the floor at considerable speed for a man of his advanced years. "It's my house, and I'll open my own front door."

"Gerry, wait," I yelped, and raced after him.

The old man flung open the front door and pulled a startled Sergeant Reynolds into a bear hug. "Isn't it great news?" he said, releasing the shell-shocked policeman from his grasp. "The postman returned from the dead!"

With this astounding statement, Gerry Logan danced in the direction of the kitchen, shaking booty I didn't want to see.

Liam Reynolds took a step back and his gaze collided with mine. "Want to tell me what's going on, Maggie? I got a call from O'Shea while I was on the ferry. He said to get straight over here and hung up. I was expecting to encounter a bloodbath."

"Instead, you encountered a stoned octogenarian," I said cheerfully. "To make your evening even better, there's a second one in the kitchen."

Reynolds groaned. "Is Lenny behind these shenanigans? Or did Gerry Logan make psychedelic poteen?"

I motioned a zipper across my lips and stood aside to let him pass. "I know nothing."

He brushed against me, and for a second, I forgot to breathe. "You know far too much, Miss Maggie Doyle. What's this nonsense Gerry was sprouting about the postman being back from the dead? Did the zombie apocalypse start on Whisper Island while I was gone?"

I led him into the kitchen where both Gerries had been wrestled into superhero underpants to protect what wasn't left of their modesty.

"I had to let them borrow my undies. I don't know what they've done with their own." Lenny trailed off when he spotted Reynolds. "Uh...it's not what it looks like?"

Reynolds surveyed the kitchen and its inhabitants. "I'd say it's exactly what it looks like."

"Liam," I interrupted before he could start reading the Logans the riot act, "Gerry was serious about Eddie

Ward. I don't know who's in the morgue, but Eddie Ward is alive. I spray-painted him green this evening, and it was definitely him."

Reynolds's stare pinned me in place. "Are you high, Maggie? I didn't think you were the type."

"No, I'm not high. I really did spray-paint him green. And," I added belatedly, "he really is alive."

"It was green hair spray," Mack added. "For St. Patrick's Day. With glitter."

Lenny nodded. "The stuff with glitter is the best."

Reynolds ran a hand through his hair. "Have you all gone crazy in the few hours I was on the mainland?"

Lenny's grin was manic. "Dude, that's just what Ward said when we told him he was toe-tagged in the morgue."

The policeman looked at Mack. "McConnell, you're an upstanding citizen, right?"

Mack squirmed. "Um, kind of."

"What the heck is going on here?"

I answered for him. "While I was out jogging, I saw a suspicious-looking guy going into Eddie Ward's house. I called Lenny, and he and Mack came to help me investigate. The intruder turned out to be Ward. He said he'd been on vacation and was astounded to discover he'd been declared dead."

Reynolds swore fluently. "If Ward is alive, who's the dead man?"

"That, my friend, is for you to figure out." I glanced at my watch. "Need my help herding this gang to the station? I guess you'll want our statements."

Reynolds surveyed the scene before him and swore under his breath. "Yes, please. The sooner I untangle your mess of a story, the sooner I can return to reality."

FIFTEEN

Two hours later, Liam Reynolds and I stood in my hallway, both in the same awkward poses we'd adopted the night he'd confided in me about the case. Despite the late hour, I was wide awake. After I'd helped Reynolds and Mack herd Lenny and the old dudes to the police station, the policeman had taken all our statements. Gerry One and Two hadn't made a whole pile of sense, but a patient Reynolds had done his best to coax their stories out of them. Gerry Two remained adamant that Gerry One had been at his house on the night of the murder, playing Xbox and discussing a new recipe for poteen. To my surprise, Reynolds had made no mention of the brownies or the nudity. Once all the paperwork had been taken care of, he'd driven me home to Shamrock Cottages.

"Are you hungry?" I asked, shifting my weight from one leg to the other.

His rumbling stomach answered my question. "It's almost eleven."

"No matter. I'll fix us omelets, and maybe a cocktail." I grinned at his look of alarm. "Even I can manage an omelet."

"If you do the food, why don't I fix the drinks?"

"Deal."

He headed into the living room, and I soon heard the clink of bottles. I switched on the light in the kitchen and grabbed the ingredients to make cheese and ham omelets. Despite my brave words, my cooking skills hadn't improved much since I'd started working at the Movie Theater Café. I could just about warm up soup and not burn scones and muffins that my aunt had prepared ahead of time. Still, omelets were easy, right? There had to be a reason they were included in beginner cookbooks. With the aid of my phone and the internet, I soon had a recipe and got to work.

Two minutes later, the piercing screech of the smoke alarm brought Reynolds running into the kitchen, clutching a tumbler in each hand. "Seriously, Maggie? Not again." He reached up and switched off the alarm while I, red-faced, dumped the smoking frying pan into the sink.

I plastered a cheerful look on my face and gestured to the plate of cheese I'd prepared for the omelets. "I guess we'll have to stick with sliced cheese."

"Sliced cheese is fine." Reynolds grinned and handed me one of the glasses. His fingers brushed mine. This time, neither of us jerked away. His gaze slid to my mouth. "I made Old-Fashioneds with an extra dash of maple syrup."

"Sounds delicious." My voice had an uncharacteristic breathy quality. I prided myself on my self-control, but whenever I was close to Reynolds, it went AWOL.

When he took a step nearer, the spicy aroma of his aftershave tickled my senses. This close to him, it was all too easy to forget my past and very near future and focus on the present. "Maggie, I—" he began in his whiskey-soaked voice. His phone vibrated with a shrill ring tone. Reynolds took a deep breath and stepped back. He glanced at the display and muttered something in Irish that I was pretty sure wasn't polite. "I'm sorry. I have to take this call."

"No problem. I'll be in the living room."

I sat in my favorite armchair and waited. My heart pounded in my chest. *Calm down, Maggie. Time to play it cool.* Falling for Liam Reynolds would be all too easy if I let my guard down. He was funny, charming, smart, and sexy. In short, everything a woman could want. But he was also Irish, a father, and determined to make Whisper Island his home. I didn't know where I'd be in a couple of months, let alone what I wanted to do with the rest of my life. I cast my mind back to those long-ago summers on the island when I'd been so sure of my path and confident I'd achieve anything if I worked hard enough. Aged twenty-nine with a failed marriage and a lackluster career behind me, I knew better.

Through the wall separating the kitchen from the living room, Reynolds's voice was a low rumble. I couldn't hear what he was saying, but I could guess it wasn't a conversation he cared to have. A few minutes later, he joined me in the living room. His face was paler than it had been a moment before, and the shadows beneath his eyes appeared darker. He slumped onto the armchair opposite mine and took a sip of his cocktail.

"They're good," I said, determined to break the silence. "We should commandeer your services for the cocktail hour at the Movie Club."

"Gladly. My mother ran a cocktail bar in Dublin. I grew up with these recipes."

"Liam Reynolds, man of mystery, finally reveals something about his past," I teased, but I could see it wasn't the moment for levity.

Liam stared into his glass without seeming to see the amber liquid. "What a day. I thought I'd impress the district superintendent with a swift case wrap-up. Instead, I found myself herding two stoned octogenarians wearing nothing but superhero underpants, *and* it transpires that my murder victim is a John Doe. The boss is furious. That was him on the phone just now."

"It sucks. Especially the superhero underpants part."

This elicited a reluctant laugh from Reynolds. "Yeah. The scene at Gerry Logan's house was surreal. When I catch up with him tomorrow, I'm going to have a stern word with your pal, Lenny. Even if poteen played a role in tonight's shenanigans, the smell of hash brownies pervaded the kitchen."

I bit my lip. "Listen, Liam, I'm sorry I didn't mention the Logans' rift with Ward. I'd only just found out about it from Lenny. If I'd believed any of them were involved in the murder, I'd have told you about it right away."

He took a long drink from his glass and met my eyes. "I felt like a fool because I'd confided in you about the case, but that was on me. I should never have shared that information with a civilian."

Guilt seared a hole in my stomach. He'd taken a risk by confiding in me, and I'd broken his trust by not returning the favor. "You needed someone to talk to, and you knew I had the professional experience to understand."

"Looks like O'Shea has won." Reynolds took another sip and eyed me over the rim of the glass. "My career on Whisper Island is over before it had a chance to begin."

I took in his pinched expression and the defeated slump of his shoulders. "Don't say that. Surely the district superintendent will understand why you assumed the dead man was Eddie Ward?"

His weary expression conveyed little optimism.

"He's livid, Maggie. I held a press conference. I stood up in front of my peers and superiors and a whole bunch of press, and I told them we'd charged two men with the murder of Eddie Ward. Tonight's revelation makes the force look bad, and it's my fault."

I winced. He was right. It was his case and his responsibility to correctly identify both the victim and the killer. "Well, the dead dude just happens to be someone else. And the murderer probably isn't Carl Logan."

"Exactly. But who?" He slapped his thigh. "I didn't like it when we couldn't locate Ward's dental records. Turns out he grew up in the Traveller community and moved around a lot. As an adult, he's avoided going to the dentist because he's afraid of drills."

"Hence the lack of dental records."

Reynolds nodded. "Exactly. And his medical records listed a weight and height consistent with the dead man's, as well as an identical blood group. The only fly in the ointment was the pathologist's insistence that the dead man was diabetic, and Ward's former doctor in Galway knew nothing about that—but he'd only met the man twice."

"All of this points to an honest mistake on your part, Liam," I said, placing my glass on the coffee table. "And it also points to a murderer who went to a lot of trouble to disguise the identity of the victim and throw suspicion on the Logans."

He exhaled sharply. "Yeah. The sheer amount of

evidence against Carl and Gerry Logan gave me pause, but most criminals aren't the masterminds we encounter in crime fiction. A murderer dumb enough to leave a breadcrumb trail is more the norm than the exception."

"I know, but in this case, I'm convinced the Logans were framed."

"In the light of tonight's revelations, I agree. But where do I go from here? The district superintendent has given me seventy-two hours to sort out this mess and find the real killer." He glanced at his watch. "Five minutes ago. That means I have less than three days to save my job." He gave a bitter laugh. "And you can be sure Sergeant O'Shea won't lift a finger to help me."

Judging by O'Shea's past behavior, he'd do everything in his power to make sure Reynolds didn't solve the case. "Why are you so determined to stay on Whisper Island? I can understand you wanting a change from working in London, but why here?"

"For my daughter." His worried expression softened, and his love for his child shone through with every word. "I want her to have the sort of summer holidays I had as a child. My grandparents lived on the coast in Kerry, and my brother, sister, and I went to stay with them every year. We swam in the sea daily, rain or shine, and had freedom we didn't have in Dublin. I want that for Hannah."

"Isn't she still in London?"

"Yes. My ex-wife got primary physical custody, and I get her for school holidays."

"Why no weekend visitations? Because you moved away?"

A pained look flitted across his face. "The opposite way around. I wanted shared custody and to have Hannah live with me every weekend. When I didn't get it, I decided I'd make sure she had a nice, safe place to spend her holidays, and that I had a job that was less intense than my previous one."

A light bulb dawned. "That's why you didn't get shared custody. Your job."

"Yeah." His lip curled in disgust. "My ex is a lawyer and a very good one at that. I didn't stand a chance in the negotiations. And I could hardly argue her point about me being a workaholic. I was dedicated to the job, and crazy hours are part of the deal."

"I'm sorry." I'd known plenty of cops whose marital breakdowns made it hard for them to get shared custody. It wasn't a slam-dunk reason not to get it, but when it came to a dispute, it was easy for the former spouse to argue that the cop worked long and irregular hours and came home stressed and irritable.

"Don't be sorry." Reynolds gave a long sigh and leaned back in his chair. "It was my fault our marriage broke up. Being a homicide detective in London isn't exactly a low-stress occupation. I often worked weekends and holidays, and I had a tendency to take the job home with me."

"You're not the first cop to do that," I said gently. "It's hard to switch off from the horrors of the day and talk about everyday, quote, unquote, normal things."

He nodded gravely. "The last straw for my wife was when I had to run out of Hannah's seventh birthday party because I got a tip-off that the child killer I was chasing had been spotted at a shopping mall. I caught the guy and got promoted, but I came home to find my stuff in suitcases outside the house and the locks changed."

"Ouch. I'm wincing on your behalf." Actually, I was furious on his behalf. Okay, cutting out on their kid's party sucked, but anyone who married a homicide detective knew what they were getting into.

"Yeah. It wasn't pleasant." He grimaced. "Unfortunately, the judge took my wife's arguments on board, and I couldn't come up with a convincing rebuttal. As a homicide detective, I couldn't guarantee I wouldn't be working weekends. I could have arranged a babysitter to look after Hannah, but as my ex pointed out, that's not the point of having shared custody."

"No, it's not." On this point, his ex was correct.

"At least this way, I can schedule time off for when she's with me, or arrange for her to attend a summer camp while I'm at work. Except for this case, Whisper Island isn't exactly a hotbed of crime."

"You must miss her like crazy."

"Every minute of every day. We Skype, but it's not the same as seeing her regularly." A smile of pure pride spread across his face. "Still, she's happy and doing well in school, and she's looking forward to her first visit to Whisper Island." His frown returned. "Assuming I'm still here, that is."

"You will be. A lot can happen in a case in seventy-two hours," I said, but my forced optimism rang false even to my ears.

"True, but knowing the identity of the victim kind of helps. At the moment, all I've got is a pile of evidence pointing to Carl and Gerry Logan, and a motive that tonight's revelations have smashed to smithereens."

"If you'll let me, I'll help you. Whoever did this has to be familiar with the Logans in order to know enough about them to frame them so cleverly."

"I can't ask you to help me, Maggie. You're—"

"A civilian," I finished. "Then don't ask. Just turn a blind eye when I dig for info where you can't. I don't want to give details, but I'm working at the hotel at the moment. Let me talk to Carl's coworkers. He isn't a man with a lot of friends outside of work. One of them has to know something that can help us."

"Okay, but promise me you'll be careful. No putting yourself in danger like the last time."

"You were with me the last time," I reminded him. "You'd have kept me safe."

"Through a hail of bullets? We're lucky we weren't all shot." He drained his glass and stood. "I'd better go. And you'd better get some sleep."

I followed him into the hall and opened the door. He stepped outside but lingered on the doorstep. In the moonlight, his fair hair appeared silver. "Thanks for the drink, Maggie."

I gave him a mock salute. "Any time, sergeant. Sleep well."

When I closed the door and locked up for the night, it struck me how much I'd miss Reynolds if he lost his job and had to leave Whisper Island. I liked his company and enjoyed having him as a neighbor. And it wasn't just Reynolds's presence I appreciated. These last few weeks had provided me with a glimpse of an alternate future, one that didn't involve me returning to San Francisco and picking up the pieces of my old life. Now that I was no longer someone's guest, I had room to spread out and make myself at home. How was I going to feel when the end of May rolled around and it was time to move on?

SIXTEEN

The morning after Eddie Ward returned from the dead, my car refused to start. After several attempts to coax the engine into life, I took a peek under the hood, but my novice eye could see nothing wrong.

"Car trouble?" Liam Reynolds strode over to join me. The bags under his eyes and the involuntary yawn told me all I needed to know about how he'd slept— about as badly as I had.

"Yeah." I glared at the car. "I should have listened to my aunt and bought a car on the mainland."

"Jack Logan of Zippy Motors has quite the reputation." Reynolds's grin enlivened his tired face. "O'Shea told me the guy's a constant thorn in the side of the Inland Revenue. He knows every trick in the book to get out of paying his fair share of tax, and has invented a few more."

"Jack Logan hiding cash doesn't surprise me in the

least. He drives a flashy car for a guy who sells and rents wrecks to unsuspecting tourists." I stared gloomily at my car's innards. "But right now, all I want is for this wreck to last a couple more months."

"Want me to jump-start it?"

I regarded him with hopeful eyes. "Would you?"

"Sure. Hang on a sec."

A few minutes later, my car wheezed into life. "Thanks," I called through my rolled-down window.

"No problem. I'll see you later. And Maggie?" A crease formed on his brow. "Be careful."

"I'm always careful." With these words, I waved to Reynolds and shot out the gates of Shamrock Cottages. Despite my tiredness, I used the drive to the hotel to sift through the scant information I'd gathered on the ghost. I groaned. After days of asking questions and getting Philomena to dig for info, I had two days left to crack the case, or I'd be out a couple of thousand euros.

After I'd pulled into a free space in the hotel parking lot, I whipped out my phone and dialed my aunt's number. Philomena answered on the first ring. "Oh, hello, Maggie. I was expecting a call from Jack Logan."

I laughed. "Don't tell me you and John want to buy one of his cars. I had to get Sergeant Reynolds to jump-start my Zippy Motors special this morning."

"Oh, no. I don't want to *buy* one of his dreadful fleet. John's work van broke down and we need to rent a replacement fast. I left a pleading message on Jack's voice mail." She sighed. "I suppose he'll charge us a small ransom, but we're desperate. It's the start of the building season, and John has a job to finish by April. But enough of my woes. How are you?"

"Not bad." Also not good, but I left out that part. "I was wondering if you could do some more digging for me. Do you know where I could find a copy of the plans for this extension the Greers want to build?"

My aunt chuckled. "In my house."

It took me a moment for the penny to drop. "Oh! Is Uncle John involved in the project?"

"No, but he put in a bid. The Greers turned him down flat. They wanted to hire a fancy construction company from the mainland."

"Could I swing by your place after work and take a look at those plans?"

"No problem, but aren't you working at the café tonight? If so, I can bring them by on my way home from work."

"Really? That would be great. I'm due to start at six."

"Okay. I'll see you then. Have a good day, Maggie."

"You, too." I disconnected and got out of my car, deep in thought. I wasn't sure what brainwave I expected a bunch of building plans to trigger, but I figured it was worth a shot. Philomena's mention of my uncle being turned down for the job of building the hotel's new extension also bothered me. I knew business was tough for him at the moment. Being turned down for a potential windfall like the hotel project gave him and my aunt a reason to hold a grudge against the Greers. But I couldn't see either John or Philomena clanking chains and wailing. They were the pragmatic type who'd indulge in a dedicated grumble, and then move on.

Lisa was on duty at the reception. She glanced up when I walked in. "Hasn't Mrs. Greer told you to use the staff entrance?"

Her snooty attitude chose the wrong morning to pick me as its victim. I glared at the woman. "Actually, Melanie told me to report at the reception each morning so she can decide what floor I'm working on that day."

Lisa sniffed. "It's most irregular. Our floating staff usually report to Mrs. Dennehy, the head of housekeeping."

"It's not for either of us to question our boss's decision, now is it?" I snapped. "And it's not your place to boss me around."

Lisa's lips tightened, and a pink flush stained her prominent cheekbones. "No need to fly into a strop. I'll call Mrs. Greer now."

A moment later, Melanie appeared, looking harassed. Before I'd started working at the hotel, I'd assumed Melanie was a lady of leisure. She owned a restaurant in Smuggler's Cove, but I had the impression that its day-to-day operations were taken care of by the restaurant manager. I'd guessed her role at the hotel was of a similarly non-involved nature. I couldn't have been more wrong. Although Paul held the title of hotel manager, Melanie appeared to be the one doing all the work. This revelation gave me a grudging respect for the woman, although I'd never understand why she'd chosen to stick with Paul and their marriage after all he'd put her through. But what did I know about breakups when kids were involved? Maybe Melanie was willing to put on a front for their sakes.

"Come into the office, Maggie," she said now. "We can discuss where I need you to work today."

This last bit was for Lisa's benefit. Judging by Lisa's expression and her words to me earlier, the receptionist suspected there was something odd about my employment at the hotel.

In the office, Melanie gestured for me to take a seat. "How is the investigation going? You only have two more days to solve the mystery."

A fact of which I was uncomfortably aware. "It's going. Under other circumstances, you'd be glad to know your staff is a tight-lipped bunch."

"They aren't usually," she replied frankly. "This ghost business has them scared. Even those who don't believe in the supernatural have the sense to know they're being terrorized."

"The only piece of information I've managed to discover is that your new extension isn't popular."

Melanie screwed up her nose. "It's not *my* new

extension. I was against the idea, but Paul and my father-in-law are determined to go ahead with it."

"What's your objection?" I asked, genuinely curious.

An ironic smile played on Melanie's mouth. "As you're well aware, the hotel has been in financial difficulties for several years. I think we should concentrate on making what we have profitable rather than throwing money we don't have at yet another building project."

"Has the spa and beauty center not worked out? That was the most recent extension, right?"

Melanie sighed and some of her hauteur appeared to deflate. "It's doing all right, but it's heavily reliant on local trade at this time of year. Apart from buying holiday and birthday gift vouchers, the residents of Whisper Island simply can't afford pricey beauty treatments. We'll see an uptick in trade during the summer months, but we need a plan to bring in more revenue all year round."

"Seeing as we're being frank with one another, who do *you* think is behind the hotel ghost? You must have a hunch."

A bitter laugh escaped her lips. "Ironically, my money was on Carl Logan."

"Carl?" My eyebrow shot up. "Why would he want to put his own job at risk?"

Melanie stared at her hands for a long moment

before saying in a strained voice, "You're aware that Paul hasn't been faithful to me."

I was aware Melanie's husband had been repeatedly unfaithful to her as he'd been to me all those years ago. "I heard something about him having an affair with a hotel guest when I was investigating your mother's murder," I said gently. "That can't have been easy for you."

"A hotel guest?" Melanie snorted. "Is that what Paul told you? I'm sure he's charmed the knickers off several hotel guests over the years, but the woman he was planning to leave me for was Carl Logan's wife."

I sucked in a breath. "Carl Logan has a *wife*? Lenny never mentioned him being married."

"They were only married for a short time. It was a whirlwind romance that fizzled within a few months of taking their vows. They separated a couple of years ago. Carl acted like the separation was no big deal, but I believe it bothers him more than he'd care to admit."

"I doubt Carl was pleased when he found out Paul was having an affair with his ex, but we know Carl can't be behind the hotel ghost."

Melanie sighed. "If only we could wrap it up that easily, but given that the 'hauntings' continued after his arrest, we'll have to look elsewhere."

"Carl will be released on bail soon," I said. "With the motive for him killing Eddie Ward collapsing, the courts will be more likely to let him out, especially if it's likely that the evidence against him was planted."

"I'll be glad to get our head chef back. Carl's a prickly personality, but he's an excellent cook." She stood, indicating that our meeting was at an end. "I'm putting you with the cleaning staff on the third floor today, Maggie. You can report to Mrs. Dennehy."

As I went out the door, a thought occurred to me. "Melanie, where is Carl's estranged wife now? Does she still live on the island?"

A catlike smile crept over Melanie's face. "Oh, yes. In fact, you just spoke to her this morning."

It took a moment for me to get the message. I darted a glance at the blond-haired receptionist, and closed the office door again. "Lisa?" I asked, incredulous. "Your hotel receptionist is the woman Paul almost left you for?"

Melanie inclined her head. "Lisa doesn't know that I know about her affair with Paul. At least this way, I can keep an eye on her."

And make her life a living hell. Suddenly, the receptionist's uptight manner and clipped tones took on a new light. Clever, malicious Melanie.

As I made my way to Mrs. Dennehy's office to report for duty, I observed Lisa's perfectly made-up face pale at the sight of me. Here was a woman with a grudge against Paul Greer and his wife. Had Lisa decided to take revenge by terrorizing the guests?

By the time my lunch break rolled round, I'd discovered precisely zero new information. Mrs. Dennehy, not being in the know about my undercover role, paired me with Zuzanna again, and worked us like dogs.

During my break, I took my sandwich and mineral water outside to enjoy the sunshine. Zuzanna sat on a bench beside Bernadette from the kitchen, smoking and picking at a container of salad. Despite our linguistic differences, I decided to try to see if Zuzanna had any information to share.

"I miss all the fun," I said cheerfully. "I hear the haunting that happened the day before I started work here was particularly spectacular."

"The one the same night as the murder?" Bernadette shrugged. "It was no more dramatic than the previous ones."

Zuzanna's eyes widened. "Lots of staff quit. Lots of guests scared."

"Who'd want to scare the guests?" I asked. "And don't tell me you believe in ghosts."

She regarded me with a look of scorn. "No ghosts. Only in head."

I leaned forward. "So what do you think is going on, Zuzanna? You were there when I found the hidden speaker. Who would want to scare away the guests?"

"How I know? Maybe they want to dig. That makes sense."

I glanced at Bernadette, who looked equally baffled by this statement. "Dig for what?"

"I study archaeology in Warsaw. I come to Ireland to improve English."

"Yes..." I circled my hand in a gesture for her to continue.

"Rich history on this island. Lots of places to excavate."

"Are you saying that there's a place of archaeological significance on the hotel grounds?" Philomena had already mentioned a potential site to me, but I didn't share that tidbit with my companions.

Zuzanna shook her head. "I not say nothing. I only say what I read."

"Back up for a sec. You read something about the land near the hotel?"

"There was an interesting article in the *Journal of Irish Archaeology* last year." She caught my surprised look and flushed. "I read English better than I speak."

"Go on," I said. "What did the article say?"

"There are a lot of potential excavation sites on Whisper Island. It mention one near here with fairy tree. Excavation permission not granted in the Sixties. This hotel has fairy tree."

The wheels in my mind were whirling. Philomena would be able to find recent editions of this archaeology journal that Zuzanna had mentioned. She might even have copies at the library.

"Are you coming out for drinks tonight?" Bernadette asked, cutting through my thoughts.

I blinked. "Drinks? No one mentioned drinks."

"We're meeting at Murphy's Pub in Smuggler's Cove," Bernadette said. "Do you know it?"

"I think so. It's down by the town's harbor, right?"

"That's the one. We're meeting at eight. There'll be a crowd of us. You're welcome to come."

"So you're not patronizing the hotel bar?" I teased.

Bernadette roared with laughter. "Not likely. The Greers are very strict about staff not visiting the bar and restaurant in our free time. We might lower the tone, don't you know."

"That would suck," I said dryly. "Okay. If I can swing it, I'll drop by. I'm working at my aunt's café until nine. If it's not too late, I'll come after I lock up."

Bernadette waved a hand. "No problem. Come whenever you have time. It's just a casual get-together to celebrate Lisa's birthday."

My sandwich turned to sawdust in my mouth. The last person I wanted to hang out with after a long day at work was Lisa. She'd made her dislike of me clear. However, I couldn't miss an opportunity to chat to hotel staff away from the hotel and observe their interactions with one another. I plastered a smile onto my face. "I'm looking forward to it."

SEVENTEEN

After my shift at the hotel finished, I raced to the café to take over for Noreen. When I walked in, my eyes widened. The café was packed. With the exception of the more popular club nights, I'd never seen the café this full. I weaved my way through the tables. My heart leaped when I spotted Sheila Dunphy, the president of the Whisper Island Folklore and Heritage Society, drinking tea with the Spinsters and Sister Pauline. The four women were deep in conversation, but they looked up and smiled when I walked past.

When I reached the counter, my aunt was mopping sweat from her brow with a handkerchief. "Boy, am I glad to see you. The St. Patrick's Day tourists have started to arrive."

"It's nice to see the café buzzing." I slipped behind the counter and put on my red-and-gold apron with the Movie Theater Café logo.

"Despite being rushed off my feet, I managed to bake all the muffins and scones you'll need for the rest of the day, and a pan of leek-and-potato soup is simmering on the stove."

"Excellent. Thanks, Noreen."

My aunt eyed my figure critically. "Make sure you have a bowl of soup yourself. And cut a slice of my cheese bread to go with it. You look like you haven't been eating."

I laughed. "Just because I haven't been consuming the large quantities you served me while I was staying with you does not mean I'm not eating. I eat plenty, trust me."

"Well, make sure you eat something here," she said firmly. "I don't want you wasting away on the job."

I regarded my less-than-firm midriff. "I'm unlikely to starve, Noreen."

"Oh, before I forget..." She shrugged into her coat. "Philomena called. She said to tell you she has to take John to the doctor this evening, but Julie will call in with whatever it was you asked her to give you."

I suppressed a smile at my aunt's unsubtle rebuke at not knowing everything on Whisper Island. "I asked her to show me the plans for the hotel extension."

"Oh, that." My aunt's voice dripped with disdain. "A disgrace, if you ask me. I don't hold with fairy trees, but I object to trampling all over places of historical significance."

"Have you heard about this supposed archaeological site under the fairy tree?"

"Oh, yes. That rumor has floated around for years."

"Do you know what's supposed to be there?" I asked. "Is it a valuable site?"

"Allegedly, the remains of a medieval leper hospital lie under that land." My aunt nodded to the Spinsters' table. "You should ask Sheila Dunphy to tell you more. She knows all about that sort of thing."

"I thought she was the president of the Folklore and Heritage Society?"

"She is, but she led the protest against excavating the site back in the Sixties. She earned quite a few enemies in the process." My aunt laughed at my surprised expression. "Sheila's older than she looks. She must be in her seventies by now." Noreen patted her pockets and eventually located her glasses.

I fished her purse out from under the counter and handed it to her. "Don't forget your bag."

"Thanks, love. Give me a call if you need anything."

"Okay, but I should be fine. Enjoy your evening."

After Noreen had left, Sister Pauline came over to the counter and paid for her tea. "I need to get moving, but the others would love another pot of Earl Grey."

"Sure," I said as I handed the nun her change. "By the way, weren't you at the Whisper Island Medical Centre when Mack delivered meds last week?"

"Yes." The elderly nun frowned. "I heard a

rumor that one of the medications was stolen. Does it have anything to do with the man who was murdered?"

I glanced around the café and lowered my voice. "Yes, but please keep that information to yourself."

Sister Pauline gave me a knowing smile. "You wouldn't happen to be doing a little investigating, Maggie?"

"Of course not." I grinned and winked at her. "This is a matter for the police."

"And yet you were the one who caught Sandra Walker's killer."

"With a little help from you, Bran, and Sergeant Reynolds."

The smile on the nun's face widened. "I haven't had that much fun in decades."

Personally, getting shot at wasn't among my fave activities, but whatever floated her boat. "You must come over to the cottage with Noreen. You haven't seen it yet."

"I'd love to." She sounded genuinely delighted to be invited. "Let's set a date after St. Patrick's Day."

"It's a plan. Have a nice day, Sister Pauline."

"You, too, dear."

When the nun closed the café door behind her, Miss Flynn waved me over to their table. "Hello, Maggie, dear. Can you bring us a plate of scones with the tea?"

"Sure." My gaze settled on Sheila. "Aren't you the

president of the island's Folklore and Heritage Society?"

Sheila smiled. "I am indeed. Are you thinking of joining us?"

Heck, no. "Maybe," I lied. "It's hard to fit in all my interests with juggling two jobs."

The lines on the older woman's face deepened. "Noreen said you were working up at the hotel."

"That's right. I'm just helping out until St. Patrick's Day."

Sheila's mouth formed a hard line. "It's no secret that I'm not a fan of the Greers."

"I heard something about an extension and a fairy tree, as well as an archaeological site underneath it."

Her eyes met mine, and I read a mixture of despair and outrage in their pale blue depths. "They're planning on cutting the tree down. I've fought three successful campaigns in my lifetime to save that tree, and I won't lose this time."

"From my understanding, the planning permission has already been granted," I said gently. "It's as good as done."

She grunted. "The war's not over. I intend to appeal."

Miss Flynn squeezed my hand. "Best get that tea, dear. Sheila gets very upset at the mention of the hawthorn tree."

I took the hint and prepared a pot of Earl Grey tea in the manner the Spinsters had taught me when I'd first started working at the Movie Theater Café. On autopilot, I arranged a basket of the Spinsters' favorite scones and added a ramekin filled with strawberry jam and one filled with clotted cream.

Sheila's face lit up when I brought their tray. "A scone will be the perfect addition to our tea party."

I arranged scones on plates while Miss Murphy poured out three cups of tea.

I'd just returned the tray to the kitchen when the bell above the café door jangled. When I emerged from the kitchen, the Two Gerries were seated at their preferred table. Gerry One clutched his head in his hands, and his friend didn't look much healthier. "Hello, you two. Any more adventures with brownies?"

"Never again," Gerry Two said. "Slept better than I had in years, but I woke up with an awful headache."

"I think that batch of *poitín* was a little strong." Gerry One tugged at his mustache. "I'm glad we had Lenny's brownies to soak it up."

I swallowed a laugh. "What can I get you this evening?"

"Two coffees," Gerry Two said, "and make them Irish. We're celebrating."

"Oh? Has something happened with the case?"

Gerry One beamed. "Carl was released on bail this morning. He's not out of the woods yet, but they've apparently identified the dead man and can find no connection between him and my grandson."

"That's excellent news. So who's the dead guy?"

"Some fella from Liechtenstein called Alex Scheffler or Scheffel," Gerry One said. "Never heard of the chap and I have no idea why he was on Whisper Island wearing Eddie Ward's uniform."

"Bizarre." Although I was fascinated by this revelation, the Two Gerries wouldn't know any more about the dead man, so I changed the subject. "By the way, I'm going to Lisa's birthday party this evening. You don't think Lenny would mind?"

Gerry One looked surprised. "Carl's Lisa? Why would Lenny care? Sure, Carl and Lisa were only married for about five minutes. They've managed to work at the hotel for the last couple of years without killing each other."

"I didn't think Lenny would mind, but I wasn't sure what the family dynamic was."

"Nonexistent as far as I know. Carl never mentions her."

"Have they filed for divorce?"

Gerry's bushy white eyebrows drew together to form a V. "I don't know about that. Doesn't it take a few years to go through in Ireland?"

"I believe so." Four or five years, according to Julie. The thought of being stuck with my odious ex for that long gave me the shivers. "Thanks for the feedback. I wanted to be sure it would be okay with Lenny. I'll go fix your Irish coffees."

By the time I'd delivered two perfect Irish coffees

to the Two Gerries, Julie had arrived, rather breathless. "Mum said you wanted to look over the plans for the hotel's new extension. We don't know if these are still accurate, but here are the plans my dad received when he wanted to bid on the project."

"Thanks, Julie. I appreciate you taking time out of your evening to drop these off."

Her expression was glum. "No worries. I should have gone for a run, but I didn't feel like it."

"What's up? Bad day?"

"Something like that." My cousin scrunched up her nose. "In the staff room at lunchtime, Oisin Tate said that he and Mandy Keogh are now officially an item. So I guess all my training for the Runathon was for nothing."

"Don't say that. You've toned up and gotten in great shape. Even if you started the training with the intention of impressing Oisin, you've done an amazing job. I just know you're going to rock Friday's race."

She managed a wan smile. "Thanks, Maggie. I couldn't have done it without your support."

"All I did was go with you."

"That was exactly what I needed. Knowing I had someone to train with at least a couple of days a week made me more motivated to go on my own on the other days."

I nodded. "Accountability works."

"I'm being silly to be this disappointed." She sighed and shoved a stray auburn lock behind her ear. "It's not like I know Oisin all that well. He was just one of the very few decent-looking single guys on the island."

A thought struck me. "Hey, do you want to join me tonight at Murphy's Pub? Some of the crowd from the hotel is meeting for drinks to celebrate Lisa's birthday."

Julie glanced up in surprise. "Lisa, Carl's ex? I wouldn't have thought you two would get along."

I laughed. "We don't. One of the girls was talking about it and said it would be fine if I came along."

My cousin perked up. "Do you think Marcus, the sexy massage therapist, will be there?"

"I don't know, but Marcus strikes me as the kind of guy who goes to every party."

"All right. I'm sold."

"Julie," I began, but stopped. I understood my cousin's determination to find a man, but her tendency to latch onto bad ones worried me. My terrible taste in men was enough for the both of us. Finally, I said, "I like Sven. He seems like a nice guy."

"Yeah," she said noncommittally. "He's okay."

I glanced over at the Two Gerries' table. The men were occupied with their Irish coffees and their daily fight over the *Irish Independent* crossword solution. The Spinsters and Sheila Dunphy were busy with their tea and scones. No one else in the café knew us. Nevertheless, I lowered my voice. "What do you know about Carl Logan's marriage?"

"Only that it's over. His mum wasn't too happy that he got married so fast. I think he'd only known

Lisa a couple of months." Julie leaned closer. "Last I heard, Lisa was pretty chummy with Paul Greer, but it ended last summer."

"I heard about that. Lisa's kind of uptight. Do you think she's the type to hold a grudge?"

"Against who?" My cousin frowned. "Carl or Paul?"

"Both."

"I don't know, but I can't see Lisa terrorizing hotel guests with banshee wails, can you?"

"No," I replied with a laugh. "But what about Carl? Could she be the one framing him for the murder?"

"That's a hop, skip, and a jump away from accusing her of being the killer." My cousin eyed me shrewdly. "Why would Lisa kill a total stranger and pass his body off as Eddie Ward's?"

"If she did, she can't have acted alone," I mused. "Most of Lisa's height is in her high heels. She can't be more than five two and she's skinny as a rail. She doesn't have the strength to drag a corpse around."

"That's true, but Lenny said the dead guy was poisoned. They do say poison is a woman's weapon."

I laughed. "Only in books. I came across a few male poisoners during my time on the force."

"Either way, I can't see Lisa staging such an elaborate murder." Julie shook her head. "She has the brains to plan one, but she couldn't carry it out."

But she could have had an accomplice. I sighed. I

had less than two days left to solve the case of the hotel's hauntings, and less than three to help Reynolds find a killer. I'd dealt with tougher odds in the past, but I wasn't feeling optimistic. I needed to call Reynolds and find out what he knew about the dead man. First, I had a drinks party to attend.

EIGHTEEN

"Thanks for helping me clean up," I said two hours later as I locked and bolted the café door.

"No problem." Julie followed me down the sidewalk.

I nodded to my car, which was parked in its usual spot in front of the café. "Let's walk. It's not far from here to the pub."

We strolled down to the harbor, passing the familiar shops and businesses of Smuggler's Cove, and the library where Julie's mother worked. Murphy's Pub was located on a small side street off the harbor. When we walked in, the place was packed.

I scanned the crowd. "Wow. I didn't expect it to be this busy on a Wednesday night."

"Looks like half the hotel's staff are here," Julie said, "plus a few other familiar faces." She waved to a table in the far right corner.

Günter, our Unplugged Gamers pal, held a pint of Guinness to his lips. He waved when he saw us. "Come and join us," he shouted. "We have spare seats."

Julie and I battled our way through the crowd. When we reached Günter's table, I recognized several of his companions. Sven and Marcus from the hotel sat across from him, and Günter sat between Zuzanna and Bernadette.

Sven removed his coat from a stool near the edge of the table. "Think you two can squeeze onto one stool?"

"Nonsense." Günter stood and made his way to a neighboring table. A moment later, he returned with a triumphant expression and a second stool in his arms. "Now we are all comfortable."

"Always the gentleman," Marcus said.

Was it my imagination, or was there an edge to Marcus's tone? I eyed the man carefully, but his expression remained placid. I looked around the room. "Where's the birthday girl? I should go over and say hello."

"She's standing by the bar with Jack Logan," Julie said with a laugh. "I think she'd be delighted to be rescued."

I took another look and my eyes widened. Sure enough, there was Lisa. She was dressed casually in jeans and a loose shirt and wore far less makeup than she did at work. The less fussy look suited her. At her side stood Jack Logan, Lenny's car salesman cousin, with his trademark smirk in place. In contrast to his smug expression, Lisa wasn't smiling. In fact, she looked as though she'd been sucking on lemons. "I'll get our drinks and say hi to Lisa. What do you want, Julie?"

"A vodka and tonic, please." My cousin's attention was on Marcus, and she appeared to be oblivious to Sven's attempts to chat her up. She pointedly ignored Günter, and he returned the favor. Ah, well. I'd done my best. If my cousin was determined to chase after a guy my every instinct told me was bad news, that was her choice. I'd be here to pick up the pieces when it all fell apart.

I maneuvered my way through the throng and touched Lisa's arm. She sprang back, and I read alarm in her eyes. She shifted her gum from one cheek to the other, reminding me that I never had mentioned the gum business to Reynolds, but now that we knew the dead man wasn't Eddie Ward, him being diabetic wasn't an issue.

"Hey," I said. "I hear it's your birthday. I hope you're enjoying your day."

A shuttered expression hid whatever emotion she was feeling. "Yes, thanks," she said in a dull monotone. "It's been very nice." She sounded as though she were on her way to her execution.

"Can I buy you a drink to wish you a happy birthday?"

"That's okay, I—"

"I insist," I said smoothly. "I'm about to order drinks for my cousin and me anyway. What would you like?"

"A red lemonade," she murmured, studiously not looking at Jack Logan.

Red lemonade was an Irish phenomenon that I recalled fondly from my childhood. "I haven't had that in years. I think I'll order one for myself."

After I'd placed our order, Jack addressed me. "How's the car, Maggie? Is it zipping you around the island like our slogan promises?"

I gave an unladylike snort. "Yeah...when it doesn't need to be jump-started."

Lisa choked on a laugh.

Annoyance flickered in Jack's eyes but his smile never wavered. "Nonsense. You're probably not used to driving a stick."

"I drove a stick for years, Jack. We do have them in the U.S., you know." I turned to Jack's companion. "Do you want to join us, Lisa? A bunch of us have seats in the corner. I'm sure we can squeeze in one more." I was being rude but I didn't care. And when even snooty Lisa jumped at the lifeline I'd thrown her, my opinion of Jack sank lower.

"Thanks," she whispered when we walked toward the others. "I'd been trying to come up with an excuse to get away from him."

"He seems pretty fond of you."

She rolled her eyes. "Trust me, the feeling isn't

mutual. I never liked Jack Logan. Even his own family isn't fond of him."

"Seriously?" I feigned surprise. "His grandfather doesn't seem to mind him."

"Oh, Gerry likes all his grandkids. I meant that Jack's cousins don't like him."

"Oh, I see."

"Jack has no class," Lisa continued. "He even propositioned me on my wedding day—to his cousin. Seriously, who does that?"

We reached the others, and Julie and I pushed our stools together to make space for Lisa. Despite her red lemonade containing nothing stronger than sugar, Lisa became more animated the more she drank.

After warming her up with small talk and low-grade island gossip I'd gleaned from the café, I cut to the chase. "I hear Carl got bail today."

Lisa swallowed and took a gulp of red lemonade. "So I heard. The idea of him killing anyone is just plain crazy. He's not the violent type."

"Hopefully, all charges will be dropped soon," I said, "once the police figure out the dead man's identity and find the killer. I'm convinced Carl was framed."

Lisa was silent for a moment. "I know. I've been turning it over in my head. For someone to go to such lengths to pin the murder on Carl, they have to have a serious grudge against him."

"Can you think of anyone who falls into that category?"

Lisa gave me a sly smile. "Apart from me, you mean?"

"Well...you are his ex-wife."

"Estranged wife," she said softly, "not that the distinction makes much difference. But no, I didn't frame Carl, nor would I want to. And why would I kill a man I'd never met?"

"We don't know who the man is. Maybe you had met him."

"I doubt it. And I certainly haven't killed anyone."

She was convincing. I had to give her full marks for presenting her defense. However, I couldn't shake the sensation that Lisa wasn't being entirely honest with me. She was holding something back. Now maybe that something had no bearing on the case, but I wanted to know what it was. "Can you think of anyone who'd like to see Carl go to jail?" I asked. "Anyone with a grudge?"

Lisa shook her head. "I've thought about it since Carl was arrested. He's got a hot temper but he's all bluff. I can see him insulting someone, but not enough for them to form a grudge that strong."

Now that I had Lisa talking, it was time to steer the conversation in the direction of the other mystery that I was nowhere close to solving. "Between Carl's arrest and the ghost, there's been a lot of drama at the Whisper Island Hotel lately."

"There's no such thing ghosts." Lisa's gaze flickered in the direction of the group around the table, all deep in conversation about football results. The movement was too quick for me to guess who Lisa had been looking at, but there had to be significance to that eye movement right after I'd mentioned the hotel ghost.

I got straight to the point. "Who do you think is behind the hauntings?"

This time, Lisa's eyes remained on her glass. "Someone who doesn't want the new extension built."

"I'd guessed that much," I said dryly, "but there appear to be a number of contenders. The Folklore and Heritage people don't want the fairy tree cut down, and apparently, archaeologists want to excavate in that area."

"All sound reasons not to want the Greers to build there," Lisa said in the bland monotone she'd briefly lost during this evening's conversation.

"Can you think of another reason someone would want that land left alone?"

To my surprise, she nodded. "It's quite obvious when you think about it."

"Uh, it is?"

She cast me an amused look. "The island's farmers have been plagued by animal rights activists pulling ridiculous stunts. What's more ridiculous than wailing like a banshee and clanking chains?"

"The tree," I whispered. "It's not the fairy tree legend they care about. It's the tree itself."

"That's my bet," Lisa said.

"You might very well be right." I leaned back in the

stool and scanned the faces around the table. Günter was into hiking and healthy living. Sven and Marcus had extolled the virtues of using natural beauty products. Bernadette specialized in the hotel's vegan and vegetarian menu options, but being vegan didn't automatically make her an activist. Zuzanna had told me she'd studied archaeology and therefore had a potential interest in the archaeological site. My gaze slid to the woman beside me. Julie was right. Lisa did have brains. If she were the one responsible for sabotaging her ex-lover's business, she'd cleverly put me off her scent.

At eleven-thirty, the pub's manager announced it was closing time and we all filed out into the cold night air. Julie and I walked in the direction of the Movie Theater Café where we'd parked our cars.

"I'm looking forward to tomorrow." At my blank expression, my cousin added, "Our trip to the mainland? Are you still on for that?"

Oh, heck. I'd forgotten all about the broken projector and Lenny's plan to deal with it and question his black market tech pal on the same day. My stomach clenched at my lack of progress in the two cases, but I read the disappointment on my cousin's face. "Sure," I said brightly. "I'll be there. We're catching the one o'clock ferry from Carraig Harbour, right?"

She nodded, her expression happier. "That's right. I'm looking forward to a relaxing day out."

My smile felt rigid. Relaxing was the last thing I felt capable of doing.

"By the way, Mum said you'd emailed her about ordering an archaeology journal."

My mood brightened. "Yeah. Did she find it?"

"Sort of. They don't have a copy on Whisper Island. She could request an interlibrary loan, but it would be faster if we went by the university library when we're in Galway tomorrow."

"That's a great idea. Thank you."

"No problem." Julie shifted her purse to her other shoulder. "I'd better get going. I'll see you on the ferry."

"See you then. Sleep well."

After Julie had jogged down the street to where she'd parked her car, a voice called out, "Hey, Maggie. Can I catch a ride with you?" Günter lumbered up to join me, his blond hair white under the street lamp.

"Sure. Are you still staying with my aunt and uncle?"

He nodded. "For the moment. I'm looking for a place to rent."

I cast an amused glance in the direction of Julie's car. She lived several houses down from her parents' place. He could have easily asked her for a ride. "Hop in," I said. We drove the short distance from the café to my aunt and uncle's house on the outskirts of Smuggler's Cove. "I think Lisa had fun," I said to break the ice.

"Yes. The crowd from the hotel is always a laugh,"

Günter said. "I asked Sven and Marcus about Eddie Ward, back when we all thought he was the murder victim, but neither of them knew anything interesting. Now that the dead guy turns out to be someone else, I guess it's not relevant."

"I guess not." I slowed the car and turned onto my aunt and uncle's street. "It must be nice for you to speak German with Marcus."

"Yeah. There are only two people on the island who speak German well enough to chat with me in my native tongue." Günter grinned. "But Marcus's German amuses me."

"What do you mean? He's German, isn't he?"

"Oh, no," Günter chuckled. "He told me he was from Bavaria, but that's nonsense. His Bavarian accent is terrible."

My heart lurched in my chest. "Are you saying he can't speak German properly?"

"Define 'proper.' We have many dialects in Germany, and even more in German-speaking countries like Austria and Switzerland. Marcus speaks High German with me and tries to flavor it with a Bavarian accent. My bet is that he's from Switzerland."

My mind turned over this new information. "Why would Marcus lie about where he's from?"

"I don't know. Maybe he wanted a clean slate when he moved to Ireland. I know I did."

This was the closest Günter had ever come to

confiding in me. "But you didn't lie about where you're from."

"True. All I'm saying is that I can understand someone wanting to forget their past, so I've never pushed it with him. If he wants to say he's German, okay."

"I guess." I stopped in front of my aunt and uncle's gate. "Night, Günter."

"Bye, Maggie. Thanks for the lift."

After he'd disappeared into the house, I drove home to Shamrock Cottages, deep in thought. What was the significance of Marcus's odd accent? Günter had mentioned a fresh start as a potential motivation, but Marcus lying about where he came from was extreme. Was the subterfuge just another oddity in my ever-growing list of weird coincidences, or did it have any relevance to the murder?

NINETEEN

I worked my last shift at the hotel on Thursday morning. When noon rolled around, I knocked on the Greers' office door. This time, Melanie sat behind the desk while Paul paced in front of the office's floor-to-ceiling window.

"So you've made no progress." Melanie's tone held no rebuke, and her expression was so forlorn that I felt rather sorry for her.

"I wouldn't say *no* progress. I found that speaker, remember?"

"But not who put it behind the wall." Her lips twisted. "We need to know *who* is behind this nonsense."

"I know, and I'm working on it. I'm going to the mainland today, and I intend to use the opportunity to check a few facts."

She raised an eyebrow. "The grapevine tells me your trip is a shopping trip."

I held my head high. "Yeah, but I can do both. The clothes shopping part won't take long."

A smug expression wiped the worry off Melanie's face. "Given your lack of fashion sense, I'm sure it won't."

I bit my tongue to stop myself from lashing out at her. Where Melanie was concerned, each tentative step we took toward building a neutral relationship was destroyed by her seeming inability to refrain from making snide comments.

"To sum up," Paul said, turning from the window to face me, "you don't know who's behind the hotel ghost, and we've wasted two thousand euros on your so-called expertise."

"I still have until midnight to crack the case," I reminded him. "That's another twelve hours."

Paul loosened his tie and returned his gaze to the window. "It's hopeless. You don't even have a suspect. I don't see what you can discover on the mainland."

"Maybe nothing of relevance, but I'm optimistic."

"At least one of us is," Melanie said tartly. "As far as I can tell, we've wasted a lot of money hiring you and we're no closer to knowing who's sabotaging our business."

I took a deep, calming breath. Melanie wasn't wrong. I had no idea who was behind the hauntings. All I had to go on was the hope that Lenny's black market pal could be persuaded to tell us who'd purchased similar equipment recently—assuming our ghost had made his or her purchase from him. It was a slim possibility, but it was all I had. "I'm confident I'll have answers for you by tonight." I held up a hand. "No, I won't share details before I'm sure, but I will say it'll come as a surprise."

It'd certainly come as a surprise to me. I hoped I exuded a confidence I wasn't feeling.

Paul and Melanie exchanged dubious glances. "Fair enough," he said finally. "Do your thing and report back to us by dinner time."

"By midnight," I corrected.

Paul sneered. "That sounds dramatic. Do you intend to wake us up to update us on your lack of progress?"

My fingernails dug into my palms, but I willed myself to stay calm. "I'm just reminding you that I have until midnight to crack the case. We had a deal."

Melanie sniffed. "A deal I'm not convinced you can make good on."

"We'll see about that." I stood. "But now, I have a ferry to catch."

In contrast to my last trip on the ferry, the sea was smooth as glass, and we made good time. When Julie went in search of a drink, Lenny took me to one side. "I had another look at the surveillance footage from the hotel. It looks like the footage from the times of the hauntings was spliced with footage from another day.

It was a clumsy job, but it would fool an eejit like Pat Inglis."

"So the real footage from the times of the hauntings was wiped out and replaced with old footage?"

Lenny nodded. "Whoever did it must have known that Pat—and whoever else works as a security guard at the hotel—doesn't watch all the cameras. If they knew what time the system was due to show certain live footage, they could plan where to stage a haunting. In the chaos after, it would be easy enough to slip into the security room and play the doctored footage over the original."

"It's still taking an enormous risk."

"This whole business smacks of someone in it for thrills, Maggie. They probably get an adrenaline kick out of it. If they were a true tech pro, they could doctor the footage remotely, but that doesn't appear to be the case here."

When Julie returned with her bottled water, we switched to neutral topics, and half an hour later, Julie, Lenny, and I drove into Galway city.

It was my first trip to Galway since I'd moved to Whisper Island and I was excited to see how much it had changed since I was a teenager. The city was home to eighty-thousand residents, almost a quarter of whom were students at NUI Galway, one of the constituent universities of the National University of Ireland. According to Lenny, the Two-Thousands had seen an influx of immigrants, most of whom had come from

Poland and other central and eastern European states. This gave the city a cultural flair that Whisper Island lacked, but during our drive from the harbor to the city center, I saw that Galway had lost none of its native charm since my last visit.

We parked in Eyre Square Centre, right in the heart of the city, and strolled across the square to a strange fountain with rusty triangles arranged in a pattern that I didn't recognize. "I remember this fountain. What's it called again?"

"The Galway Hookers," Lenny said with a grin. "You're in the Wild West now."

My jaw dropped. "Seriously? How is it meant to represent hookers?"

"Don't mind Lenny," Julie said. "A Galway hooker is a type of sailboat. The triangles represent the shape of their sails."

"That's not half as exciting as Lenny's explanation."

"To be fair, it was more of an insinuation than an explanation, but it was fun watching you leap to the wrong conclusion." Lenny checked his watch. "Want to meet back here at five? You girls can go shopping, and I'll deal with the projector and the purveyor of black market tech."

"Okay," I said. "Want to grab a bite to eat before we catch the ferry home?"

"Sounds like a plan." Lenny shifted the bag

containing the projector to his other shoulder. "See you later, ladies."

Julie and I hit the pedestrianized—and aptly named—Shop Street, Galway's main shopping thoroughfare. I recognized a few of the chain store names, but most were new to me. Thankfully, my cousin navigated us through the various stores with ease, and I was soon in possession of a spring wardrobe that hadn't completely bankrupted me.

"You're a shopping whirlwind," I said, when we emerged from a brightly lit store with particularly penetrating hip-hop music blasting in the background.

"I'm a functional shopper. I know what I like and I go straight for it."

"A woman after my own heart." I checked the time. "We still have plenty of time for me to go to the library and look up that article."

"You can't just stroll into the library, Maggie," Julie said with a laugh. "You need to apply for a card and state a reason why you want access."

My buoyant mood deflated. "Will that take long to sort out?"

"I'm not sure, but I can offer to go in for you." She whipped a card out of her purse. "I use it for research for the master's in education I'm doing online."

"Julie, that would be awesome. How far is it to walk?"

"Not far. Ten or fifteen minutes, depending on how fast we are."

I grinned. "After all the training we've done, we can move fast."

We took off at a rapid pace, speeding down Shop Street to Mainguard Street, Bridge Street, and then reaching O'Brien's Bridge. We crossed the River Corrib and strode up Nun's Island Road. "Are there actual nuns living on Nun's Island?" I asked my cousin as we speed walked our way toward our destination.

"Yes. Fewer now than there used to be, but there's still a community of enclosed Poor Clares living on the island."

"You're going to have to translate that for me. What's an enclosed Poor Clare?"

"The Poor Clares is an order of nuns. 'Enclosed' means they don't leave their monastery except for emergencies."

I stared at her, horrified. "You mean they stay locked up in their nunnery?"

"More or less, yeah."

I shuddered. "I can't imagine living that sort of life."

"Nor can I, but they chose it, so I guess it works for them. Whatever floats their boat."

We hung a right onto Gaol Road and passed Galway Cathedral. Another bridge linked us up to University Road and our destination. Julie's estimate of a fifteen-minute walk proved to be accurate. When we reached the campus, Julie marched us past a series of buildings, barely giving me time to admire the mix of modern and old architecture.

"Before we reach the library, will you please tell me what's going on?" my cousin begged. "Why was Melanie so keen to hire you of all people to help out at the hotel?"

"I guess it'll come out soon enough. I'm working undercover at the hotel to try to find out who's behind the ghost that keeps scaring away guests and employees."

"I knew it." My cousin grinned at me. "I didn't buy the whole emergency shifts at the hotel business for a second, especially after Melanie waylaid you in the lobby after our massages. If it's not too crass a question, how much are you making them pay?"

"Five and a half grand," I said, "but I won't get the second installment unless I solve the case before midnight tonight."

"Yikes. You're cutting it tight."

"Tell me about it," I said with a sigh. "That's why I'm grateful for your help."

"Okay, that's the library." Julie pointed at the modern building straight ahead of us. She made a beeline for the steps and I followed suit. At the entrance, my cousin whipped a pen and notebook from her bag. "What do you need me to look for?"

I rattled off the year and issue number of the archaeology journal. "I'm not sure if it's even worth reading, but it's all I've got to go on so far, so I figure it's worth checking."

"No worries. I'll get through this in no time. Do you want to grab a coffee while you wait? There's a coffee shop over there." She pointed across the square to a building with tables outside and students relaxing with coffee cups and sandwiches.

"Sounds good. I'll grab a latte and meet you back here."

"Okay." My cousin consulted her watch. "See you in thirty minutes. Sooner if I can swing it."

"No rush. Take as long as you need."

Julie disappeared into the library, and I made my way across a grassy verge to the café. Inside, the line to order was long, and I let my gaze drift over the groups of students while I ran through the information I had on the hotel hauntings one last time.

The next instant, my stomach leaped, and my breath froze in my lungs. Standing three people ahead of me in the line was the dreadlocked animal rights activist Liam Reynolds had arrested the night we found the dead man on the beach. And the girl he was locking lips with was none other than Zuzanna from the hotel.

TWENTY

When Zuzanna and her boyfriend broke their kiss, her adoring smile told me all I needed to know. Whether she'd staged the ghost business to prevent the archaeological site from being built over or the tree from being cut down, I neither knew nor cared. Every fiber of my being told me she was behind the hotel's "hauntings." A burning anger coursed through me. Although no one had been physically hurt during their war of terror at the Whisper Island Hotel, people had been scared. By putting the hotel's finances in jeopardy, Zuzanna had placed her coworkers' jobs at risk.

As if she sensed me glaring daggers into her neck, Zuzanna turned around and spotted me watching her. She sucked in a breath and paled to a chalky white before an angry red stained her cheeks.

I took a step toward her, blocking her exit. "Hey, Zuzanna. Have you got a moment? I'd like to talk to you about swapping shifts at the hotel."

The girl's mouth opened and shut. Her gaze flew to her boyfriend. Mr. Dreadlocks shifted his backpack to his other shoulder and gave me an insolent up and down. "Can't it wait until she's back on the island? It's her day off, after all. She's entitled to a break."

My gaze was riveted on his backpack. Out of the top, a stray cable bulged, reminding me of Lenny's various bags of tech goodies. My mind whirred, and the pieces of the puzzle clicked into place.

I smiled brightly at the young man, but he showed no sign of recognizing me from the night of his arrest. A self-absorbed sack of excrement like him wouldn't notice anyone outside his orbit. "It'll only take a minute," I said in a soothing voice. "Zuzanna and I have already discussed changing days."

The girl shot me a wide-eyed look and her mouth formed a pout. With a show of reluctance and a sulky expression that was a subconscious imitation of her boyfriend's, Zuzanna followed me out of the café.

The moment we were out of sight, I rounded on her. "It was you all along. *You're* the hotel ghost. And I'd bet you're a ghost with excellent English, too. You overdid the errors, by the way. You weren't consistent in your mistakes. When you started talking about archaeology, your English magically improved."

Her nostrils flared. "You can't prove anything. It'll be your word against mine. You won't find my fingerprints on anything that could be used as evidence against me."

"You're wrong," I lied. "You weren't careful enough when you placed that speaker inside the suite's wall. The police found a fingerprint."

"That's not possible. I wore—" She broke off and flushed a deeper red. Her hands balled into fists. "You're trying to trick me."

"Fingerprint or no, you'll still need my help if you don't want to get into a heck of a lot of trouble with the police."

"You have nothing on me," she said with a sneer. "And neither do they. Besides, why would you want to help me?"

"Because I want to cut a deal with you and your boyfriend."

Her eyes narrowed. "What sort of deal? Why would we want to do anything for you? I know you've been nosing around the hotel asking questions. You're that American who solved a murder a few weeks ago. I'll bet the Greers hired you to catch whoever's behind the ghost."

"They did, and I have." I pinned her in place with an intense stare. "Listen to me, Zuzanna. You and your boyfriend are going to be up to your scrawny necks in trouble when the police find out what you've done. Your boyfriend is already mired in legal issues. I saw him being arrested on Whisper Island."

"Jason will be fine. He has a good lawyer. He has nothing to worry about." Her chin jutted in a defiant gesture that didn't match the fear in her eyes. *Good.* I'd play on that fear.

"Even the smartest lawyer will find keeping him out of jail a challenge if the charges keep mounting."

"What charges?" she demanded scornfully. "He was attacked by a bull. Jason should be the one pressing charges against that stupid farmer."

"Your idiot boyfriend caused the death of an innocent animal by trespassing on private land. What kind of fool barges into a bullpen and scares the animals? I don't see how that's compatible with his alleged endorsement of animal welfare."

"Jason didn't shoot the bull," she whined. "It's not his fault the farmer got trigger-happy."

I gritted my teeth and tempered down my anger. "If the farmer hadn't shot the bull, Jason would have died. The man didn't shoot his own bull willingly. He did it because your fool of a boyfriend was about to get trampled to death."

Zuzanna, breathing heavily, placed her hands on her hips. "This conversation is over. I have nothing more to say to you."

"But I have plenty to say to you." I took a step closer and she shrank back, her eyes darting from side to side in search of an escape route.

"You're crazy. You've got nothing on Jason or me. You're just bluffing."

"Am I? I'll bet your arrogant boyfriend is the brain behind the doctored surveillance tapes at the hotel."

She shook her head, still walking backward. "You can't prove that."

I dogged her every step of the way. "I don't need to prove your involvement with hard evidence. One word from me, and the Greers will fire you. If the hauntings stop once you're gone, well, I'll have done my duty."

"Do you think I care about a crummy job cleaning hotel toilets?" she demanded with a sneer. "I'm only there to help Jason."

"If you want to help Jason, cut a deal with me now, before I call the Greers and the police."

Zuzanna backed into a tree and winced when the bark scraped her hands. "What deal? You can't offer us anything we'd want."

"I bet your boyfriend still has the original surveillance footage saved somewhere. He'd have needed it to doctor it and upload the replacement to the hotel's servers." I was bluffing. I had only a vague idea of how this worked, but if there was even a slim chance that the original footage from the hotel's security cameras revealed the person who'd stolen Carl Logan's knife, it was worth pursuing.

"So what if he has?" She looked perplexed. "Why do you want to see the original footage?"

"For another case I'm working on." At her stony

expression, I added, "The man who went over the cliff."

"The murdered man?" This elicited a reaction. "Do you think he's on the surveillance footage?"

"Either him, his murderer, or both. You staged a haunting the night of the murder, remember?"

She gave the barest of nods.

"My friend looked at the hotel's copies of the surveillance tapes, and he said the tapes were doctored. Thirty minutes worth was replaced with footage from the previous day. I need to know who went in and out of the hotel on that night, and I'm willing to negotiate on your behalf with the Greers and the police in order to get it."

"No." The word came in a staccato burst. "I want nothing to do with this. It's not my problem if some stupid man got himself murdered."

The girl twisted her rings and looked about her with a frantic expression. She was afraid of me, and I intended to play on that fear. After what she'd done, she deserved nothing less.

I shrugged and schooled my features into an impassive expression. "Suit yourself. If I were in your position, I wouldn't want word to get out that I had the missing footage. It could prove dangerous."

Zuzanna paled under her heavy makeup. "We'll erase it."

"Deleting it won't help you if the killer thinks you

had access to it. For all he knows, you watched it before getting rid of it."

She sucked in a breath and bit her lip. "Okay," she said after a long pause. "I'll talk to Jason, but no police. They can't know. If you tell them, we don't have a deal."

"Okay. No police—*for now*. But I need that footage. Do you want to be responsible for letting a killer escape justice?"

The girl shook her head slowly. "I'll talk to Jason and meet you here in a few minutes."

"No way. I'm not letting you out of my sight. I'll talk to Jason with you and I'm not leaving until I have that footage." I took my phone out of my pocket. "I have Sergeant Reynolds's number on speed dial. Do you want me to press it?"

Muttering, the girl stomped back to the café where her irritated boyfriend was waiting outside with their coffees. He glared at me. "That was way more than a minute."

"Shut up and listen to me before I report you to the police for breaking and entering and causing a whole lot of people a bunch of grief," I said. "Given your previous arrest, along with whatever else is on your record, I doubt you want me to do that."

The guy shot Zuzanna an alarmed look.

The girl shrugged. "She knows everything. But apparently we have something she wants."

"What could we possibly have that *you'd* want?"

he asked me with a sneer. "Are you looking for a threesome?"

Ugh. The idea of that dreadlocked reptile touching me made my skin crawl, and Zuzanna, pretty though she was, was the wrong gender to appeal to me. "No, you fool. I want the original surveillance footage from the Whisper Island Hotel from the dates and times you and your partner in crime staged hauntings."

A nervous tick twitched in his cheek. "Why? There's nothing special on it."

"Maybe. Maybe not. But it just might help catch a killer."

————

An hour later, Julie, Lenny, and I squashed into Jason's one-room student apartment. As I'd guessed, Jason turned out to be a vegan computer nerd who took an instant liking to Lenny, especially when he realized Lenny's tech savvy trumped his own. While the guys huddled around Jason's computer, Zuzanna, Julie, and I sat on the sofa bed. Zuzanna twisted her rings with such force that I was afraid she'd pull her fingers off.

Lenny looked over his shoulder, an animated expression on his face. "Hey, Maggie. I need you for this part."

I stood and joined my friend at the computer. After a moment's hesitation, and a sharp look from Lenny, Jason deigned to give me his chair.

I peered at the blurry picture on the screen. "What am I looking at?"

"This is footage from the kitchen." Lenny pressed fast-forward and then hit pause. "Know the guy next to Carl's knives?"

I snorted at the sight of the grainy footage. "Hard to tell. The Greers opted for a bargain-basement security system."

"Did you expect anything else?" Lenny inquired. "Anyone who hires Pat Inglis as their security guard is doing it on the cheap."

"Can you zoom in? I'd like to get a better look at the guy standing next to Carl's workstation."

Lenny obliged, and a familiar face came into view. I sucked in a breath.

"Do you recognize him?" Lenny asked.

Before I could comment, we both gasped. The man in the video looked around the empty kitchen before picking up Carl's knife and hiding it in his jacket.

"Oh my goodness." My hand flew to my mouth. "Marcus took Carl's knife?"

"What?" Julie exclaimed in horror. "No way."

Zuzanna gasped. "Not Marcus."

I swiveled in my chair. "You both know Marcus. Back me up here. That's him, isn't it?"

The two women leaped to their feet and peered over my shoulder at the laptop screen.

Julie inhaled sharply. "Yeah, that's him."

I turned to Zuzanna.

"Yeah," she said. "That's Marcus. I can't believe he'd kill someone."

"I don't know that he's the killer," I cautioned, "but he's got to be involved if he stole the knife used to frame Carl." I regarded Zuzanna's horrified expression with interest. "Is there something you'd like to tell us about Marcus?"

The girl slumped back onto the sofa bed and fiddled with her rings. "He gives the best massages," she offered lamely.

Lenny looked at me and raised an eyebrow.

"Who is this Marcus guy?" Jason demanded. "Some gigolo?"

"He's a massage therapist at the hotel," I said, watching Zuzanna's face as I spoke. "I don't know what else he does." *Or what he knows.* Günter's words about Marcus's fake accent played on repeat in my head.

"It's not what you think," Zuzanna said, addressing her boyfriend. "Marcus...caught me installing a mini speaker in the ballroom. He guessed I was behind the wailing banshee noises and the poltergeist activities."

Jason swore fluently. "I told you to be careful."

"Says the man who caused a bull to be shot," she retorted.

"Back up a sec," I interjected. "Marcus knew you were behind the fake hauntings?"

Zuzanna nodded. "Yes. He promised me he wouldn't tell anyone."

"And in return," I guessed, "you were to stage a haunting on the night of the murder."

She hung her head, two red spots appearing on her cheeks. "I didn't know anyone would die, I swear it. Marcus told me he wanted to play a prank on Sven. Those two are always joking around. I assumed he was telling the truth."

"Didn't you guess when the dead man was found?" Lenny demanded. "Didn't you think it was a weird coincidence?"

"Well, no. At first, everyone assumed the dead man was the Whisper Island postman. I knew Eddie Ward was friends with Marcus, but when Carl was arrested, I thought the case was closed."

"What did you think when you found out the dead man was a stranger?" I asked. "Did you ask Marcus about it?"

She shook her head. "Why would I? If a stranger was murdered, that made it even more unlikely that Marcus was involved. I honestly thought he was telling the truth about pranking Sven."

"Did he ask you how you and Jason managed to fake the surveillance footage?" Lenny asked. "He must have been aware that the times he appeared on the saved recordings would be replaced with innocent footage."

The girl scrunched up her forehead. "Yeah, he asked me, but I was vague. I mean, that's Jason's area. All Marcus wanted to know was that the original footage would be erased. I said it would." She looked from her boyfriend to Lenny and added in a defensive tone, "I didn't know Jason had the original. I thought it was gone forever."

Thank goodness for Jason's lack of tech savvy. I turned to Lenny. "Please copy the footage. We'll need to show it to Reynolds."

"Hang on a sec." My friend's fingers flew over the keyboard. "There's a working camera I haven't checked yet. It's the one near the staff entrance."

My heart leaped. "Awesome. Maybe we'll see Marcus leaving."

A few clicks later, Lenny found what he was looking for. "Okay, this is it."

He hit play, and we leaned forward to watch the action unfold. According to the time on the recording, two minutes after Marcus picked up Carl's knife in the kitchen, he walked out the staff entrance. A couple of seconds later, two other men came into view. One wore a red baseball cap pulled low enough to obscure his face. The other was a handsome, dark-haired man dressed in a summer postal uniform.

"Whoa," Lenny exclaimed. "It's the dead dude. And he still has his face." Without waiting for me to ask, he zoomed in on the stranger in the postal uniform. We hunkered closer to the screen. "Dude looked better with a face," he said.

"Most people do," I added dryly.

Julie came up to the desk and hung over my

shoulder. "Up close, he's not all that much like Eddie Ward."

"Yeah, but it was dark and the physical resemblance was near enough that anyone not paying attention would easily assume he was the real deal." As I stared at the frozen footage of the dead man, a thought occurred to me. "Lenny, do you have all the footage from that day, or just the part around the time of the hauntings?"

"I copied everything."

"So did I," Jason said. "Made it easier to find a good fit to splice the real footage with."

My heart rate kicked up a notch. "Can you check the tape from the main hotel entrance earlier that evening?"

"Sure," Lenny said. "What time do you want?"

I shook my head. "I don't know. Probably not much earlier than when we see them exiting the staff door. Let's try an hour earlier."

Lenny scrolled back and put the video on fast forward. For a few tense minutes, nothing of interest appeared on the screen. Guests came and went. Paul Greer helped a guy find a parking spot. Melanie appeared briefly on the steps and then returned to the lobby. And then, just when I was about to tell Lenny to switch it off, I saw him. "That's our man," I shouted. "That's the dead guy."

Lenny squinted at the screen. "Are you sure? I see a dude in a suit."

"Exactly. Zoom in on his face."

He obeyed and whistled. "Well, I'll be. You have sharper eyes than I do. That's him all right, but wearing a totally different outfit. Let's follow him."

My friend clicked on another file and worked his magic to bring up footage of the lobby. The guy in the suit walked up to the reception desk, had a conversation with Lisa, and headed for the stairs with a key card.

"He was a guest at the hotel?" Zuzanna demanded. "I don't recognize him."

"I doubt he stayed long," I said, my eyes not leaving the screen. "I'll bet he used the room to change into the postal uniform, and then took the staff elevator down to the kitchen area to hook up with Marcus and the guy in the red cap." I got to my feet. "We need to get back to Whisper Island and talk to the hotel and Reynolds."

"I thought you said no police," Zuzanna cried. "You promised."

"I promised I'd help you, but you must see that I can't not tell the police about where we found the missing surveillance footage."

"No way," Jason yelled. "No police."

I ignored him and focused on Zuzanna, who I'd identified as the one with a still-functioning moral compass. "Come back to Whisper Island with us, and I'll go with you when you talk to the Greers. I'll do my best to persuade them not to press charges, but you have to promise to give up this crazy campaign. In return, I'll make sure to tell the police how much you've helped by coming forward with the original footage."

Her lips twisted into an ironic smile. "I didn't come forward. You forced me."

"They don't have to know that. Point is, you provided vital evidence in a murder investigation."

She crossed her arms over her chest. "I'm not sorry about damaging the Greers' business. They're planning to build on sacred land. That fairy tree is precious, and they don't appreciate its significance. And there's the archaeological site underneath...it's a disgrace."

"That whole island is a disgrace." Jason pouted sulkily. "You have no appreciation for animal rights."

"Says the guy who got a bull shot to death," I snapped. "Save it, Jason. I have no issue with people who want to avoid animal products, but your methods are harebrained. You can't seem to tell the difference between beef and dairy farming."

"That wasn't him," Zuzanna said. "That was—"

"Shut up." Jason leaped to his feet. "Are you crazy? We swore to mention no names. Our friends are loyal to us, and we need to be loyal to them."

Lenny snorted with laughter. "Whatever. Your black market tech source, Chivers, squawked the instant I mentioned a possible connection with a murder. He gave me a long list of names that I think the police will find very interesting."

Jason's jaw descended in slow-motion. "No way."

"Yes way," I said, rolling my eyes. "I'm sure the police will catch up with the rest of your buddies eventually, but I'm more concerned about finding a murderer." I checked my watch. "Come on, guys. If we get moving, we'll catch the ferry that leaves at half-past."

TWENTY-ONE

On the ferry back to Whisper Island, the cell phone reception was lousy, and I couldn't get a working connection to Reynolds's phone. When Lenny drove out of the car elevator at Carraig Harbour, he turned to me and asked, "Where to?"

"The hotel first." I glanced in the back seat, where a tense Zuzanna sat next to Julie. "I'll try Reynolds again on the way."

Lenny took the road that led in the direction of the hotel, and I hit Reynolds's number. It rang three times. *Come on. Answer.*

"Maggie?" His voice was crackly but audible.

"Thank goodness." The words burst forth in a flood of relief. "I thought I'd never get through to you. I have news. Marcus at the hotel is our guy."

"Who?"

"Marcus Kramer. He's a massage therapist at the

hotel's beauty center spa. Have you checked your email?"

"I'll do it now. I spent the afternoon chasing down leads that proved useless."

"We had better luck." I couldn't keep the touch of smugness out of my tone.

"Is that so?" he asked in a drawl. "Wait...I see an email from Lenny."

"Yeah. With the help of one of the maids from the Whisper Island Hotel, we tracked down the undoctored surveillance footage from the hotel for the night of the murder. Lenny's marked the times you need to watch. Have you got it?"

"Hang on a sec." The sound of keyboard clicks followed. "I'm downloading the footage now. How did you get hold of this?"

I met Zuzanna's pleading gaze in the rearview mirror. "Please trust me when I say it's a long story and I'd only waste time by telling you. I'll fill you in on the details later."

To Reynolds's credit, he had the sense not to argue with me. "Okay. I have the footage and I'm playing the section you marked. *Whoa.* I see our murder victim."

"Yeah. He's also on the footage entering the hotel earlier that evening, dressed in a suit and tie. Lenny marked the section in his email to you. For now, focus on this segment and look at the soon-to-be dead guy's companions."

"He's talking to a guy in a baseball cap whose face I

can't see," Reynolds said, "and another guy walked out just before him, and turned back to say something to our murder victim."

"The visible one is Marcus from the hotel."

I heard a chair scrape. "I'm leaving the station now," he said, "and heading for the hotel. What do you know about Marcus?"

"Not a lot. He claims to be German and he's a borderline sleaze, if that's worth anything."

"Claims to be German?" A car door slammed and an engine revved into action. "What does that mean?"

"Günter says Marcus doesn't speak German like a German. Günter's guess is that Marcus is Swiss."

"Switzerland is right next to Liechtenstein, where our mysterious murder victim comes from." His voice was tinged with ill-concealed excitement. "I ran an Interpol black notice on him and found out the dead man is a convicted diamond thief named Alex Scheffel. Scheffel served seven years for a huge diamond robbery and got out last month. Great work, Maggie. If this cracks the case, I owe you one."

A smile spread across my face. "I'll hold you to that promise, sergeant."

His deep laughter rumbled down the line. "Oh, I know you will."

"Good luck, Liam. Go catch a killer."

———

"If you turn any redder, I'll use the fire extinguisher on you." I looked at Melanie for support. "You're what passes as the brains of this operation. You know I'm right."

"I know I'm not happy at your suggested solution. This creature—" Melanie gestured at Zuzanna, who sat slumped on a chair at my side, "caused considerable damage to our hotel's reputation."

I looked from her to her husband. "Your business will thrive once the public knows how you and Paul assisted the police in catching a murderer—and a murderer whose crime has nothing to do with your hotel."

Melanie pursed her lips. "Given that a member of staff is currently in custody, I hardly think we can claim to have had nothing to do with the crime."

I sighed. So far, my appeal for the Greers not to press charges wasn't going well, but I'd wear them down. "May I remind you that you guys owe me a favor?"

"All we owe you is the rest of the fee we agreed to pay you for getting to the bottom of our mysterious ghost," Melanie said. "No more, and no less."

I rolled my eyes. "Aren't you forgetting that I caught your mother's killer? Not to mention agreeing to say nothing to the police about Paul's creative accounting."

Paul's eyes darted wildly around the room and he

tugged at his tie as though it were choking him. "You promised not to bring that up again."

"Dude, you and your wife owe me big time. Don't press charges against Zuzanna, and she'll leave your employ today and not cause any further mayhem."

"Why do you care whether or not she's punished?" Melanie demanded. "You barely know the girl."

"I don't care what happens to her, but I promised her I'd plead her case if she came forward to the police with the missing footage. I keep my word."

Melanie pressed her mouth into a hard line. "She caused a lot of trouble for us, staff members, and hotel guests."

"True, but no one was hurt or injured, and no property was seriously damaged." I slid a look at Paul, who bore a striking resemblance to a constipated bear. "And if you and your father weren't so greedy, you could have planned the extension on a piece of land that wouldn't cause controversy. You had to have known building over that area would upset a lot of people."

"Extending the other side of the hotel would destroy the symmetry of the building," Paul whined. "You can see that from the plans."

"What I see is that there's no reason you couldn't have opted to build on the other side of the hotel and saved yourselves and others a whole pile of grief. Can't you at least meet with your architects again and discuss the possibility of building the extension elsewhere?"

Melanie clucked her tongue. "That's what I told Paul and his father when they first mentioned this ridiculous building scheme."

Our eyes met and, for a brief moment, I felt a connection with my teenage nemesis. She was uptight and prissy as heck, but I didn't envy her being stuck with Paul as a husband.

"So," I said, looking from Melanie to Paul, "do we have a deal?"

"All right," Melanie said finally. "If the girl leaves the hotel at once, we won't press charges. But any more nonsense, and we'll go straight to the police."

"You got it," I said. "Right, Zuzanna?"

The girl stared at her shoes, but nodded.

Melanie unlocked a drawer and removed an envelope. "This is the rest of your fee for your undercover work."

"Thanks." I pocketed the envelope and got to my feet.

"And I'll call the architects today and get them to draw up an alternative plan," Melanie added, ignoring her husband's squawk of protest. "I've had enough drama to last me a lifetime."

I gave her a small smile. "You and me both, Melanie. Come on, Zuzanna. It's time for us to make tracks. I have a race to run tomorrow and I need my beauty sleep."

TWENTY-TWO

My triumphant return home after solving not one but two cases was hampered by my car. When I turned in the gates of Shamrock Cottages, the vehicle belched exhaust fumes, and a series of warning lights pinged on the dashboard.

"Oh, come on," I muttered. "I need you to survive another couple of months." The last thing I wanted was to have to waste my money from the hotel investigation on a new car.

I chugged up the drive and pulled up in front of my cottage. Noreen was waiting for me on the doorstep, a large carrier bag in her arms.

I got out of my car and regarded my aunt's bag with a sinking sensation in my stomach. "Please tell me that doesn't contain more animals."

"Nothing of the sort," Noreen said indignantly. "Just my dirty undies."

I slow-blinked, my house key clutched in my right hand. "Uh, okay."

"My washing machine broke down and I can't get a repair person this side of the long weekend." She clucked her tongue disapprovingly. "It seems everyone has taken off for St. Patrick's Day."

"That's the tradition," I said and opened my front door. "Want to use my machine?"

"If you wouldn't mind. I had a mountain of laundry to wash before the machine broke down, and it's only gotten bigger."

"No problem." I stifled a yawn and led her into the small utility room off my kitchen where my washer and dryer were located. "Help yourself to detergent."

"Do you want me to wash your stuff while I'm doing mine? I might as well sort everything into darks, coloreds, and whites."

"Yeah, that'd be great. I need to wash my running gear before tomorrow's race." I fished all my running pants, sports bras, and sport socks out of the wash basket. "They need to go on the sports wash setting, but any delicates you have should be fine in there as well."

After we'd dealt with laundry, I made hot chocolate and filled Noreen in on the two mysteries. By the time I reached the part about the doctored surveillance footage, she was buzzing with excitement.

"I wish I'd been in on the chase," she said, a wistful

expression on her face. "I missed out the last time as well."

"For what it's worth, I haven't been involved in any chase," I said dryly. "Sergeant Reynolds will have taken care of the arrest. I just had to make a statement."

"Still, it's thrilling." My aunt beamed. "Life on Whisper Island has been so much more exciting since you moved here."

I laughed. "I don't think I can be held responsible for the murder and mayhem that's hit the island recently. It's just a coincidence."

"A happy coincidence. You were here to solve the crimes."

"To be fair, Sergeant Reynolds played his part."

"But he can't talk to people like you can. You have a knack for getting people to open up to you, whether they want to or not." My aunt leaned forward, oblivious to the hot chocolate mustache she'd acquired. "Have you considered setting up as a private investigator? We don't have one on the island."

"Lenny asked me the same question, but I doubt there's enough work to support me. These last few weeks have been exceptional."

"There's plenty of people who could do with your expertise," my aunt insisted. "I can imagine you'd get clients from the mainland who'd appreciate an outsider's help."

"I don't know about that. There's got to be plenty of P.I.s around. Why would anyone want to hire me?"

"Because you've got a knack," my aunt repeated. "And you know how to be discreet.

I tried to hide a yawn, but failed. "I'm sorry, Noreen, but I think I'd better hit the sack. It's been a long day, and I'm participating in the Runathon tomorrow."

"No problem, love. You go on to bed. If it's okay with you, I'll stay to put on another load of laundry and then let myself out. I can lock up with your spare key."

"Sounds perfect." I gave her a peck on the cheek. "Good night."

"Night, love. Sleep well."

"Thanks, Noreen. I think I will."

A few minutes later, I crawled into bed with the intention of finishing a chapter of the Agatha Christie book I was reading for the next book club meeting, but the instant I laid my head on the pillow, I dozed off.

———

When my phone rang the following morning, it wrenched me out of a deep sleep. Groggily, I groped for the phone on my nightstand and held it to my ear. "Hello?"

"Maggie?" Julie sounded distressed. "Where are you? The race is due to start in twenty minutes."

As if struck by lightning, I sat bolt upright, almost sending Bran flying off the end of the bed. My gaze fixed on my bedside clock. "Oh, heck. I was so tired last night that I forgot to set my alarm."

"If you hurry, you'll make it on time. I've collected your number from the registration booth."

I rolled out of bed and rubbed my eyes with my free hand. "Thanks, Julie. I'll get there as soon as I can."

I disconnected and ran into the kitchen, Bran at my heels. After I'd fed Bran and the cats, I found an energy bar and shoveled it in, and washed it down with water. Noreen had left laundry folded in neat piles on the kitchen table. On autopilot I reached for my running gear.

And froze.

"Aw, no. No, no, no, no." I held my running pants up, but my mind wasn't playing tricks on me. They were now small enough to fit a child. In my tired state, I'd forgotten to tell Noreen not to put them in the dryer. Swearing, I raced back into my bedroom and located a clean sports bra, regular socks, and a T-shirt. At least I wouldn't be forced to run in an underwire contraption. Back in the kitchen, I regarded my freshly washed running pants with trepidation. Could I squeeze myself into them? I stretched the material between my fingers. They still had some give. It had to be possible.

After a struggle, I managed to pull the running pants up to my thighs, but they wouldn't budge past my underwear. *Aw, heck.* I'd have to go commando. I peeled off the running pants and discarded my panties. On my next attempt, I coaxed the running pants up to my waist and checked my reflection in my bedroom mirror.

They were shorter than they'd been before their spin in the tumble dryer, and tight enough to display an undignified bulge of excess flesh around my midriff. But they fit—more or less—and I had no time to waste looking for an alternative.

Wincing at the strain on my pants, I bent down and laced up my running shoes. Once that was done, I pulled my hair into a tight bun, grabbed my running belt with its filled bottle of water, and ran out of the cottage, ignoring Bran's plaintive whine to be allowed to come along. The last thing I needed during the Runathon was Bran causing havoc, and I was pretty sure that dogs and parades were a bad mix.

A glance in the direction of Sergeant Reynolds's cottage showed me he'd already left for Smuggler's Cove. I heaved a sigh of relief. With the island's chief of police otherwise occupied, I intended to break the speed limit in my effort to bust butt and get to the race on time. I leaped into my car, gunned the engine, and took off in a shower of gravel. Thankfully, my temperamental vehicle didn't give me any trouble on the drive from Shamrock Cottages to Smuggler's Cove. I hit the gas pedal hard, only slowing to a more sedate pace once I hit the outskirts of the town.

The starting point of the Runathon was down by

the harbor, right in front of the library where my aunt Philomena worked. I parked in the first free spot I could find, and jogged the rest of the way. The town was packed with islanders and tourists, all turned out for the Runathon and the St. Patrick's Day parade that would follow.

In front of the library, Philomena and Julie stood at the starting line with the other Runathon participants. I ran over to join them, out of breath before the race ever started. "Hey," I gasped. "I just made it."

"Whoa." Julie stared at my outfit. "What happened to your running pants? Either they shrank or you've put on seven kilos since yesterday evening."

I scrunched up my nose and sighed. "Noreen happened to them."

Philomena put a hand over her mouth to stifle a giggle. "She mentioned she was going to do her washing at your place."

"Yeah, she did." I tugged at the seat of my pants. "This was the result. I couldn't even fit underwear beneath them."

"The tumble dryer?" Julie asked sympathetically. "That'll do it."

"Okay, on your marks..." A voice blasted through a megaphone and the Runathon participants took their starting positions.

"Good luck," I said to my cousin and aunt.

"You, too." Julie smiled at her mother and me. "We've got this."

A second later, the starting pistol blasted, and we were off. When we approached the Movie Theater Café, a group of familiar faces was gathered outside to cheer us on. Mack, Lenny, Sister Pauline, and the Spinsters waved to us. Uncle John and Noreen raised their glasses of green-tinged water when we jogged by.

After my initial panic to get to the race on time, I settled into a steady jog. By the time we reached the school, I was chugging along comfortably.

"Hey, Maggie."

I glanced to my left and my jaw dropped. "Sergeant Reynolds? I didn't know you were running today."

"Sergeant O'Shea and the reserves are on duty. I said I'd participate in the race unless I was needed."

I slowed to a pace that would allow me to chat comfortably. "Any news on Marcus?"

"He's behind bars, but he's clammed up and is refusing to talk."

"Ouch. Have the charges against Carl and Gerry Logan been formally dropped?"

"Yeah. That happened early this morning." Reynolds pulled a face. "Marcus was traveling under a fake German passport. We're still trying to figure out his true identity. Interpol's on the case."

"Can you think of a connection to the dead guy?"

"I can guess at one. According to Interpol, Alex Scheffel went to prison after a big heist in Berlin, and most of the diamonds were never recovered. The

German police always suspected Scheffel was a minor player in the operation, and didn't have the brains to carry out a job that complex on his own. My hunch is that Marcus—or whatever his real name is—was Scheffel's accomplice."

I turned this information over in my mind. "Why would they meet on Whisper Island? And who was the third man with them on the surveillance footage?"

"That I can't answer. Maybe Marcus has the missing diamonds, and Scheffel came after him. As for the guy in the red baseball cap, he might have had nothing to do with Scheffel or Marcus. He might have simply appeared on camera at the wrong time."

I didn't buy this theory. I'd watched the footage several times, and I could have sworn Marcus had spoken to the guy.

Before I could explore this theory farther, Reynolds's phone beeped. "Hello?" A moment's silence. "Okay. I'm on my way." He disconnected and looked at me with an expression of regret. "A fight broke out down at the harbor, and the lads need my help. Looks like I'll have to wait for another time to display my jogging skills."

"Maybe we can go jogging together some time," I said, hearing the hopeful note in my voice and cringing.

His slow-burn grin melted my embarrassment. "Sure. I'd like that. See you around, Maggie. Good luck with the race." And then he turned around and ran back in the direction of the harbor.

I sped up and rejoined my aunt and cousin. Philomena was red-faced from effort, but jogging onward with dogged determination.

Julie was fit enough to speak. "Where's Reynolds?"

"He had to go back to break up a fight."

My cousin laughed. "That's St. Patrick's Day for you. Some of those eejits started drinking at midnight."

We reached the spot where I'd abandoned my car and ran past it, heading in the direction of the beehive huts that dotted the cliffside on this part of the island. I allowed my gaze to wander, soaking up the gorgeous landscape that appeared to advantage on such a sunny day. Suddenly, out of the corner of my eye, I spotted a flash of red. A man crouched behind one of the beehive huts, wearing a red baseball cap with an identical logo to the one I'd seen on the surveillance footage. My stomach lurched, and a surge of adrenaline shot through my body. This had to be the third man.

TWENTY-THREE

"Maggie?" Julie stared at me, her brow creased with concern. "Are you feeling sick?"

"I'm fine. I just need to check something." Without waiting for her response, I left the pack of runners and took off down the hill. A ripping sound came from behind me, but I didn't stop to check what it was.

A chorus of gasps and wolf whistles followed my progress down the hill toward the beehive huts.

"Maggie," Julie yelled over the crowd. "Your pants."

My hands flew to my backside and met bare skin. "Aw, heck."

The extra pressure from my increased speed had proved too much for my shrunken running pants, and they'd voiced their objection by splitting to reveal my bare butt to the world.

Before I could deal with my clothing situation, the

man behind the beehive hut moved. In an instant, I recognized him. I sucked in a breath as Jack Logan crept around the hut and snuck inside, his red cap pulled low as he'd worn it in the video. I glanced back at the road, but the pack of runners had already passed. Moving slowly, I darted behind one of the other beehive huts. What if I was wrong about Jack? What if him appearing on the video footage was a coincidence? He'd been at Lisa's birthday drinks. Maybe he hung out with the crowd from the hotel on a regular basis.

I reviewed the info I'd gleaned about the dead man, Alex Scheffel, and the diamond heist he'd been convicted for in Germany. Scheffel and Marcus both spoke German, and they'd both appeared on the hotel's surveillance footage on the night Scheffel had been murdered. How was Jack Logan connected to them? The conversation I'd had with Günter about Marcus's odd accent replayed in my head. What had he said about speaking his native tongue? He knew two people on the island who spoke German well enough to chat with him?

My hands shook as I removed my phone from my running belt and texted Günter. He must have had his phone in his hand, because his response was instant.

Jack Logan speaks German. He's not perfect, but he lived in Berlin for a while and speaks it well enough to hold a basic conversation.

My thumbs flew over the keyboard. *Tell Sergeant Reynolds that Jack was the man in the red cap. He'll know what I mean. I'm sending you my GPS coordinates.*

Günter's reply was swift. *I'm on it.*

I slipped my phone back into my running belt and hunkered low, my heart pounding. It leaped when a twig broke beyond my hiding place. Carefully, I leaned to the side and peered around the hut. Jack Logan emerged from the beehive hut I'd seen him hiding behind earlier. In his right hand, he clutched a metal case that was caked in mud. After glancing from side to side, he slipped up the hill.

I raced around the other side of the hut I was hiding behind. Checking to make sure Jack wasn't looking in my direction, I darted across to the hut Jack had exited and ducked my head low to enter. The small space was claustrophobic. I blinked until my eyes adjusted to the darkness and whipped my phone back out and switched on its inbuilt light. I swept the light around the interior of the hut and spotted what I'd expected to see: a freshly dug hole roughly the size of the box I'd seen Jack carrying. I bent down to take a closer look, but there was nothing of interest left to see.

I stood and made my way back out of the hut. On the hillside, Jack had almost reached the road. My pulse raced as I contemplated my next move. I checked my phone for messages. There was one from Reynolds.

We're on the way. Stay where you are. Don't approach Logan!

I snorted. Jack Logan might be a criminal and a

diamond thief, but I didn't think he'd be much of a match for me if it came to arm-to-arm combat. If Jack happened to have a weapon, on the other hand, things might get trickier. I was still debating whether or not to obey Reynolds's order when I heard a car engine start. To my horror, my wreck of a car sped past with Jack at the wheel.

That low-down thieving swine. Burning with anger, I raced up the hill, totally forgetting my split pants situation. Back on the road, I scanned the terrain for potential help. The only vehicle in the vicinity was a green tractor, which was making its laborious progress over a field. I waved my arms above my head and ran toward my only source of transportation.

When I neared the tractor, my jaw dropped. The Two Gerries sat squashed onto the driver's seat, a bottle of poteen between them.

"Well, hello, Miss Maggie." Gerry One's voice sounded unnaturally high. "Aren't you supposed to be jogging in that race?"

"Your grandson is a killer," I announced and swung myself up and into the cart the tractor was dragging behind it. "And he stole my car."

Gerry One squinted at me. "You must mean Jack. The other lads wouldn't be involved in those sorts of shenanigans."

"I do mean Jack, and you need to hit the gas. He's getting away—in my car."

Gerry Two gave me a once-over. "Either I've had too much to drink, or you're half naked."

I put my hands on my hips and glared at him. "Yes, I'm letting it all hang out today. Now get with the program and drive."

Gerry One hit the gas, and the tractor lurched forward.

"How fast can this thing go?" I shouted above the roar of the engine.

"Not very," he yelled back. "When I get her up to full throttle, she can go forty kilometers an hour."

I slumped back into the trailer. Forty kilometers was around twenty-five miles. Traveling at that speed, we'd never catch up with Jack. The tractor roared across the field and onto the road where it slowly gathered speed. We soon caught the tail end of the Runathon runners, and I spotted Julie and Philomena still going strong. They looked startled to see me up in the trailer. I shaded my eyes and scanned the area for any sign of Jack and my car. "Look," I shouted and pointed at car tire tracks in the field next to the road. "He must have detoured over the grass to avoid the runners."

At the upcoming fork in the road, the runners weaved to the right, and we hung left in the direction the tire tracks stopped and turned into muddy skid marks on the road.

"By Jove, I see him," Gerry Two yelled excitedly. "He's come to grief in that wreck of a car of yours."

Sure enough, my car had skidded into the ditch at the side of the road. Smoke billowed from under the hood, and a patch of oil streaked across the road.

"I knew that snake had sold me a bad car." I pounded a fist against my palm. "I'm getting a refund before he flees the country."

"He's running," Gerry One said. "I see him up ahead. And he's not half as fast as the joggers in the Runathon. I always told him he needed to exercise more, but he was too busy playing with his fancy car to listen. The young don't listen to their elders anymore."

I exchanged a loaded glance with Gerry Two. "You do know he'll be arrested when we catch up with him?" I asked Gerry One. "He's in a whole pile of trouble."

"That spoiled brat tried to blame Carl for his misdeeds," Gerry One shouted. "And me. He was always a bad lot, but when he came back from Germany, I was willing to give him a chance. He's my grandson, after all. But this is the last straw. I'm not having anyone frame Carl and me for murder, not even my own flesh and blood. Let's go get him."

TWENTY-FOUR

The engine roaring, the tractor raced down the road toward the fleeing Jack. In the distance, I heard the wail of a police siren. Reynolds was on his way.

Jack ran ahead. Somewhere along the way, he'd lost his red baseball cap, and his sparse hair did little to conceal his pink scalp. Suddenly, a long line of people wearing running gear streaked across the road, blocking Jack's path. Julie, notable in her hot pink T-shirt, gave me a thumbs up.

Jack, recognizing that his escape route was blocked, turned and headed back in the direction he'd come from. Gerry One swung the tractor around, so that it and the trailer neatly blocked the road.

Jack, close enough now that I could see his red, sweaty face, swore and attempted to leap over the ditch. I hurled myself down from the trailer and took off after him. The Runathon runners took their cue from me, and a trail of brightly clad joggers streaked across the field Jack had chosen as his latest escape route.

Suddenly, one of the runners broke out of the pack and gathered steam. My jaw dropped when I recognized Philomena in her fluorescent orange running suit. She ran behind Jack, took a flying leap, and tackled him to the ground. Seconds later, Julie joined her mother, adding hot pink to the rolling mass of people.

I increased my speed and reached them just as Jack managed to crawl out from under them. I hurled myself on top of him, fists flying. "I want my money back, you rat. You sold me a wreck of a car, and then you had the temerity to *steal* it."

"I needed a getaway car less noticeable than my Porsche," he whined.

"The fact that it broke down on you just when you needed it to drive a few miles is poetic justice," I yelled, "but I still want a refund."

"I'd say paying you back is going to be the least of Mr. Logan's worries," said a dry voice behind me. "I like the bare-cheeked look, by the way. Are you starting a new running fashion trend?"

I rolled off Jack and jumped to my feet. Sergeant Reynolds stood grinning at me, beside a goggle-eyed Sergeant O'Shea. My cheeks burned under their scrutiny. For the first time since the adrenaline of the chase had kicked in, I was squirmingly aware of my naked behind.

"She's running around the island half naked," the older policeman said, outraged. "We ought to charge her with indecent exposure."

"Given that Ms. Doyle has just helped us to apprehend a probable murderer, I'd say her bare buttocks are the least of our concerns." He winked at me, and my cheeks grew even hotter.

Reynolds dangled handcuffs in front of Jack Logan. "According to your German police record, you know the drill." Snarling, Jack held out his wrists, and Reynolds snapped the manacles into place. "I got a call from Interpol. It turns out your pal Marcus is Marco Trezzini, a Swiss citizen from Ticino. According to Interpol, Trezzini was on the run for embezzling funds from his company but has no record for jewel heists. Care to share how he came to be involved with the murder of your former partner in crime, Alex Scheffel?"

"I'm not saying a word," Jack snarled. "You've got nothing on me."

I kicked the metal box on the ground on the spot Jack had been lying. "Oh, yeah? Then you won't mind if we take a look inside."

Jack emitted a choking sound.

I raised my eyebrow at Reynolds, but he nodded. "Go ahead and open it, but use gloves." He tossed me a pair of rubber gloves, and I slipped them on. The clasp on the metal box gave on my third attempt. I flipped open the lid and inhaled sharply even though I'd known what I'd see.

A collective gasp sounded from the gathered crowd. We all stared at the diamonds sparkling under the sunlight.

Reynolds turned to Jack. "Still sticking to your story that you know nothing?"

Jack's nostrils flared. He looked from me to his grandfather, who was standing at the edge of the crowd, glaring at his grandson.

"Don't look to me for help, boyo," Gerry One said. "And don't expect me to visit you in prison. Whatever about you trying to stitch me up for a crime I didn't commit, I can't forgive you for trying to frame Carl."

Jack flushed an angry red that spoke more of embarrassment than shame. "I don't care what you country bumpkins think of me. I was the only member of the family who made something of himself. You're over eighty and still living in the same ramshackle house your grandparents built."

Gerry One jutted his jaw. "I'd rather be honest and live on a low income than be a rich crook."

Reynolds jerked Jack forward. "Let's get moving. Show's over, folks. Thanks to everyone who aided today's arrest." He cast me a look and winked. "Later, Maggie."

———

The aftermath of Jack Logan's arrest proved to be anticlimactic, as was often the case after high-octane situations. Philomena and Julie dragged me back to Smuggler's Cove, where they found clothes for me, before we returned to watch the parade wind its way through the town. Later, we ate fish and chips by the harbor and drank more than I was used to in true St. Patrick's Day fashion.

By six that evening, I was, to quote my Irish relations, wall-falling tired and more than a little drunk. Philomena and Julie poured me into a taxi and gave the driver directions to Shamrock Cottages. When I'd finished fastening my seat belt, the taxi driver, who was used to St. Patrick's Day debauchery, handed me a plastic bucket.

I squinted at it. For some reason, I was having problems seeing straight. Maybe that fifth Leprechaun's Gold cocktail had been a bad idea after all. "It's green," I said redundantly. "You're getting into the festive spirit."

"I came prepared," he said with a grin. "This is my seventeenth time working on St. Patrick's Day."

I must have nodded off during the drive from Smuggler's Cove back to my cottage, for I suddenly found myself being hauled out of the taxi by the driver and propped up on my doorstep. "Are you all right to get in, love?" he asked.

"Definitely." I reached for my purse and, on the

third attempt, succeeded in counting out the correct fare plus tip.

The taxi screeched off into the night. I struggled to my feet and wrestled the key out of my purse. All I wanted to do was have a bath and fall into bed. Maybe not in that order.

I'd just inserted the key in the lock when my senses alerted me that I wasn't alone. I whirled around and scanned my surroundings. "Hello? Is anyone there?"

A shadow emerged from between two of the empty cottages. Lisa from the hotel walked up to me, hollow-cheeked and red-eyed. I sobered up immediately. "What's wrong?"

She dabbed at her eyes with a tissue. "May I come in? I need to talk to you, Maggie."

I blinked past my surprise and pushed open the door to my cottage. "Sure. Come on in. Can I offer you a coffee? I could do with one." Especially if I needed to sober up and concentrate.

"I'd love a coffee." Lisa followed me into my small kitchen and sat in silence at the table while I fixed a frothy cappuccino for her and a strong black coffee for me. Bran raced from the living room to sniff our guest but judged her unworthy of his interest. He lay beside my chair and settled his face on his paws.

"So," I said, sliding our coffees onto the table and taking a seat. "What's going on?"

She slid her gum to the other cheek. "I heard you arrested Jack."

"News travels fast," I said, taking a sip from my mug. "And *I* didn't arrest Jack. That was the police."

"Well, you apprehended him. That's what people are saying." Lisa wound the tissue around her hands in a nervous gesture that I doubted she was aware of making.

I raised an eyebrow. "Why do you care about Jack being arrested? I'd have thought you'd be more concerned about Marcus. Isn't he your friend?"

"I don't care about Marcus." She waved a hand in a dismissive gesture. "It's Jack I'm worried about. He and I were...close...and I'm afraid he might say something about me that could be misconstrued." She twisted her lips into a bitter Cupid's bow. "He was upset when I broke up with him. It would be like him to be vindictive."

I cast my mind back to the night in Murphy's Pub when I'd seen an uncomfortable exchange between Lisa and Jack. "Jack was your lover?"

Lisa bowed her head with the grace and piety of a martyr. "Yes. He didn't mention it to you?"

"Well, no. Buying a useless car from Jack was the extent of our relationship."

"I wasn't sure. I know you're friends with his cousin and close to his grandfather."

Even my alcohol fuddled brain recognized when someone was fishing. *Okay, Ms. Lisa. Two can play at that game.* "Are you still involved with Jack?"

She shook her head. "That ended years ago. You

know by now that he was a crook in Berlin. We met when I was working there."

"Do the Logans know you and Jack were an item? More importantly, does Carl know?"

Lisa reared back. "Goodness, no. He'd be horrified."

"Then why are you telling me?"

She bit her lip. "Because I need your help. I'm worried Jack will try to blame me for the murder. It wouldn't be the first time he's shoved the blame onto someone else. Sergeant Reynolds trusts your opinion."

"Alex Scheffel," I said, shifting the pieces into place. "Jack let him take the fall for the diamond robbery in Berlin."

Lisa nodded. "Alex was a minor player. All he did was trail a diamond dealer who was staying at the hotel where he worked."

"Were you also working at the hotel?"

Lisa frowned. "Oh, no. I was a pharmacy assistant at an English-language pharmacy in the center of Berlin. The position at the Whisper Island Hotel is my first job as a receptionist. They hired me because I'm good with languages."

The coffee in my mouth suddenly tasted bitter. A pharmacy assistant would know the effects of sodium nitroprusside. But how did Lisa get hold of the vial that went missing from the Whisper Island Medical Centre? Wait...hadn't Mack mentioned a blond woman was among the patients in the waiting room on the day he made the delivery? He hadn't known her name, but he'd said she was about our age. Lisa wore a lot of makeup, but I judged her to be no more than a couple years my senior.

"Tell me more about this diamond robbery," I said to buy time. "What role did Scheffel play?"

"None beyond supplying Jack with the information about where the diamond deal was to take place. Jack and his gang arranged the robbery. They knew Alex would squeal the moment the police caught up with him, so it was either kill him or frame him."

"And Jack opted to frame him." I leaned back in my chair and regarded the woman across from me. She flinched under my scrutiny and reached for another piece of gum. When she pulled the package from her purse, I sucked air through my teeth. It was the brand of gum that I'd seen on the passenger seat of the postal van. It might mean nothing, but could Lisa's be among the jumble of prints forensics had found in the van? If she had no police record, her prints wouldn't be in the system. I glanced down at Bran. His eyes were closed and he began to snore. While I was sitting here with a killer, the dog my aunt had insisted would protect me snoozed at my feet. *Some guard dog you've turned out to be, buster.*

"Why do you think Jack will try to frame you?" My palms were sweaty as I slipped my phone out of my pocket under the table with one hand, while I faux-casually held my coffee mug with the other. I hit

Mack's number and paused. Would Mack know who Lisa was? Even if he'd seen her at the Whisper Island Medical Centre the day he made the delivery of pharmacy supplies, would he be able to put a face to a name? No, I wasn't thinking clearly. Mack could wait. I needed to contact Reynolds.

"Jack always tries to frame someone for his crimes. Fool that I was, I came to Whisper Island in the hope that Jack and I would reunite." Lisa gave a delicate sniff. "When I saw that wasn't going to happen, I got together with Carl. The marriage was doomed before it ever began. I didn't love Carl, and he figured out pretty quickly that there was someone else, but he never found out it was Jack."

I leaned back in my chair and snuck a glance at my phone's display. I opened a new message to Reynolds and hit record. "Lisa, did you help Jack arrange Alex Scheffel's murder?"

She reared back as though I'd struck her, and a hand fluttered to her neck. "Of course not."

"You're going to have to work harder than that if you want to convince me." I hit send and prayed that Reynolds would check his phone soon and get his behind back to Shamrock Cottages in time to save me from the psycho sitting across from me. I switched my phone to silent in case he tried to call me. Sure enough, the display flashed with an incoming call a moment later. I hit the green button and focused on Lisa. Please let Reynolds have the sense to stay silent.

"I'm going to ask you again. Did you kill Alex Scheffel?"

No sound from Reynolds, but the call was still connected. A message flashed.

I'm on the way. Keep her talking.

"I came here to talk to you because I was afraid Jack would try to push the blame onto me. I thought you'd understand the position I'm in." Tears glistened in her eyes, unshed. "He's pressured me from the moment I came to the island. It's because of him that my marriage to Carl failed."

"Jack doesn't strike me as the sentimental type. I'd peg him as the use-'em-and-lose-'em kind of guy. Why would he care if you hooked up with his cousin?"

Lisa bristled and a hint of anger flashed in her cold gray eyes. She was a cool customer, but underneath that controlled exterior lay a red-hot temper. Somehow, Alex Scheffel had aroused her anger and she'd poisoned him. But why? What did Scheffel have on Lisa for her to want him dead?

I took a deep breath. "Lisa, if you want me to help you, I need you to be honest with me. What did Jack pressure you to do that he can use as leverage against you?"

Her eyes narrowed in suspicion, but after a pause, she took the bait. "He asked me to get Carl's knife from the hotel kitchen. I didn't know what he wanted it for."

My chest swelled and I struggled to keep my breathing even. The news of the doctored surveillance footage hadn't been released to the public. Only the police, Zuzanna, her boyfriend, Lenny, Julie, and I knew about it. A lot of people, sure, but none of us were close to Lisa, so there was a strong chance that she had no idea I knew Marcus was the one who'd stolen Carl's knife.

"When did you take it? On the night of the murder?"

She shook her head. "No. I wasn't working that night. I snuck into the kitchen during my morning shift and stole it then."

Liar, liar, pants on fire. I kept a straight face. If Lisa wanted to drop a hint about how she'd inadvertently helped Jack to murder Alex Scheffel, she'd chosen the wrong clue to drop. I recognized bait and switch when I saw it, and that was totally what Lisa was trying to do. By telling me she'd taken the knife, a weapon that had not actually killed the murder victim, she was hoping no one would connect her with the sodium nitroprusside that was the true cause of death.

Lisa widened her eyes. "So will you help me, Maggie? I'm desperate."

Desperate...the one true word she'd spoken during our entire conversation. Yeah, I'd help her...all the way to the police station. Which, if my hunch was right, was exactly where Lisa wanted to go.

I cast her my most understanding cop look. "Sure I'll help, but you need to come to the station with me now and talk to Sergeant Reynolds. You have no need to worry about Jack. He's in custody."

And so was the box of diamonds that I was pretty sure my unexpected guest wanted to steal. I'd watched Reynolds lock them in the police station's safe. How did Lisa intend to get to them? I glanced at her purse and swallowed hard when I saw a telltale pistol-shaped bulge. Yeah, a gun would do the trick, especially in Ireland where most cops didn't carry firearms. I knew from a previous case that the police on Whisper Island had none.

The woman blinked back fake tears. "Thank you, Maggie. I've been so frightened. It's a relief to get this off my chest."

She stood up and looked at me expectantly.

I sat frozen, and the phone in my lap burned an imaginary hole in my pants.

At the sound of Lisa getting ready to leave, Bran leaped to his feet and knocked against my leg. As if in slow motion, my phone slid from my lap and tumbled to the ground.

Please land face down. Please, please...ugh.

My heart slamming against my ribs, I stared down at the glowing display that showed my phone was currently on a call with Liam Reynolds. A horrible silence descended over the kitchen for one tense second. Then, with a hiss, Lisa pounced on my phone and disconnected the call from Reynolds.

"You contacted the police?" she snarled. "They were listening in all this time?"

Slowly, I got to my feet and inched my way to the back door.

"Don't even think about it." Lisa whipped the pistol out of her purse and aimed it at my heart.

I tasted bile. How long would it take for Reynolds to reach me? Another fifteen minutes? If Lisa had her way, I'd be dead before then. "You wanted me to go with you to the station to find the diamonds. Why did you need me?"

"Why do you think, you fool? I needed a hostage so that the police would give me the diamonds and let me off the island."

I stared at her, genuinely perplexed. "You could have used anyone to be your hostage. Why pick me? You must have waited for me to get back from town. Why go to all that trouble when you could have used someone else?"

She sneered at me. "You might have brains, Maggie Doyle, but you have no common sense. I needed someone Liam Reynolds cares about. Someone he'd lose his cool to protect."

"But Liam and I are not an item. We live next door, but that's it." *Now who's the liar, Maggie?*

Lisa's laugh was as sharp as shards of broken glass. "I know men. I saw the way he looked at you today when you caught Jack."

My head jerked up. "You were there?"

"Oh, yes. I was one of the runners. I saw the whole thing." Lisa jutted her chin and her pretty face twisted into a scornful expression. "I watched you and your flabby bottom chasing after Jack, and him desperately trying to conceal the box. And Reynolds putting the diamonds—*my* diamonds—into the police car."

I ignored the insult about my behind and focused on solving the mystery—and saving my life. The fire extinguisher was beside the back door. If I could only get to it... "Did Jack hold out on you? Did he not give you your fair share of the loot?"

She snorted. "Do you honestly think Jack would have thought to hide the diamonds in a tourist attraction that gets trampled over all year round? Burying them in the beehive hut was my idea." Her jaw tightened. "The snake must have followed me to find out where I'd stashed the box."

I took a deep breath and sidled toward the back door. *Two more feet...* I stretched out my arm.

"Stop right there." Fury suffused Lisa's face, turning it into a contorted mask. "I'm the one in charge here. I say when—"

The front door opened with a crash. On instinct, Lisa whirled around, forgetting to keep the gun aimed at me. *Amateur hour.*

I darted to the back door, grabbed the fire extinguisher, and charged at my wannabe killer. We fell to the floor in a screaming heap at the precise moment my unexpected visitor barged into the kitchen.

An orange-haired, green-bearded Lenny stared down at us from under an enormous leprechaun hat. "Hey, dudes. What's up?"

TWENTY-FIVE

Lenny's dramatic appearance, in every sense of the word, distracted Lisa sufficiently for me to prize the pistol out of her talons and hurl it across the kitchen.

"You bitch," she screeched and scratched me with her long nails.

"Whoa, dude. Not cool." Lenny lurched sideways, showing me that he'd had as much to drink as I had.

I whacked Lisa on the arm with the fire extinguisher and she screamed in pain. She fought me like a wildcat, clawing and pulling hair.

"If you have a weapon about you, Lenny," I said through gritted teeth as Lisa clawed at my eyes, "now's the time to use it."

My friend considered this for a moment and then his face lit up. "Man, I got just the thing."

With the speed and dexterity of a Wild West

gunslinger, Lenny pulled two cans of glitter spray out of his backpack, popped the lids and let loose.

Lisa screamed when the spray hit her face. In a glitter-filled haze, I rolled out from under her and struggled to my feet. Blinking through my glittered eyelashes, I staggered over to the spot the pistol had landed and picked it up.

Breathing hard, I aimed it at Lisa through blurred vision. As long as she stayed writhing on the floor, there was a good chance my shot wouldn't go astray. "We need a rope to tie her up," I wheezed.

Lenny, also coughing, nodded and pulled off his crazy hat. "We can use my leprechaun legs."

A laugh bubbled up my throat. "Go for it, buddy."

When Liam Reynolds ran into my kitchen five minutes later, he found a trussed up killer covered in glitter with her feet bound with leprechaun legs and her wrists tied with Bran's leash.

"Yo, dude," Lenny drawled. "Have you come to join the fun?"

Reynolds took a step back at the sight of us. "Please tell me you two took a taxi. I can smell the alcohol fumes from here."

"Of course," I said confidently, not at all sure how Lenny had arranged transportation from Smuggler's Cove to my cottage.

"Granddad gave me a lift," Lenny supplied, beaming. "Julie told me Maggie had gone home early, and that just won't do on her first St. Patrick's Day in

Ireland." He reached down and pulled several more cans of glitter spray from his backpack and a bottle of Gerry Logan's infamous poteen, dyed green for the occasion.

"Oh, no," I groaned. "No more alcohol. The only drink I'm fixing is coffee."

Liam handcuffed Lisa and hauled her to her feet. "Have an espresso toast for me, Maggie. With the station cells full to bursting, I don't think I'll be home anytime soon."

———

After the drama and the excess alcohol, I slept like a rock. When I rolled out of bed the next morning, I had less of a hangover than I deserved, but I still hadn't felt this lousy since spring break my freshman year of college. After an extra-long shower, I dragged myself into the kitchen and fixed an extra-large, extra-strong coffee to match. I'd just taken a seat at the kitchen table when my doorbell rang.

I managed to place my mug on the table without spilling its contents—a major win in my shaky condition—and staggered to the front door. I remembered that I was still wearing my bathrobe the instant I opened the door.

Reynolds stood on my doorstep carrying a paper bag bearing the Movie Theater Café's logo. "Whoa,

Maggie. You look like I feel. What happened to your hair?"

"King of the compliments," I said dryly, but stood aside to let him in. "Genetics happened to my hair. My curls always look like this before I tame them with products and a blow-dryer."

He tugged a loose curl and stretched it to its full length. "Wow, it's long."

Was it my imagination, or had his voice grown deeper? Our eyes met and the desire I read in this matched my own. I cleared my throat and stepped back, putting space between us. "I hope that bag contains one of Noreen's scones."

"Four, actually." Reynolds grinned and gave me a slow perusal that made my cheeks burn. "I thought you might have the munchies."

"You're hilarious," I drawled and tightened the belt of my bathrobe. "What I have is a splitting headache."

"Well," he said as I led the way into the kitchen, "I've got news that'll cheer you up."

I raised an eyebrow in disbelief and switched on the coffee machine. "Lisa made a full confession?"

He laughed. "No such luck. Her partner in crime, Jack Logan, squealed loud and clear. He gave us enough dirt on Lisa to make building a case against her child's play."

After I'd fixed Reynolds an espresso, I took the seat opposite him. "Come on. Don't leave me in suspense."

His expression grew serious. "Before I get to the

story, I owe you my thanks. If it weren't for your help, I'd be out of a job and a home."

"You brought me scones." I took a deliciously crumbly bite. "Give me the low-down on what the suspects said and we're even."

He grinned. "Obviously, this is all off the record—"

"I can keep my mouth shut. You, of all people, should know that."

"I do know that, Maggie, and I appreciate it. Okay, this is what we've pieced together so far. Lisa was the brains behind the diamond robbery."

"I guessed as much. So Jack Logan and Alex Scheffel worked for her?"

"Yeah. They had a deal that if one of them was caught, the others would save part of the loot for them for when they got out of prison. Hoping to make good on this deal, Scheffel tracked down Jack and Lisa when he got out of prison. He showed up unannounced on Whisper Island three days before the murder."

"I bet Jack and Lisa weren't thrilled to see him."

Reynolds grimaced. "That's an understatement. After playing it safe for several years, they'd been carefully laundering the diamonds over the last eighteen months. They had no intention of sharing the proceeds with Scheffel, but they didn't want him to go to the police with dirt that could put them behind bars."

I sifted through what I knew. "So Jack and Lisa formulated a plan to get rid of Scheffel. On the

Wednesday before the murder, Lisa invented an excuse to make an appointment at the Whisper Island Medical Centre at a time she knew Mack made his weekly delivery of medicines. Somehow, she managed to steal a vial of sodium nitroprusside."

Reynolds nodded. "You've got it. And because they're greedy, Lisa and Jack's exit plan included another get-rich-quick scheme that involved robbing the hotel safe right before payday."

I rolled my eyes. "Can you believe the Greers still pay most of the staff wages in cash? How crazy is that?"

"Totally bonkers, but I don't think they'll be doing that again after I tell them what Lisa had planned."

"You haven't mentioned Marcus," I interjected. "Where does he come into the story?"

"I was about to get to him," Reynolds replied with a grin. "You're impatient."

"Hey, I just want to get to the good stuff."

"As it turns out, Marcus isn't involved with 'the good stuff', as you put it. At least not directly. He's exactly who he says he is—an embezzler on the run using a false passport. He had nothing to do with the heist in Berlin, and he didn't meet Jack and Lisa until he moved to Whisper Island."

I frowned. "Then how did he wind up stealing Carl Logan's knife?"

"Two words: 'Lisa' and 'blackmail'."

"Ah ha," I said. "Lisa found out about Marcus's criminal past and used it to her advantage."

"Correct. Through Marcus, Lisa found out about Eddie Ward's planned leave. She forced Marcus to get hold of the postman's van and manipulate the records to show that Ward was supposed to work that night. Then she planned her and Jack's exit from Whisper Island. When Marcus let slip that Zuzanna was the poltergeist, Lisa told him to make her schedule a haunting for the night of the murder."

"Okay. Back up a sec. I'm getting confused. What did Lisa and Jack plan for the night Scheffel died?"

Reynolds laughed. "Not what happened, that's for sure. A wealthy guest was supposed to be staying at the hotel. Lisa believed the woman would keep her jewels in the hotel safe. In addition to the jewels, she knew Paul Greer had put a large quantity of cash in the safe, and she planned to take the lot." Reynolds smiled. "Or rather, she planned for her two goons to do it for her."

I mulled this over for a moment. "So we have Jack and Scheffel robbing the hotel safe and using the post van as a getaway vehicle. Where's Lisa when all this is happening?"

"Waiting for them near Carraig Harbour. She wasn't working that night. They intended for Scheffel to drive the van on and off the ferry while Lisa and Jack hid in the back. From a distance, Scheffel could pass as Eddie Ward, and the ferry staff weren't likely to look too closely late at night."

A thought occurred to me. "Ask Lisa if she hung out in one of our neighboring cottages while she was waiting for her cohorts to collect her. When I got home after finding the body, the doors of Number Four were open. In all the chaos after, I forgot all about it."

Reynolds pulled out a notebook and scribbled a few words. "Thanks. I'll check that out."

"So what happened next?" I demanded, leaning forward and clasping my mug between my palms.

"As you know, the hotel safe robbery didn't happen. When Zuzanna staged her haunting, several staff members ran into the Greers' office to get away from the clanking and the wailing. Jack and Alex couldn't get anywhere near the safe, and had to make a getaway through the staff exit. They bumped into Marcus in the hallway and forced him out the exit and into the van. I don't know if they intended to kill him or scare him, but Marcus assumes the former."

"What happened to the knife Marcus stole from the kitchen?"

"According to Marcus, he produced the knife once he was in the van and tried to escape. Somehow, Jack wrestled the knife off him, but Marcus managed to open the back of the van and jump out. He fled and the others, presumably deciding they had no time to waste going after him, kept going to the point they'd arranged to meet Lisa."

"And somewhere near there, Scheffel died," I finished. "But why *then*?"

"I'm no doctor," Reynolds said, "but my guess is his diabetes played a role. Lisa had no intention of letting

Scheffel live. She wanted to get rid of him as soon as they reached the mainland. Knowing he liked to drink, she poisoned a bottle of Gerry Logan's poteen with sodium nitroprusside. She intended for Scheffel to drink it slowly, as one usually does with strong spirits, and not die immediately. Unfortunately for Lisa and Jack, a couple of key items on their getaway plan fell apart. One factor was the storm blowing in earlier than expected and the ferry being canceled as a result. This meant that they had no way off the island."

"Unless they took a boat and sailed," I suggested. "They could have tried to escape that way."

Reynolds shook his head. "Jack was a good sailor. He knew the attempt would be suicidal."

"So Jack and Scheffel had to drive around the island trying to figure out what to do?"

"Given the timing, they must have done a loop around the island at least once. That still shouldn't have been enough time for the poison to kill Scheffel, but Jack said Scheffel was getting through the bottle of poteen faster than he'd anticipated, plus diabetics process medication differently. Whatever happened, Scheffel died at the wheel, and Jack panicked."

"And being the rat that he is, he decided that if he couldn't get rid of the body easily, he'd cover his behind by setting up his cousin and grandfather as suspects. He had Carl's knife, and Gerry's poteen. Arranging the rest would have been easy."

"He even had his grandfather's ax with him,"

Reynolds said. "He'd taken it from the shed earlier that day in case he needed it for the robbery."

"Ugh." I put my mug down with a clatter. "If Jack wasn't behind bars, I'd go to the station and punch him."

"You'd have to get in line behind Lisa and the entire Logan clan," Reynolds said dryly. "Lisa was livid when she discovered Jack had been stupid enough to stab the body. He didn't have the smarts to know a pathologist would guess the wound had been inflicted after death. It was Lisa who insisted Jack plant the empty vial of sodium nitroprusside in Gerry Logan's bathroom."

My fingers curled into fists. "Add her to the list of people I'd like to punch."

"Remind me never to get into your bad books. You have a temper." Reynolds reached out and tugged at one of my stray curls, and his fingers brushed against my cheek, sending a delicious shiver down my spine. "What do you say, Miss Doyle? Want to go out for dinner with me sometime? We only have a couple of months left before you leave the island."

"About that..." I lowered my voice to a sultry whisper. "I might be staying longer."

A slow smile spread across his face, revealing his dimples. "That's great news."

"And there's more. We're going to be in the same line of work." I paused for dramatic effect, relishing his puzzled expression. "I've decided to set up business as a private investigator."

As Liam Reynolds's face transformed into a worthy imitation of a *Scream* mask, my laughter floated through the cottage. I had a feeling the next few months on Whisper Island were going to be fun.

—THE END—

A NOTE FROM ZARA

Thanks for reading ***The Postman Always Dies Twice.*** I hope you enjoyed Maggie's second adventure on Whisper Island! Maggie and her friends will be back for more murder and mayhem in ***How to Murder a Millionaire***.

Join my **mailing list** and get news, giveaways, and a FREE digital Movie Club Mystery story. Join Maggie and her friends as they solve the mystery in *To Hatch a Thief*.

http://zarakeane.com/newsletter

Happy Reading!

Zara xx

Would you like to try Maggie's Brandy Alexanders that she made in ***The Postman Always Dies Twice***? Here's the recipe—poison not included!

BRANDY ALEXANDER COCKTAIL

- 1 oz (30ml) brandy (often a good quality cognac)
- 1 oz (30ml) dark crème de cacao
- 1 oz (30ml) cream
- 1 square melted dark chocolate (55% cocoa solids recommended)
- Ground nutmeg to garnish

1. Melt the chocolate.
2. Pour all the ingredients into a cocktail shaker.
3. Add ice and shake vigorously.
4. Strain the ice out of the cocktail.
5. Dry shake the cocktail vigorously (i.e.: shake a second time, but without ice).

6. Strain into a cocktail glass and garnish with a light dusting of ground nutmeg.

Maggie's tip: If you'd like sweeter taste, use white crème de cacao instead of dark, and substitute the square of melted dark chocolate with white.

The Movie Club Mysteries continue in *How to Murder a Millionaire*.

Armed with her newly issued private investigator's license, Maggie Doyle is on the case...of a sheep that went missing twenty-two years ago. When she trips over a dead body on the first day of the investigation, Maggie realizes there's more to this cold case than a fight over lamb chops.

An invitation to spend the weekend with her grandmother's oldest friend and her family, the super wealthy Huffingtons, gives Maggie the perfect excuse to sniff out the killer. After the family patriarch is electrocuted in the swimming pool, Maggie finds herself embroiled in yet another murder inquiry. With the body count rising, can Maggie catch the killer before they strike again?

EXCERPT FROM *HOW TO MURDER A MILLIONAIRE*

Whisper Island, Ireland

When I rolled out of bed at the butt crack of dawn, I had no idea my day would start with a missing sheep and end with a dead dude in a crotchless mankini.

Averting my gaze from the dead guy's man junk, I kneeled beside the body and felt for a pulse. As I'd expected, there was none. The man's skin was cold to the touch, indicating he'd been dead a while. I stood and scanned the barn for clues, but the cause of death was obvious: the rake sticking out of his chest was hard to miss.

I swore under my breath. How the heck could this be happening to me again? In the five months since I'd swapped my cheating ex and crumbling career in the San Francisco PD for life on a remote Irish island, I'd stumbled into two murder investigations. Becoming involved in a third was *not* on my to-do list.

Swallowing a sigh, I reached for my phone and hit speed dial.

My neighbor, and not-so-secret crush, answered on the second ring. "Sergeant Reynolds, Whisper Island Garda Station."

His deep rumble and Irish accent affected me like a comforting blanket. "Liam, it's me. You're not going to believe what I've just found."

"Maggie?" He groaned. "Aw, no. Why didn't I check caller ID?"

"That's a lovely way to greet the woman who cooked you dinner last Saturday," I said indignantly. "You could muster up a little enthusiasm."

"When said woman only contacts me at my work number to report finding dead bodies, I have good reason to be wary."

"Well, actually..." I let the words hang in the air a moment.

"No way." There was the sound of a chair scraping the floor on the other end of the line. "Don't tell me you've found another one."

"It's not like I *plan* to find dead people. It just sort of...happens." I didn't add that this particular corpse *happened* to be wearing a lime green mankini that hadn't been designed with swimming in mind. I'd let Reynolds enjoy that sight when he got here.

He muttered something in Gaelic that I was pretty sure I didn't want translated. "Tell me who's dead and where you are, and I'll get over there right away."

"Jimmy Wright is our vic." I rattled off the address of the Wright farm. "It's a thirty-minute drive from the station, give or take."

"I know the place. That's where I had to arrest an animal activist a few months ago. You sure Jimmy's dead?"

I regarded the rake sticking out of the farmer's chest and the pool of blood staining the straw beneath his body. I tasted bile, and my grip on the phone tightened. "No doubt about it. All he's good for now is fertilizer."

"Once a cop, always a cop, right down to the black humor," he said in a bone-dry tone. "I'll be there in forty. If no ambulance is required urgently, I'll swing by the Whisper Island Medical Centre on my way to the Wright farm and get Dr. Reilly to join me."

"You do that. And bring a forensics kit," I added as an afterthought. "It looks like murder."

"Why am I not surprised? You have a magnetic attraction to people who die unnatural deaths."

I tried to muster some righteous indignation, but failed. He had a point. I did have an uncanny nose for murder. "I'll see you soon."

"Wait a sec, Maggie." Reynolds's voice deepened a notch. "Promise me you won't touch anything. Your P.I.'s license doesn't give you permission to trample all over crime scenes."

Trample all over the place? What did he take me for, an amateur? "Sure thing, Sarge," I drawled. "I'll stay out of the barn."

I disconnected before Reynolds's sharp mind guessed my intentions and ordered me off Wright's property.

Shoving my phone into my purse, I exited the barn and jogged across the farm courtyard. Although it was gone eight-thirty in the evening, the sun still shone brightly, and would do so until around ten o'clock. Just as I'd had to get used to the longer hours of darkness during an Irish winter, I had to adjust to the longer hours of sunlight now that it was June.

When I reached my new car, I pulled my keys from my pocket. I say "new", but the vehicle was my cousin's cast-off. Julie had sold it to me for a steal when she'd upgraded to an SUV last month. I opened the passenger door of the MINI, trying to ignore the wobbly door handle. There was a reason the car had been cheap, but I'd spent the last of the money from my successful investigation into the Whisper Island Hotel hauntings on rent, equipment for my new profession, and my day-old private investigator's license. Besides, the MINI was an improvement over the last rust bucket I'd driven.

I reached under the passenger seat and grabbed my mini detective kit. In the glove compartment, I located a pair of disposable rubber gloves, plastic overshoes, a cover for my hair, and a can of pepper spray. The latter was probably overkill—experience told me Jimmy'd been dead a while. I didn't think his killer was lurking on the farm, but I wasn't taking any risks.

I glanced at my watch. I had around thirty-five minutes before Reynolds arrived. I could spend it sweating in the barn with Jimmy Wright's earthly remains, or I could sneak into his house and start the investigation I'd been sent here to conduct. As long as I didn't have to pick the lock, I was golden.

ALSO BY ZARA KEANE

MOVIE CLUB MYSTERIES

TIME-SLIP MYSTERIES

ABOUT ZARA KEANE

USA Today bestselling author Zara Keane grew up in Dublin, Ireland, but spent her summers in a small town very similar to the fictitious Whisper Island and Ballybeg.

She currently lives in Switzerland with her family. When she's not writing, Zara loves knitting, running, unplugged gaming, and adding to her insanely large lipstick collection.

Zara has an active Facebook reader group, **Zara Keane's Ballybeg Belles**, where she chats, shares snippets of upcoming stories, and hosts members-only giveaways. She hopes to join you for a virtual pint very soon!

zarakeane.com

THE POSTMAN ALWAYS DIES TWICE

Copyright © 2017 by Sarah Tanner

Published 2017 by Beaverstone Press GmbH (LLC)

EBOOK ISBN: 978-3-906245-46-1

PRINT ISBN: 978-3-906245-49-2

Lightning Source UK Ltd.
Milton Keynes UK
UKHW010431200221
379081UK00002B/809

9 783906 245492